GW00457863

Me, myself and

ANASTAZJA

Annette De Burgh

Copyright © 2023 Annette De Burgh

All rights reserved worldwide. No part of this publication may be replicated, photocopied, redistributed, held in a retrieval system, or given away in any form without the prior written consent of the author or the terms relayed to you herein.

This is a work of fiction.

Names, characters, businesses, descriptions, places, events and incidents are either the products of the author's imagination or used in a fictitious manner. Any resemblance to actual persons, living or dead, or actual events, is purely coincidental and unintentional.

This publication is available in both Kindle and paperback format in all global territories from Amazon.

Dastardly and Muttley © TM Hanna Barbera and Heatter-Quigley.

Author website
www.annettedeburgh.com

Annette De Burgh is on GoodReads.com

This book is dedicated to all care givers, whoever you are and wherever you are.

It is also dedicated to all the carers who looked after me in my home, all of whom showed me so much humanity and good grace at a time when I really needed it – to each and every one of you, I say, Thank You.

Annette De Burgh

The only thing worse than being talked about
is not being talked about.

Oscar Wilde

Annette De Burgh

ONE

'The ambulance will be here in half an hour, Anne.'

The voice was authoritative and laced with a clipped northern accent. It belonged to Fiona, one the many staff nurses on the acute stroke unit of the university hospital. Fiona had a friendly manner, and as she approached the hospital bed situated near the window which overlooked the Warwickshire countryside she could see there was no immediate response from the occupant in it, so she carefully made her way closer. Observing the still form, she saw the elderly lady open her eyes and look towards her.

'You'll be home soon. I've spoken to your son and everything is in place,' smiled Fiona as reassuringly she touched Anne's right hand and smiled.

Without expression, Anne turned to look out of the window. 'What?' she said cautiously, her voice a little faint. Then she returned her gaze to Fiona, saying, 'Well, at least it's not raining.' There was a deep resignation in the tone as Anne glanced down at the bed in which she lay. Under the bed sheets she could see the form of her body, and while they were still her limbs, she had little or no control over them, especially her right side, which remained stubbornly stiff and unresponsive despite the hospital's best efforts to improve matters with physiotherapy. Anne's speech, however, was returning and although she could now be understood, gone was the authoritative tone that her friends had come to know so well.

Ninety-one-year-old Anne was of small build, with short white hair and a good skin complexion that betrayed her age. Her appearance was unremarkable, but her character and personality were something else entirely.

Anne gave a resigning sigh, for despite her incapacity and the traumatic effect of recent weeks – the shock, the annoyance and the frightening times she had experienced – Anne knew only too well that many more difficulties and obstacles lay ahead. This was to be a long road to a recovery that was never going to be complete. It was not that she was unprepared for all the challenges that awaited her, for the sad realisation was that not only would her once busy and active life come to an end, but that life itself, for her, would never be the same again. The era of travelling, restaurants, shopping and community meetings had, overnight, been taken from her. It was now make do and mend, as her mother had frequently said. No use dwelling on the past was another one of her mother's favourite sayings, and this was something Anne had given thought to in recent days.

While the sayings were very true, they were hard to live up to.

Anne's newly found predicament had all happened so quickly, as so often life-changing events do. Anne was a well-known and outspoken member of her local community; she was also respected for being the founder member of a social group which now boasted over four hundred village members. Anne was never one to shy away from conflict, always the one to instigate an argument and never one to allow her views to be ignored.

Anne was a flawed and complex character, you either got on with her, accepted her peculiarities and at times unconventional way of looking at life, or you took offence at the earliest opportunity – usually within five minutes of meeting her.

Anne had moved into this village, situated in the Heart of England, from Scotland more than thirty years ago and had witnessed the ever-changing development of the surrounding areas. She had, with her late husband John, downsized from a successful life in Scotland to this small village, and to a smaller house which was not commensurate with the lifestyle they could enjoy if they so wished. The house and village were respectable, but neither John nor Anne harboured any ambitions to remain there, intending instead to move on to Falmouth, but they soon found themselves becoming integrated into local life, putting any thoughts of a further move on hold. It was a decision Anne had always regretted.

Anne was always the first to join some sort of action committee to try and remedy the ever-increasing list of problems that beset residents of the village. Sometimes her endeavours with others were successful, other times fruitless. No matter what you thought of Anne's opinions, deep down she always had the best interests of the community at heart and would give a great deal of her time to help.

Anne never dwelt on her past – it was chequered but mostly successful. Voluntary work had been her life; John, the vice-president of a global American corporation, would spend much of the year travelling overseas without her. Anne had no option but to forge her own identity, otherwise she would have drowned in the sea of John's corporate existence.

Her voluntary work started out as giving advice in a local bureau for under-privileged families, then she moved on to a coveted role on the Scottish Juvenile Court, before being appointed a magistrate for the city of Glasgow, and then Coventry. Anne was never a rule-follower, and despite her fellow magistrates taking everything so seriously, Anne developed a more tolerant approach and had a certain sympathy and understanding for some of the accused and their predicaments – namely homelessness, addiction and poverty.

Anne had always been a writer, even during her young adult years, and today she could boast of having written a number of novels that had sold reasonably well, especially in America.

Anne was a rebel, even when she was at school. There were no particular subjects that she enjoyed or excelled at, and she was usually towards the bottom of her class when any form of examination was taken. It was because of this that Anne had been kept back a school year to give her a chance to catch up with her education. It did not turn out that way, for Anne, when she actually bothered to go to school, was simply not interested in the subjects or – more tellingly – none of her teachers were able to inspire her to learn.

In contrast, Anne's father Edward had been a fastidious and measured man: a stockbroker who had fought in the First World War, where he had become horrifically injured by losing a leg, then had simply had to go on with his life with a diligent and quiet attitude. He became very disabled but Anne could never recall a time when he complained. Edward had many interests, photography being the main one, and became knowledgeable and competent with all his self-taught skills. Anne realised that she had to take a leaf out of her father's book to face the enormous task that lay ahead within her own life.

Anne's mother Peg, as she was often referred to, was a machinist in a factory sewing clothes. Peg gave Anne little educational inspiration, but she was a clever and intuitive woman who, when her husband returned from the war injured, took it upon herself to save the family home and make sure there was enough money on hand to pay the bills every month.

They were never what you would call wealthy, but Peg was a good money manager and, like her mother before her, she looked after all the family finances because Edward was frequently hospitalised.

I always turn a pound over twice was another of Peg's sayings, and this ethos had also rubbed off on Anne's son David.

Now, as Anne lay on her bed in this modern hospital ward, she briefly reflected on how life had changed for her father in almost an instant – very like her own experience that day.

Edward kissed Peg goodbye one morning, left for work, walked down the road to the bus stop and travelled into the city reading the *Liverpool Post*. He arrived at his office at the normal time. By mid morning he was alone, when suddenly he got up and fell to the floor. He never recovered from the heart attack, despite being taken to the Liverpool Infirmary, where he was pronounced dead on arrival. From then on, Anne and Peg were on their own, with survival at the forefront of their minds.

Peg took many months to recover from the emotional shock, so it was left to Anne to take up the reigns, becoming the sole breadwinner and taking over the running of the house. She even sold her treasured bicycle to raise money.

Now Anne would be reliant on her son David, who John had recognised as being measured and fastidious like his grandfather. David didn't suffer fools gladly, and was always able to spot one; he was good at finance and organising, and because of this Anne had no qualms in putting her well-being in his hands. Once David was told what was required to assist Anne's transfer from hospital to home, he sorted all the details and was determined to do the right thing by his mother. Equipment and house alterations were all dealt with. David also sourced the services of a home care agency, but not before he had checked the care agency's financial health via Companies House to reassure himself they were not a fly-by-night organisation that would be here today and gone tomorrow. David rarely took anything at face value.

David was also a stickler for doing the right thing, and – to keep things absolutely legal – a lasting power of attorney from the Office of the Public Guardian was acquired, with David's solicitor to act as co-attorney in the event of his own incapacitation. David did not need any financial assistance from his mother, and this made the whole decision a lot easier for Anne. Quite simply, Anne trusted her son and it was not a trust that was misplaced.

Anne's life-changing experience came one January evening as she was preparing for bed. Looking out of her bedroom window at the illuminated rear garden, as she did most nights to reflect on the passing day, she suddenly felt unable to move. Anne knew immediately that she was having a stroke. She was able to call for an ambulance and tell the call handler that the key had been left for the cleaner in the key safe by the front door – and opened the electric gates. Then she fell to the floor, just like her father had done so many years earlier.

The ambulance arrived within ten minutes and the crew were able to locate the key. Climbing the stairs quickly and efficiently, they found Anne lying motionless on the floor of her bedroom. Preliminary checks indicated extremely high blood pressure and an inability to talk. Anne was placed on a stretcher and put in the ambulance, and the house was locked up before she was then blue-lighted to hospital where she was given life-saving treatment. The doctor in charge had no option but to call David and inform him that his mother had suffered a serious stroke and might not make it through the night. David got in his car and made his way to the hospital.

The following month was a traumatic time for all concerned. Anne's condition remained critical and dangerous, as indicated by the red dot next to her name on the patient information board that David glanced at every time he visited the hospital ward. This infamous red dot remained in position for weeks indicating that Anne was still considered to be in danger. It was only in the fourth week that the red dot changed to yellow, indicating less danger.

Although Anne was termed a 'stroke survivor', she had been left seriously incapacitated by what had turned out to be a very large hemorrhagic stroke, and the prognosis for a full recovery was practically zero. This new, disabled Anne would replace the energetic, independent Anne. It was a tough call for all concerned.

Gone was Anne's steely personality and her strong, independent voice, and in its place came a weaker voice and an elderly lady who was a hundred per cent dependent on others. Although the hospital predicted that Anne's speech would return, and it had started to do so, the predicament in which David found himself was difficult, for Anne was not the sort of person who would fit well into a nursing home, nor did David think it would do anything to aid what little recovery she could make. So David decided – with Anne's agreement, and after taking into account all of Anne's requirements – that a live-in carer would be the most appropriate way of taking care of his mother. This would mean that Anne could live in the comforting and familiar surroundings of her own home. But even with the appointment of a suitable live-in carer, the task was not to be underestimated, for Anne – despite her disability – could, at times, be difficult to get on with.

Anne's house was considered reasonably large, situated in what the villagers referred to as a prestigious lane. It was comfortable and warm with ample suitable accommodation for any live-in carer. Anne had voiced her concerns to the matron of her hospital ward, saying she was unsure about a stranger living with her, and – despite reassurances from the matron and hospital nurses that all care agencies are properly checked – Anne remained doubtful. But for Anne, the alternative did not bear thinking about, so she pinned her hopes on having a middle-aged English woman to look after her – someone who could stimulate her with conversation and who would be capable of looking after her, both physically and mentally. She also wanted a good, wholesome cook.

David had contacted four different care agencies and had decided on one particular company on the basis that the receptionist who answered the telephone was both polite and reassuring, and so a representative from the care agency had visited Anne in the hospital. They also had a rendezvous with David and visited Anne's home to check whether the house had everything that would be required. It was then down to the agency to find a suitable person, and for David to express his views on who it should be.

Over her recent weeks in hospital, Anne had often wondered what type of person would suddenly become integral to her life.

She envisaged a homely, rotund woman who wore an apron and busied herself with daily chores and interesting gossip. Someone who was well read and had travelled would also be a bonus. Anne always loved to get out of the house and David had investigated purchasing an adapted motor vehicle, which would enable Anne – while still sitting in her wheelchair – to get out and about, so the carer would have to be a competent driver, but more importantly someone who could listen. It seemed a long list, and would such a person really choose caring as a career? Please, Anne secretly thought to herself, don't give me somebody foreign!

The care agency had offered Anne an opportunity to meet the proposed carer before hiring them, but Anne – difficult as ever – had declined the offer, suggesting a week's trial instead. This was agreed to and, according to the manager, a suitable carer had been hired. They would meet each other for the first time that morning.

Anne was now becoming impatient. After spending weeks on the hospital ward, she was getting tired of the hustle and bustle, the comings and goings, and the general melee that surrounded the acute stroke unit. The staff and the nurses were all very nice, but she had had enough of them and wanted to get back home to her 'new normal'.

The ward served morning tea at eleven, and today was no different, but just as Anne was starting to tentatively sip the hot liquid she noticed two figures in green uniforms standing in the ward doorway. One of the nurses was pointing towards Anne's bed. Then the matron arrived and directed a warm smile at Anne.

'Here is your transport, Anne,' the matron announced.

Anne gave a small, grateful acknowledgement and, with her left hand, placed her spectacles on her nose, watching as the nurses collected all her personal belongings from the side cupboards and put them into a large carrier bag. This bag seemed to hold all of Anne's possessions and hopes for the future.

Ironically, and hopefully as a sign of brighter days ahead for Anne, the duration of her stay in the hospital had coincided with some lovely winter sun, albeit with cold mornings, which had lasted for many weeks and continued well into March. It was a relief for David to travel to the hospital in such uplifting weather. Added to that, the nights were getting lighter, but the outlook for Anne still remained uncertain. The two ambulance drivers, a man and a woman, introduced themselves by their first names. Once Anne had been transferred on to the ambulance stretcher, she was then taken through the corridors of the hospital, making her way to ground level in the lift before being made comfortable inside the ambulance. Two other nurses from the ward accompanied Anne down to the ambulance and said their goodbyes. One of the nurses – with whom Anne had developed a keen friendship – held her hand and wished her good luck. For the first time in two months Anne was outside, and she felt the invigorating spring air circulating round her face. Anne took a deep breath, as if all the tension of the last few months was being released, and she silently thanked God that she had made it through one of the most traumatic and dangerous periods of her life – and that she had escaped the hospital.

However, Anne knew only too well that her real journey had only just begun, and that she would be on it for the remainder of her life.

Once Anne was positioned in the ambulance and all the necessary documentation had been filled out, they began the journey home, with the female ambulance attendant driving and the male attendant in the back looking after Anne and chatting to her. Her journey consisted of a short stint on a motorway, then another ten miles along country roads before Anne came to the familiar surroundings of her village. As she looked through the darkened windows of the ambulance, she could see that nothing had really changed and everybody was still going about their business as normal. The ambulance then turned into her road. Suddenly a sense of trepidation engulfed her and she wondered what the future really held. Would she be able to stay at home, or would the inevitable happen and she would be placed in some God-almighty care home? The thought of being in one of those places – with indifferent staff, a small room and nothing to look at but her wardrobe and the television – filled her with absolute fear, and she asked David to promise that she would not be sent to one. Everything was suddenly a terrifying thought.

David had decided to meet Anne at home

rather than travel with her in the ambulance. That way he had a chance to talk to the care agency once more, and to show them around the house, pointing out the equipment that had been installed and answering any questions that were outstanding. He had yet to meet the full-time carer who would be looking after his mother, so he agreed to stay on until she came, despite having to travel back north that afternoon. For David, seeing his mother being brought into the house on a stretcher from an ambulance was quite unnerving; all he could remember was her fiercely independent personality and her capable mindset. But now it was his turn to step up to the plate and give her the best care possible. He was aware of horror stories of home carers abusing their elderly patients, robbing them of their possessions and giving slap-dash care, and this had played on his mind during the process of finding a carer. He took it upon himself to have surveillance equipment installed that would make sure everything remained above board. There were seven outdoor cameras and ten indoor cameras on a network, with sound recordings that he could access from anywhere in the world via his phone or laptop. There were no hidden cameras – everything was visible – so if any carer was stupid enough to step out of line they only had themselves to blame. A female friend also had full remote access to this system as well. Despite being miles away, this gave David control and reassurance. He hoped he would never need to use these devices to prove a point, but they were there nevertheless. The house was also gated to prevent any unwanted visitors, and the outdoor areas were illuminated throughout the night.

Anne was pushed through the spacious hall and into the main living room, which had everything Anne needed to be comfortable, with space either side of the bed. The ambulance staff placed Anne on her bed and collected their equipment before saying their goodbyes and wishing Anne luck.

'You have a nice view of your garden,' one of the carers said, but Anne did not reply. She suddenly felt apprehension about whether this decision was the correct one and asked to speak to David alone.

Shortly after Anne had spoken to David, two carers from the agency came in and introduced themselves formally to Anne. They were middle-aged women, one called

Prue and the other Fran. They were both competent and friendly, and they quickly put Anne at ease, even engaging her in a brief chat. Anne was relieved, for these two carers were the type of person she'd had in her mind's eye and she now looked forward to meeting her live-in carer with renewed confidence.

Anne suddenly became tired from the journey and the events of the morning, so she closed her eyes and nodded off. But she was only asleep for a few minutes before she woke again and glanced around her once-familiar room and noticed that her bookcase, which had contained books by her favourite authors, was gone. A coffee table with a beautiful Chinese rug underneath – gone. Comfortable easy chairs dotted around the room – gone. Her lush green carpet – gone. In their place was a sterilised electric hospital bed, a menacing looking hoist and a newly laid laminated floor. The bed sheets were unusually coarse and she was lying on some type of air mattress. Oh, the indignity of it all, she thought. Prue and Fran busied themselves around the bed. David was on a video call in the dining room – Anne could hear his voice but could not see him. Suddenly another car drove up the drive and two more women got out, they opened the front door and came into the lounge. They introduced themselves as the manager of the care agency, a polite and personable woman who seemed used to dealing with people, and a senior called Adele – bossy but knowledgeable. David came through to the lounge to speak to both of them.

The manager touched Anne's hand in a reassuring gesture before saying, 'We've got a lovely girl to look after you, Anne.'

'What?' Anne frowned. 'Girl?'

The manager continued, 'Yes, she's lovely and can't wait to meet you.'

Anne was surprised that the girl was not already there, and she asked why.

'We like to give people a chance to settle back into their home before being introduced to their carer. It's just the way we do it,' the manager explained.

Anne did not necessarily agree, but she held her tongue. As to the sort of person it was going to be, she could only hope, but the description already given did not raise her hopes.

As she was thinking those thoughts, a white car drove up the drive and parked next to the garage. There was a slight pause before the driver's door opened and a young, attractive, blonde-haired woman wearing sunglasses emerged.

Annette De Burgh

TWO

It was mid autumn and Anastazja looked across to the village square from the door of her parents' shop in Gdynia, Poland. The weather was a little grim, the summer sun had disappeared and the mundanity of her life returned. Anastazja lived with her parents above the family's general store, which had been passed down the various generations of her family. Her father and mother now worked there seven days a week, twelve hours a day. Turning, Anastazja caught her reflection in the glass-fronted shop doorway, noticing her hair drawn back into a ponytail, her face with light touches of make up and her eyes – behind ever-present dark glasses – piercing and beautiful. Anastazja, or 'Stasha' as she was preferred to be called, always wore dark glasses, and they somehow added to her attraction, for she was a slim twenty-seven-year-old who had the agility and appearance of someone much younger. She was a keen athlete, and enjoyed cycling, hill walking and – whenever she could – swimming in the Baltic Sea, which surrounded the area where she lived. She was an eye-catching young woman whose appearance attracted admiring glances from both sexes.

However, despite initial appearances, Stasha was not entirely happy within herself and was far from contented. She glanced back to the interior of the shop wondering what else her life had in store. How odd it was that she returned here after leaving some years ago. For some, it was regarded as an ironic failure to return to their childhood bedroom after a failed relationship, and this was the difficult and depressing position that Stasha now found herself in.

Men! Why was everything their fault? It was a familiar thought of hers.

Stasha had met Filip three years ago and romance soon flourished. Filip was tall, handsome, of slim build and – as Stasha had remarked at the time – nicely spoken. His family were like hers, respectable and hard working; they owned a small hotel in the next town, and Filip worked in the hotel and did general labouring work at weekends. It was hardly a stellar career for him but he was content, and more importantly he loved Anastazja and couldn't believe a woman like her had fallen for someone like him.

It was not taken for granted that she would marry Filip, but over the eighteen months of courtship it was perhaps inevitable that they would become engaged and a wedding would be planned. Stasha wished to travel the world then settle down, plant roots and think about starting her own family, so the two families got together and began to plan the wedding. A traditional Polish wedding had been planned carefully – a date had been set and a venue booked, and the excitement was building.

Stasha did not consider herself an unintelligent woman, for she had studied well at school and gained good qualifications, and she had gone on to university to study media. She had also taken an English course and now spoke the language competently. To supplement her income Stasha worked in the family shop and also at a restaurant situated not far away at weekends and some evenings. She was prepared to put in the long, hard graft, build some savings and put down some foundations. It all seemed so well planned and well thought out and, as Stasha was an only child, the day she married Filip was going to be extra special. It was something for everyone to look forward to.

Around twenty months into their relationship Stasha discovered some slight cracks developing between herself and Filip; they were not necessarily red flags but they indicated to Stasha that she and Filip were perhaps not on the same page about various things. She tried hard to ignore her gut feeling that all was not well and attempted to compensate for certain failings. Filip was not as ambitious as she was and seemed quite content to work at the hotel all his life. Housing was another bone of contention, with Filip talking of a flat and 'a wait' before starting a family. Stasha wanted more; she had seen what was on offer in other countries and ultimately wished to get to the UK, where she had heard – rightly or wrongly – that the pavements were paved with gold and there were opportunities aplenty.

But again, differences with Filip surfaced once more when it became clear that he wished to remain in his native country.

It was therefore perhaps inevitable that Stasha's engagement to Filip broke down, and this left Stasha without any direction. Worse still, there was no longer any wind in her sails.

After licking her wounds, Stasha decided to pursue her dream of getting to the UK. Staying in Poland meant Groundhog Day, and she wished for more challenges and felt she was better than merely waiting on tables. So she began the task of collecting the paperwork from the British Embassy in Warsaw for an electronic travel authorisation visa and then visiting the passport office to check she had the correct documents. Once granted, Stasha could enter the United Kingdom.

Stasha did worry about how immigrants would be viewed in the UK, but it was not something she would dwell on, for she would earn her place in their society by working and paying tax – and that was good enough for her.

But there were some doubts, especially after learning about the experiences of other young women from her town who had made the exact same journey. The main contention was that accommodation was difficult in the UK, with landlords demanding large deposits for what turned out to be mediocre properties. More worryingly, the jobs that were on offer were not anything to get excited about. There were suggestions from parents whose children were already in the UK that she could look for work in a factory then move on from there. It was not the career Stasha had envisaged, but beggars could not be choosers.

So with her heart broken and not mending quickly, and her future unsettled, Stasha set up a new life in the UK using savings she had set aside for the wedding, only to find – once there – that the warnings she had received about life in the UK were correct, for it seemed to be anything but a land of golden opportunities, especially for low-skilled people like herself. Stasha soon discovered that the grass was not always greener on the other side, for her concerns regarding UK housing stock had been – if anything – underestimated; in reality, the accommodation offered to her was tired, overpriced and crammed, with landlords being very uncompromising. When doing her sums in Poland, Stasha had expected that thirty per cent of her earnings would go on rent; however, in reality it worked out at fifty per cent of her take-home pay – this was as far removed from the utopia she had envisaged as it could possibly be.

She thought that her qualifications would get her into some office work, administration, hotels or something similar, but it was not to be. Numerous interviews resulted in numerous disappointments. She had come full circle – after listening to the pitfalls of finding work in the UK and believing that it would not happen to her, she found herself working those infamous shifts at a non-descript factory that supplied other manufacturing plants across the West Midlands. It was mind-numbingly boring.

Stasha also experienced the high living costs of the UK, so she reluctantly agreed to more permanent shift work that started at eight o'clock every morning and did not finish till three thirty in the afternoon.

The work entailed working in a factory that assembled luxury car seats, and her job was to test that the electric mechanisms were working correctly by moving the seats back and forth and up and down. During the day, she must have looked at a couple of hundred car seats, all similar and all doing the same thing. Monotonous was not the word for it and she hated it. While there was a chance for mixing and communication with fellow workers, albeit only at break times, Stasha found she had little in common with her workforce, despite being polite and friendly. Other than a few male workers, she hardly spoke to anyone. The irony was that she was working at testing luxury car seats – but it was her intention, one day, to actually sit on one as the owner of the car.

So it was a vicious circle. Although she had achieved part of her ambition, the reality was a dreary treadmill day after day.

It got worse. Stasha's zero-hours contract, often given to unskilled workers who could easily be replaced, offered no security, no future and no reasonable way to plan her financial life. It was a hand-to-mouth existence, living pay packet to pay packet with little opportunity to save any meaningful amount. Stasha knew she was not getting paid what she felt, as a person, she was worth, and it was a source of irritation to her and a continued disappointment – she felt she had let herself down. Despite the upheaval of the move, the breakup of her engagement and all the work it had taken to relocate, the basic facts were that she was doing the same type of work that she could have easily obtained in Poland. She had not progressed, just landed herself in another country. So life in England had not gone according to plan. Why had she thought it would be different for her? She should have taken note of other young adults from her town who had returned after experiencing the pitfalls of UK life – surely she would not go back to her parent's shop with her tail between her legs?

As if there was not enough on her plate, Stasha also found that making friends was hard; there seemed to be many social clubs offering all kinds of experiences, but Stasha was a reticent person and found making new acquaintances difficult, although many wanted to be her friend. Usually, some deadbeat guy would try and chat her up anywhere from the supermarket to the local petrol station, but she had already worn that type of T-shirt – and had got rid of it.

She bought a small non-descript white car on finance, started to re-decorate a house that wasn't hers and – on impulse one Saturday afternoon, after she had decided she needed some company – decided to rehome a cat, and so paid a visit to a cat shelter. There were a great many cats looking for new homes, but the one she settled on was a beautiful eight year old female black tortoiseshell, with orange eyes, who had come in that morning and whose elderly owner had recently passed away. The cat was already called Daisy, a name Stasha would keep.

It was a new relationship for Stasha, for *you are never alone when you have a cat,* and Stasha cherished the time she had with this new 'person' in her life.

Every afternoon, once her job was complete, she would drive the twenty-mile journey home along busy roads; then, once home, came the ordeal of trying to find a parking space outside her house on the narrow terraced street. Then, once inside, she was greeted by a cold, empty house, save for the gentle welcoming purr of Daisy, who would always be sitting on the window ledge or the stairs waiting for her. But the evenings were empty and Stasha knew she had to make some effort by joining local clubs and local communities; her neighbours were also from foreign countries and, while polite and friendly, they didn't wish to know her and she didn't wish to know them.

Stasha, despite already having an enviable, slim figure, decided to join a gym, but after being on her feet all day at the factory, the last thing she felt like was spending an evening working out and watching everybody else trying to lose weight and become fit – especially when she did not need to. However, in the end she did attend the gym and made one 'semi friend' who went for a coffee with her after her session. But it was nothing more than two people meeting for a chat.

Then Stasha decided to take up cycling, so she spent some of her savings on a lightweight bicycle. She pedalled off with renewed enthusiasm only to realise that it was a lonely hobby, so she decided to join a cycling club and become part of a group. There she met a nice group of people who we were friendly and accommodating. The only problem was that it exhausted her!

She also entered the local city's annual marathon and her run was completed in a respectable time. Halfway through the run, she had felt increasing fatigue but her steely personality helped her gain a second wind and the remaining part became enjoyable. Stasha was no quitter; she hated disappointing herself and was someone who always liked to have the ball in her court, who would argue her point to the very death. She hated to be beaten and it was this determination that drove her to try and make her new life in England a success. To some extent her dream had been achieved, but something was still missing, for she often felt unfulfilled and unhappy.

More than anything, Stasha wished for company and started to think of other jobs that would bring her into contact with more suitable people. This was slightly hindered by the fact that she felt self-conscious about her country of origin, and she sometimes felt people were unnecessarily judging her, saying that she was over here taking their jobs. Someone once shouted 'go home' at her and, although it was said in jest, it struck a chord and hurt her feelings.

Thinking about her new career, she had dismissed a lot of possible jobs. Then one day she noticed an online advert for live-in carers. The job required you to help people in their own home. It seemed quite interesting and she mulled it over for the next few days while working on auto-pilot at the factory. She emailed the company and was granted an interview. The job entailed much more than merely making cups of tea and sandwiches – the work that the agency required was highly responsible and very underpaid, with very high expectations. For Stasha, it was certainly very different to the job at the factory but, despite the low rate of pay, there was a humane element in being a carer that attracted her. Here was a situation where she could help somebody else while at the same time helping herself. Perhaps she would look after a sweet old lady with lots of interesting stories to share. That would be nice.

She had telephoned her mother to discuss her indecision about whether to continue at the factory or apply for this position. Her mother, Stefania, ever sensible with her advice, had pointed out the difficulties involved; there would be intimate personal care involved with the patient which she might find hard, and she might be called on unexpectedly at night and at other times. Then there was the patient; she had decided she did not want to be looking after a man, and that she would much prefer a woman – but what would happen if they didn't get on? Although Stasha had a soft personality and a quiet voice, she was no pushover and could be like a dog with a bone if she felt she was in the right. Stasha was sure that the person she would be looking after would be grateful and welcoming. Perhaps it was a win-win situation.

Stefania had also pointed out that there would be a lot of confinement in the job, and that on some days she would not even be able to leave the house. And how would she continue with her hobbies, like her cycling? Maybe the house would be cramped, dirty and unwelcoming. There was so much to think about.

Ten days passed with Stasha's mind going back and forth. Should she or shouldn't she? Then one evening at nine o'clock she decided she would become a full-time carer. The following morning she contacted the agency again and they asked for a further interview and references. Police checks and other paperwork took another ten days, before she was given a uniform, training and phone numbers and was told what to do in an emergency. During the training, she learned how to move a patient by hoist, check their position in bed and do personal care. She shadowed other carers for a week to understand what was expected. It was challenging, but Stasha knew that she would be quite good at the job, for most of it was common sense. Now it was up to the agency to match her with the right patient.

There was another period of waiting before the care agency got in touch with her to say there was an elderly woman who had been in hospital for many weeks. She had suffered a major stroke and was looking for twenty-four-hour care. The one proviso was that there would be no pre-emptive meeting, so Stasha was asked to come to the house on the first day to start work on a short trial basis without seeing the patient first.

Other carers would be involved with the patient's daily routine – so it would not be just the two of them.

Stasha was given the address and the name of the patient, and on the following Saturday afternoon she drove to the house out of curiosity. To her surprise it was on a tree-lined lane comprising houses with long drives and expensive cars, which had a general feeling of affluence. The village was also pleasant. Suddenly Stasha asked herself whether she could really do this. These people were an unknown to her and they had garages that seemed to be bigger than her house. Her mother's ever-present advice always reassured her, so she decided to text her. She had to think about what to say, for Stasha's mother wanted to learn the English language as well as her daughter had, so she insisted Stasha texted her in English, which was not easy at times.

STASHA > STEFANIA
Been to see my new client's house, not what I had thought, not sure now

But Stasha's curiosity was ignited, and now – with the name and address of the patient – she sat down one night and searched her name on the internet. Much to her surprise, the person she was looking for appeared at the top of the search engine. She clicked on the first result and was immediately taken to her website, for she was a writer who had written numerous publications, including novels. There was also a picture of her – she looked younger than her age. Stasha found her books for sale with glowing five-star reviews on numerous web outlets, and she seemed to have a large following in the USA. This all surprised her, for it was not what she had anticipated, and after seeing the house and the road she knew that this was not the sort of proposition she had previously considered – in her mind, this patient might be fussy, demanding and impossible to get on with, as well as rude. Stasha admonished herself for being so prejudiced, but somebody like that could be hard work.

As always, she telephoned her mother and asked her to look at the websites. Her mother was encouraging and said it would be an interesting experience for her. Stasha felt a little more confident, but deep down she knew there could be troubled waters ahead – this patient could either be someone very amicable and easy to get on with, or she could be someone who would want her own way and would not be afraid to express her opinions. Stasha hoped it was the former, as she could do without a battle of wits. So, still with her broken heart and with arrangements made for Daisy to be looked after by a neighbour, Stasha packed the possessions she needed for the three weeks, got in her car and made the short journey to her new patient's house. There was a sense of trepidation as she turned the car into the drive and drove up to the front door.

STASHA > STEFANIA
Arrived. Wish me luck!

STEFANIA > ANASTAZJA
Deep breath!

She adjusted her sunglasses, that were actually mildly tinted, in the rear-view mirror and opened the car door. She was welcomed with a smile from one of the managers who had come out to meet her. Stasha was quickly put at ease.

She entered the house. A spacious hall

greeted her and she immediately felt the warm atmosphere. She was directed into the lounge and saw the hospital bed with a figure lying on it.

THREE

Stasha was shown into the uncluttered lounge, which featured a dual-aspect window and, at the far end, doors that led to a comfortable conservatory. It was a warm, welcoming room and not what Stasha had expected. She glanced down at the elderly figure in the bed.

Stasha quickly assessed Anne. She looked as if she was in her mid seventies as opposed to ninety one, and Stasha considered her a woman of small stature. Suddenly Anne's eyes looked her up and down with immediate suspicion.

The manager broke the silence and said, 'This is Anastazja.'

'Call me Stasha,' Anastazja said in an attempt to break the ice, but Anne frowned and did not hold out her hand to meet Stasha's.

There was an immediate awkward atmosphere that was felt by everyone in the room.

'Stasha?' Anne said with quiet disapproval in her faint voice. She frowned. 'It sounds like some kind of disinfectant.'

'Short for Anastazja.' Stasha shot another

smile at Anne but it was not reciprocated and, feeling suddenly unsure, she glanced at the manager for reassurance.

'We all shorten our names,' the manager said by way of an explanation, but Anne disregarded the statement and continued to cast a scornful eye over the young woman.

'What is your name?' Anne said the words slowly and with a deliberate intonation on each word.

'Anastazja,' came the reply.

Anne quickly assessed the foreign accent saying, 'Then that is what I will call you.'

It was not a good start, for this comment immediately got Stasha's back up, but Anne was not finished.

'And where on earth do you come from?' came the waspish question from Anne.

The manager stepped in with a comforting response. 'She is from Poland, Anne.' The statement was meant to derail Anne's line of questioning, but it failed to do so.

'Have you been a carer before?' Anne persisted with the difficult questions, her voice now gaining more strength and determination. 'You look like you have just come off the catwalk.' Anne coughed, and gently shook her head.

Stasha was dismayed, for she suddenly felt the atmosphere turning very quickly to open hostility. She did not like this woman and was considering walking out.

Fran and Prue returned from the kitchen and said their goodbyes, saying they would see Anne sometime in the week.

Anne watched them leave before saying to Stasha, 'And what makes you think you can be my carer?'

Stasha knew she had to give a convincing answer. She steadied herself and rested on the side of Anne's bed rails, leaning towards Anne, 'I wished for a more fulfilling career.' It was a short answer and Stasha knew it had thrown Anne for a second or so.

'And what was your previous career?' Anne said with emphasis on the word career, for it was obvious that Stasha had not had one.

'I worked in a factory,' Stasha replied. She realised that it sounded very different from being a carer.

'And tell me, Anastazja, did you wear sunglasses in the factory where you worked?' It was a biting query.

Stasha shook her head.

'Well take them off in my house,' came

Anne's abrupt reply.

It was not a good start for both of them. Anne and Stasha had got off on completely the wrong foot and, while Stasha was prepared to indulge Anne and shrug off this awkward initial meeting, Anne did not feel the same way. On first acquaintance Anne did not like Stasha; she thought she was too young and had no experience of being a carer, and that she was someone with whom she would certainly have nothing in common. Anne had the choice to reject this carer immediately and ask the care agency to find someone else, and with this in mind she asked to speak to David alone.

The manager and Stasha went into the kitchen while David and Anne discussed various things. After ten minutes it was decided that Anne would give Stasha a chance, with provisos, and Stasha was informed that sunglasses were not to be worn in the house, there was to be no loud music and no visits from boyfriends, and no inappropriate clothing was to be worn.

One thing that did surprise Stasha was that Anne had requested that she did not wear a uniform. 'I am not in a care home,' Anne had said.

Stasha was, however, infuriated by the stipulations that were put before her. She had only been in the house ten minutes and immediately it was like she was back at school. This was not what she had wanted and again it crossed her mind to walk. The brief exchange she had had with this so-called 'patient' was enough to test anyone's patience and she asked herself whether she was up for the mental fight she was now envisaging with this difficult elderly woman.

With this thought in her mind she asked to be excused and went back to sit in her car. Once inside she texted her mother:

STASHA > STEFANIA
Nightmare

Shortly after the text was delivered, her mother telephoned her, and they both spoke about the new predicament Stasha suddenly found herself in.

'I don't like her,' Stasha said simply down the phone, 'she's Middle England and a snob.'

Stasha's mother listened to her grievances and reassured her that as it was early days (like twenty minutes), urging her to try and persevere with the situation. She did, however, admit that first impressions did count and were always difficult to overcome.

Within half an hour of meeting each other, neither Anne nor Stasha had liked the other, and neither had wanted the arrangement to continue. Stefania eventually managed to cajole her daughter into giving it a try, so Stasha, like Anne, accepted the situation. Both of them had been persuaded to compromise a little and accept each other – but how long would that last?

Stasha went back into the lounge, and tried to eliminate the bad feeling, but Anne could not read the situation and said, 'You're not what I was expecting.'

Stasha shrugged, 'I think I am aware of that, Anne.' There was clipped tone in the voice. Stasha's defences were up.

Anne raised her eyebrows, 'Can you make a decent cup of tea?'

Stasha attempted a smile to remove any of the discomfort she felt. The atmosphere was so tense it was palpable, but she walked forward towards the bed and involuntary touched Anne's hand. 'I will try my best, Anne,' she said.

The manager smiled at the action and then David came in and offered to show Stasha the house. Stasha quickly replaced her sunglasses on to her nose and the managers accompanied them. David showed Stasha all the door locks, security system and key codes.

The house surprised Stasha. It was well furnished with lots of pictures, but what was more apparent was the warm and welcoming atmosphere. It was clean, tidy and well maintained. David was outgoing and trusting, and he showed Stasha how to operate the electric gates, and how to understand the house alarm and all the other appliances. He then said something that gave Stasha a start.

'The house,' he said in a Scottish accent, 'both inside and out is covered with cameras and audio recording equipment, which I can access from anywhere in the world. It is for your safety and my mother's security. There is also a female friend who also can access the cameras and recordings remotely.'

Stasha frowned, 'You'll be listening and watching us?'

'Everything is recorded and kept for a period of time. This way there can be no misunderstandings.' David's tone was adamant, and he continued. 'Nothing is secret – it is all out in the open. I rarely watch anything and never listen, but it is there if I wish to.' As an afterthought, he added, 'If anything is disabled, I will immediately be notified on my phone.'

David moved them out into the garden, and Stasha was shown the keys for the greenhouse and shed and the garden furniture before they all returned back to the lounge where Anne had fallen asleep.

Stasha's bedroom upstairs was large with built-in wardrobes. It had been recently decorated, and there was an en-suite shower room, a toilet and a view over open fields at the back. The rest of the upstairs comprised empty bedrooms and what looked like a large office that had been cleared of papers and files – everything was well decorated with some interesting pictures. There was a second staircase and the whole house seemed warm, with the central heating on, even on such a warm day. It was a reasonably large house and Stasha could not help but think how self-indulgent it was, given that Anne could not even go upstairs. Surely having such a property was a little selfish. Stasha reckoned it would be worth quite a bit. Stasha thought of her own parents, whose living conditions were crammed and at times uncomfortable. How unfair life was.

The managers said their goodbyes, David had one last chat to Anne and then the house was empty – just Anne and Stasha were left.

Stasha sent a text to her mother.

STASHA > STEFANIA
Cameras everywhere, not pleasant

'Anastazja!' Anne called from the lounge.

Stasha went in to see her, but before she could say anything Anne asked once again for her to remove her dark glasses.

Reluctantly, Stasha removed them, but she was less than thrilled at the request, and Anne was less than thrilled that she'd had to ask again.

'I would like a cup of tea and some cake?' Anne asked, not seeing the look of concern on Stasha's face

'There's no cake in, I'm afraid.'

Stasha saw Anne's face drop.

'No cake?' Anne said in disgust, and Stasha merely shook her head and shrugged. 'Not a very good start is it?' Anne pointed out, but Stasha replied saying she'd only been in the house for an hour or so and hadn't had any time to get food in. 'But you're meant to be looking after me, Anastazja,' answered Anne.

Stasha had to bite her lip at the way Anne said her name. She wanted to tell Anne that it was her family's responsibility to make sure the house was full of food before she had arrived. But most of all she just wanted to leave.

Anne suggested that Stasha go out to the shops and buy something.

'I can't leave you on your own,' came the reply.

Anne snapped, 'Well just make me a cup of tea then.'

Stasha went back to the kitchen and quickly texted her mother.

STASHA > STEFANIA
I am not staying

Stasha prepared her first cup of tea for Anne. She took particular care doing it and delivered it to Anne on a bed tray. She smiled as she placed the tray carefully over Anne's knees and sat her up in the bed.

'I don't use a cup and saucer. Bring it in one of my mugs please,' came the reply.

Dutifully Stasha returned to the kitchen, opened one of the cupboards and retrieved a large mug into which she poured the hot liquid from the cup. She then returned and placed the mug on the tray in front of Anne before going back and retrieving her own cup of tea, for she knew this was the first chance she would have to speak to Anne properly. But Anne was not finished with criticism yet.

'Far too hot,' Anne said as she almost spat the liquid out, and for the second time Stasha returned to the kitchen and put some more milk into the mug. When she returned this one, Anne's expression showed she was not enjoying the taste of the tea. Stasha stood in front of Anne's bed and attempted a disarming smile. She also noticed that Anne was having difficulty drinking from a cup and made a mental note to see what other options were available.

'You don't look your age,' Anne remarked.

'I could say the same about you,' Stasha replied, but there was little response from Anne.

'So you're single?' Anne asked as she glanced over Stasha's figure and hands.

'It is complicated.' It was all Stasha wished to say at this stage.

'Life usually is,' Anne said under her breath to try and make it sound humorous, but it did not work and it only served to irritate Stasha.

'Have you done anything like this work before?' The questions kept coming, as Anne was now curious about this slim, blonde young woman in front of her. In Anne's mind, Stasha did not look like a carer, nor did she act like one. But, in her favour, she did have a relaxing voice. 'Do you know what I like to eat?' Anne asked, now heading for safer ground.

Stasha shrugged and Anne suggested that she read through the notes on what she could and couldn't eat again. Stasha repeated that the kitchen cupboards were bare.

'Well I suggest you log on to the supermarket and get some home deliveries arranged,' Anne suggested, 'can you do that?'

Stasha made to leave the room and as she did she heard Anne mutter under her breath, 'You couldn't hit the ground with your hat.'

Anne's off the cuff remark infuriated Stasha and she snapped, "What did you say?" her tone indicated her displeasure at what she considered was a disparaging remark, but Anne merely shrugged and said nothing.

Stasha went upstairs to retrieve her laptop and returned to the lounge to start the laborious task of setting up a supermarket account in Anne's name using Anne's credit card as payment. Then came the equally laborious task of asking what Anne wanted to eat. It was a guessing game to see what Anne liked and, at this initial encounter, no clear answer was forthcoming.

After unpacking Stasha went to the kitchen – which was spacious but a little dated – and looked into the cupboards to see if there was anything to eat. She telephoned the care agency office and explained the situation. The reply that she received was along the lines of 'sort it out yourself.'

Stasha managed to cobble together a makeshift meal. For her first evening she would present Anne with a bowl of soup and cheese on toast. It was not the meal Stasha wanted to give, but beggars could not be choosers, and it was the only thing she could manage using the contents of the cupboards. Tomorrow morning a supermarket delivery would arrive and she would be able to gauge what Anne liked and disliked, but in the meantime it was merely a guessing game.

So their first few days passed with each of them trying to get to know the other. It was a difficult process, for Anne liked to nap in the morning and at length in the afternoon. Stasha found her to have intelligence and, despite her years, Anne had remained sharp and knowledgeable. It was to be an uphill struggle. Unfortunately for Stasha, a battle of wits had started to materialise; this was not something Stasha had taken into consideration when applying for the job. Anne, it would seem, was no little old lady.

Stasha had sent numerous texts to her mother:

STASHA > STEFANIA
I just don't like this woman

STASHA > STEFANIA
She is rude!

STASHA > STEFANIA
A most ungrateful person

Stasha had decided to arrange twice-weekly supermarket deliveries so as to keep Anne's food fresh, but even this had been fraught with problems, since Anne's credit card had been declined due to an expiry date issue, and they could not locate the replacement. David provided his, but Anne kept changing her mind about what she wanted, so large amounts of food were ordered but not wanted – something Stasha disapproved of. The whole process of ordering food should have been a twenty-minute task, but with Anne's indecision the whole episode had lasted an hour.

Slowly, the two of them were getting into a routine together, although Stasha felt there was an undercurrent in their fledgling relationship, mostly on Anne's part. What did surprise her was that Anne offered to buy all the food Stasha chose for herself on the weekly shop – mainly expensive vegetarian dishes and some nice cheeses. It seemed like an uncharacteristically thoughtful gesture from Anne, but then Stasha knew she had still not got a proper read on this woman.

The routine in the house was starting to establish itself, for it was evident that Anne did not like change, and so Anne's breakfast, mid-morning snack and lunch were basically the same day after day.

Their interaction was still stilted, with large gaps of silence peppered throughout their conversations. Stasha had answered all Anne's questions at least twice over. Neither woman would back down, and more often than not Anne would say, in her weak, croaky voice, 'Anastazja'. Hearing the name spoken like that had started to grate on Stasha's nerves and only renewed her resolve to wear the dark glasses around the house even more.

'I've asked you to take those glasses off when in the house,' Anne said on one occasion.

Stasha swiftly replied, 'I will take them off when you start calling me Stasha.' There was a challenging tone in her vice and short pause from Anne.

'Well, we will be both waiting a long time, won't we, Anastazja,' Anne admonished.

In these early days, it had taken Anne a few days to become accustomed to her house, and she found it strange that she would never go upstairs again. Anne had asked David about having a stair lift installed and he, in turn, had contacted the hospital and asked for their advice. The reply was that such a device would be unsuitable for Anne, so nothing had been installed. This meant that only the ground floor and garden were accessible to her. Anne tried not to think of Stasha upstairs on her own. She wondered how everything was. Were the rooms tidy? Were the carpets hoovered? She didn't know. Sharing her home with Anastazja was difficult. Anne found her moody, unresponsive and quite deliberately awkward at times, but the rigid routine that was emerging might be of benefit to both of them.

Every morning Stasha would wake at six thirty and glance at the portable CCTV monitor to check if Anne was comfortable before showering and preparing herself for the day ahead. This time in the morning had become precious to Stasha, as Anne was still asleep, and it allowed her to prepare the house and herself for what would undoubtedly be another day of point-scoring, with Anne trying to belittle her at every turn.

The latest criticism was that Stasha had not been fitting the pillowcases correctly. Stasha had been too quick and sometimes put the pillow cover on inside out, and more often than not with the flap incorrectly positioned. It was a small detail that Anne had started to observe each morning and it began to irritate her. If a job was worth doing …

'It's not how you do it, Anastazja,' Anne would say repeatedly, deliberately saying the name slowly. Through gritted teeth, Stasha would remove the offending pillowcase and re-fit it properly; it was all time consuming and totally unnecessary in her eyes.

'You wouldn't do as a chambermaid, Anastazja,' Anne had taken to saying as she perched in her wheelchair observing Stasha as she struggled with the bed sheets while the other carers tidied the room. Anne knew that Stasha was in charge when the other carers were present and deliberately played on this by finding nit-picking faults with various things Stasha was doing.

Mentioning 'hospital corners' was another one of Anne's favourite put-downs. 'Don't suppose you have ever heard of them, have you, Anastazja?'

Stasha was absolutely sick and tired of Anne using her Christian name in the way she did. She wanted to scream at her to stop doing it and continued to ask on numerous occasions to be called Stasha, but the request was still stubbornly refused. Why do this? Why would Anne not call her by her preferred name? It was all so petty, she thought.

'No, I haven't heard of hospital corners, but I'm sure you're going to tell me what they are,' Stasha replied in a polite but peeved manner.

Angelika was the other carer who had helped out that morning, another eastern

European from Lithuania who – amazingly – Anne got on with. Angelika was more intelligent than she let on, a good efficient carer who always struck the right balance. She noted Stasha's irritation and stood back, becoming amused at the scene. The atmosphere was not pleasant. Angelika felt that Anne was being a little harsh but she also felt that Stasha was mishandling the situation.

To Stasha, it felt oddly contradictory that Anne got on with Angelika, and also with another eastern European called Ligi. Ligi was a no-nonsense character that Anne had immediately warmed to. Ligi handled Anne well, and always with respect. She was someone you could never ignore, a lively and charismatic woman who soon became a welcome member of Anne's care team.

All of this irritated Stasha even more, and fuelled her suspicions that Anne was deliberately targeting her for fun.

'Sheets folded under each other to make a corner around the bed,' Anne said.

'Well, thank you for telling me.' Stasha bent down again and redid the corners of the bed. 'Happy now?' she asked and looked at Angelika, who smiled but would not be drawn on saying anything.

Breakfast was served and Anne read the paper.

'Is she still calling you Anastazja?' Angelika asked outside as Anne was busying herself with her breakfast.

Stasha nodded. 'She does it deliberately as she knows it annoys me, but I put my sunglasses on and that annoys her.'

'How are you getting on with her?' Angelika said.

Stasha didn't wish to disclose too much. 'It's difficult, Anne's very demanding, but I won't give in to her,' she replied stubbornly. 'She hates it that I come from Poland, but is okay with you and Ligi.' She rolled her eyes and shook her head in despair.

As Angelika left, Stasha sent a quick text to her mother.

STASHA > STEFANIA
Can anyone dislike someone as much as I do Anne?

When Stasha returned to the dining room to check that Anne was having her breakfast, she was met with the usual frown and the complaint that, 'My tea is too cold.'

Dutifully Stasha returned to the kitchen and

put some warm water into Anne's tea.

'You're very sulky this morning,' Anne remarked as Stasha returned.

'I didn't have a very good sleep, there's a lot on my mind.'

'Probably looking for another job,' Anne said under her breath.

Stasha shrugged, not wishing to be drawn in to another verbal sparring match, so she left and went back to the kitchen to tidy up.

'What job would you like to do Anastazja?' Anne attempted to shout from the table to Stasha in the kitchen. It was faint, but Stasha picked up the question and returned to the dining room.

'I like this job,' she said quietly, and there was a hint of sarcasm in her tone which did not go unnoticed by Anne, who raised her eyebrows. 'I like looking after you,' Stasha continued. There was a touch of a sardonic smile on Stasha's lips and she momentarily stepped back from the situation. She had won that round.

Part of Stasha's routine was to find time to speak to her mother every night, relaying the day's events and how – in her opinion – Anne had treated her. She would tell her mother all the little digs the Anne had managed to get in and how at times she felt worn down by the constant criticism and difficult atmosphere. The lack of a thank you or any type of gratitude was difficult to take, and she knew deep down that Anne didn't like her that much. She recalled how another carer called Lacey had said in a reassuring voice that Anne very much 'needed' her, and there was a difference.

The other bone of contention was Stasha's use of latex gloves; they were blue and very noticeable, and for some reason Stasha had started wearing them all the time in the house.

'Is my house that dirty, Anastazja, that you feel you need to wear those gloves all the time?' Anne had remarked one morning.

Stasha did not reply.

'I would prefer that you removed them, especially when you're serving my meals,' Anne said, 'we're not in an operating theatre.' Anne laughed at her own remark, but Stasha pretended not to hear and left the room.

Then started the petty arguments over television. Anne liked to watch soaps, which surprised Stasha; it seemed to diminish Anne's intelligence to become engrossed in daytime soaps with meaningless stories and ridiculous characters. When something came on the television that Stasha would like to watch, Anne – more often than not – would rake up any excuse to interrupt Stasha from watching it, whether it was to get a hot water bottle, a glass of water, a cardigan or some toast, any excuse would be used to stop Stasha concentrating on the programme.

Although there was a second sitting room with another large smart TV, Anne had asked Stasha to stay with her in the evenings, as she did not like watching television on her own.

When Stasha seemed to be interested in a programme and Anne wasn't, Anne would ask for the remote control to be passed to her, then she would struggle with one hand to switch the television off. If Stasha complained, Anne would say, 'It's my television.'

It was one of Anne's most hurtful remarks, and she was unaware of the despair in Stasha's eyes. Stasha refrained from retaliation, she just reluctantly held her tongue and did whatever Anne wanted. But it got under her skin.

The other carers who visited the house were a mixture of middle-aged and young women; all seemed good at their job with varying levels of dedication and compassion. Some were memorable, others were not.

Adele, who had seen Anne on her first day, had asked Stasha why she became so rattled when Anne called her by her full name.

Stasha looked over her shoulder to make sure Anne was not listening before saying, 'I am only ever called Anastazja by my mother, and she says it in a particular way that is comforting and welcoming. When Anne says it it just grates on my nerves, and I feel it is an intrusion on my feelings when she will not abide by my wishes and call me Stasha.'

Adele raised her eyebrows; she'd not realised how hurt Stasha felt over this particular matter.

Stasha now looked at the clock, and she knew the time was coming for yet more personal care to be done at lunchtime; these calls interspersed her day and the personal care of any patient was a difficult and intimate procedure, both for the caregiver and the patient. Dignity was the most important thing, and although Stasha had been trained for this procedure, it had been mentioned that various problems could arise, so preparation and a calm head were key. The environment had to be relaxed and the patient's needs had to be met with the minimum of fuss. It was not pleasant work and was mostly overlooked or underestimated when one considered the job of carer.

Stasha momentarily cast her mind back to the first time she attended to Anne's needs on her very first day. It was obvious to anyone that Anne and Stasha had not had the easiest of starts, and now Stasha had to do the most intimate personal care imaginable after only three hours in the job and several waspish exchanges with Anne. She was petrified and felt sick at the prospect of what lay ahead.

The tea call was Stasha's first time with Anne and she waited nervously for the other carer to arrive; since Anne was so severely disabled, two people had to attend to her. In preparation for this and with shaking hands, Stasha gathered all the things she needed together, but she still felt a growing apprehension and a sense of nausea. Yes, she had shadowed other carers to learn the best procedure, but now, when she was in charge, it all seemed very daunting. Her mother had said to her that when she eventually had a baby she would have to do the same thing, but Stasha had pointed out the babies could not answer back. That was what she was anxious about – what on earth would Anne say to her if she messed it up or hurt her?

It all seemed such a long way away from working in the factory, but she knew that if this part of the job was not for her then her career as a carer would be over before it began. Stasha was relieved when the other carer arrived – it was Prue, the one who had welcomed Anne back to her house that morning. Prue was pragmatic and offered guidance but Stasha still had to do all the personal care herself. So she prepared the specialist cream, a new incontinent pad, toilet rolls, wet wipes, clean towels, waterproof bed pads, latex gloves, replacement trousers and hot water.

Prue gave Stasha visible encouragement and reassurance, Stasha pulled on her gloves, stood over Anne's bed and slowly pulled the bed sheet back, then began to remove Anne's trousers.

At this stage, Anne's eyes never left Stasha's face.

Stasha was shaking with nerves, but she was determined to see this task through. Gently, and hopefully with care, Stasha went about the personal assistance that was required – she was helped by Prue talking to Anne, but Stasha was nervous and it showed in the manner in which she carried out the task. Prue guided her, but Stasha felt nauseous and momentarily closed her eyes. Quickly, she pulled herself together and the nerves soon passed; Anne was freshened up and made comfortable before being hoisted back into her wheelchair.

Anne turned to Prue and said, 'Thank you.' Prue smiled gratefully back at her. But there was no such gratitude for Stasha, who began to help Prue clear up and put everything back in its place ready for the next time – which was in four hours.

Suddenly Stasha felt a strong sensation of wanting to vomit. She could not hold it in any longer, so she dashed out of the room, through to the kitchen, out through the back door and into the rear garden. Once outside, Stasha bent over and vomited all over the patio – then she regained her composure, attached the garden hose to the tap and washed away all the sickness.

Prue came out to the garden and placed a comforting arm round Stasha's shoulders saying, 'You'll get used to it.'

Stasha would have given anything to hear a thank you or a well done from Anne, but it was clear none was forthcoming. Now with more calls under her belt, Stasha felt more confident – it showed in her growing competence – but there were still no favourable comments from Anne.

The afternoon went reasonably well, although Stasha was very wary of Anne's sudden changes of mood, and her unpredictability. At five minutes past five she saw headlights coming up the drive and she knew it was the second carer coming to help with the tea time call – it had not seemed as if much time had passed since she had done Anne's personal care at lunchtime. But all was not lost, for the care agency had contacted Stasha shortly after she had started working at Anne's to inform her that on some occasions two carers would attend to Anne's personal care so that Stasha could go and do something else. Why there had been this change of instruction was not clear, but it was very welcome.

This evening it was the turn of Lucy and Sallie to attend to Anne's needs. These were a same-sex couple. Sallie – or Sal, as she was known – was the manager's daughter. She had a genuinely caring and considerate manner – an attentive carer who always had the patient's best interest in her mind. Lucy was experienced and efficient. Both women were good, stimulating company, and Stasha realised they would soon be integrated into Anne's care routine, and that would be no bad thing.

As Stasha prepared the evening meal in the kitchen, she could hear the laughter from Anne as both Sal and Lucy were talking to her. Sal took Anne into the dining room in the manual wheelchair, and it was not long before Anne started to watch the early evening television.

However, the continued lack of courtesy from Anne had started to irritate Stasha more and more. Yes, she was the caregiver, but she was also a human who had feelings; common courtesy cost nothing and she was surprised that a woman like Anne, living in the area she did, lacked this very basic decency. Stasha pondered on this as she busied herself with the evening meal. Why would a woman like Anne feel that saying thank you was so beneath her? It was two simple words, and Stasha had heard Anne saying those very words to the district nurse and to other carers – in fact, anyone but her.

The food Stasha served always generated a

few negative comments; Anne merely pushed the plate away when she was finished. Stasha often wondered if Anne considered her a servant? After loading the dishwasher and cleaning the kitchen surfaces in preparation for dinner, Stasha began to feel disillusioned and uncertain about whether she had chosen the right path. She looked back to the dining area. Anne was engrossed in a television programme. She wondered what it was about Anne that got under her skin so much, and that had affected her so vehemently and so early in their relationship. Was it, perhaps, more of a failing on her part? Maybe Stasha thought so little of herself that all she craved was appreciation. It was true that Stasha was tremendously disappointed with the course of her life – wiping an old woman's bottom in her large house was not something she had envisaged. She momentarily felt disgusted with herself and Anne's ivory-tower attitude did not help.

Was Stasha jealous of Anne and the life she undoubtedly had? Was she resentful? Or was it that Stasha was *waiting* to be insulted? Was she *waiting* to be irritated, and was she *waiting* to be offended? Would she, in the end, be disappointed if Anne turned round and gave her a compliment?

Or did she just want, more than anything, for Anne to like her?

Did Stasha have a chip on her shoulder, as an immigrant employed in someone else's house? Why are you over here taking our jobs? It was a question she could not answer, despite reading the thoughts of everyone she came into contact with.

It was dinner time, and the food was served. They ate in silence.

'That was awful,' Anne said as she pushed the half-eaten meal away – beans on toast was not something she was used to and was not something she would eat. 'Terrible,' Anne continued in a matter-of-fact voice and Stasha shrugged.

'Well you must tell me what you want,' Stasha replied as she cleared away.

'You must learn how to cook,' Anne retorted. 'Soggy beans on soggy toast doesn't cut it,' she said in a faint voice.

Stasha shut her eyes and counted to ten. More criticism from Anne. Would it ever cease?

'What's for afterwards?' Anne asked, and Stasha felt there was a certain mockery in the voice as Anne added, 'Don't say ice cream.'

Stasha pursed her lips. 'Rice pudding?' she offered.

'Out of a tin?' Anne asked.

'Well, I have not made it myself,' Stasha retorted as she left the room.

'Probably because you couldn't,' Anne said under her breath.

Back in the kitchen Stasha couldn't muster the inner strength to argue, but then she could not find the tin opener, so they could not have rice pudding after all. In desperation, Anne agreed to have ice cream.

So passed another meal with Anne picking her way through the food and turning her nose up at vanilla ice cream that had been in the freezer since the year dot.

'You must tell me what you want,' Stasha said, for she was getting tired of preparing food that was neither appreciated or eaten.

'Well it's hard, isn't it, Anastazja?' Anne placed a deliberate emphasis on her Christian name, so that it would not be lost in the tense atmosphere, 'When you can't cook. I mean, you can open a tin and heat the contents, but that's not really cooking, is it?'

Stasha stood impassively in front of Anne with her arms crossed, 'Not easy when you change your mind every day, Anne.' Stasha raised her eyebrows. 'We will sit down and do the day menu again,' Stasha suggested, but Anne did not reply. Instead she heard Anne mutter under her breath that it was no surprise she was still single.

'I beg your pardon?' Stasha said, 'What was that you said?' Stasha's eyes were hostile but Anne said nothing. This time, however, Stasha was not going to let it go. 'You made a personal remark about me, Anne.'

Anne shook her head.

'You know nothing about me,' Stasha replied.

'Well I know you can't cook.' Anne raised her eyebrows, as she watched Stasha search for something appropriate to say.

'You know nothing about my life.' Stasha was now like a dog with a bone.

'You're single,' Anne retorted, 'Nobody wants you.'

There was a pause and Stasha turned on her heels and left the room after collecting the dishes from the table.

But Anne was not finished. 'I am not ten,' she said. 'I want something more than ice cream, for that seems your sole suggestion.' Anne paused. 'You should be more prepared.'

Stasha heard the remarks. She entered the

kitchen and slammed the dishes down on the table. 'You're a white, middle-class English woman who acts like a ten-year-old,' she said under her breath. She was weary of Anne's back-stabbing comments and was beginning to form an even stronger dislike for her, which she knew would have to be kept in check. How she wished right now that she was back working at the factory.

They sat watching the remainder of the six o'clock news, as ever in silence.

Anne surveyed the sulking Stasha and assessed her. She was undoubtedly an attractive young woman, with a nice smile and good teeth – but to Anne it was that chip on her shoulder that loomed large and was ever noticeable.

'Why are you single?' Anne asked again out of the blue.

Stasha shook her head, "It's been complicated.'

'So you keep saying,' Anne replied. 'Maybe it was your cooking or lack of laughter.'

Stasha continued to eat the remainder of her yoghurt but refused to be drawn into another edgy conversation.

'I'll have another cup of tea,' Anne said, somewhat disappointed that Stasha would not rise to the bait. 'A better one than this afternoon, please.'

Stasha went to the kitchen and busied herself with the dishwasher and cups. She poured a strong cup of tea, went back into the dining room and placed the mug of tea in front of Anne. She waited and secretly counted to ten. Sure enough, Anne could not refrain from criticising.

'Not milky enough,' Anne said.

Later, when they were sitting down in the early evening, Stasha decided to turn the tables on Anne. 'I've seen you online,' she said and was rewarded with a look of surprise on Anne's face.

'You've been nosey,' Anne said.

'I've seen what you have written,' Stasha could not resist saying.

'Stasha, I am watching television,' Anne suggested, ignoring Stasha's curious questions and ending the conversation.

FOUR

Stasha often wondered why life seemed so unbalanced and unfair. The situation with Anne seemed to increase this irritation by each passing day. Anne, so middle class and ever so complacent, in her mortgage-free home with a seemingly never-ending supply of central heating and electricity, while there were so many fighting to stay above the breadline. Anne's house, for example, was a family home which would be more than suitable for at least five people, although Anne was the only occupant. Stasha thought of her own house, a small rented two-up two-down with basic furniture, which was not particularly warm. Perhaps it was this resentment that Anne was picking up on; maybe Stasha was showing signs of the green-eyed monster. But she felt that she was in the right, and she was still baffled that the other carers, especially the younger ones, seemed to receive a far better reception from Anne that she had ever received.

Anne usually bedded down at around ten o'clock and was sound asleep within ten minutes. With personal care done and medication finished for the day, Stasha retreated to the second sitting room, where she would spend the rest of the evening alone.

But on one particular evening, Stasha had decided to have a good look around the house. Anne was asleep, so she started upstairs. The office and study had some lovely autographed pictures, but there were no personal documents lying around and she knew that David had cleared everything away. There were two desks, as well as some laptops, computers and bookshelves, but nothing that sparked her interest. All of the filing cabinets were empty, and the drawers had nothing in them.

The rest of the upstairs consisted of bedrooms and a laundry room, and there were boxes containing books and other paraphernalia. It was all tidy and clean. Since Anne felt the cold, the central heating was on upstairs as well as downstairs, despite nobody being up there during the day, and Stasha had had to turn down the radiator in her bedroom because it was so hot, especially with the unseasonal warm weather outside. There was a second staircase, more toilets and a large bathroom.

The house also had Wi-Fi, CCTV, electric gates, electric window blinds and three garages that seemed to have once housed cars, but which were now empty, and there was an overall feeling of space. Such a large house for just one elderly woman. Satisfied that Anne was asleep, Stasha took a few photographs of the inside of the house and, together with the ones she had taken outside the previous day, she sent them to her mother. She soon received a text back.

STEFANIA > ANASTAZJA
Very nice – keep your head up

Stasha made herself a light supper and sat down with her laptop. She occupied her time doing some personal work and social media.

Stasha was thankful that Anne slept soundly for most of the night, enabling her to get a good sleep as well. The house was quiet of a night, since it was situated back from the road, so no lights came through the bedroom windows and there were few cars passing outside. There was only a humming sound from the office and the sound of the central heating switching on and off. Then there was the grandfather clock that seemed to chime all night long at ridiculous inaccurate times – Stasha found it an unnecessary distraction.

So Stasha's new day consisted of getting up to make sure Anne was comfortable, but not waking her, and then getting ready for the first two carers to arrive at nine o'clock to wash, clean, undress and dress Anne before placing her in her wheelchair, then propelling her into the dining room for her breakfast.

David had left a list of items that had been purchased and were due for delivery, or had been delivered. The list seemed endless, with Anne having the choice of either an orthopaedic manual wheelchair or a fully adjustable electric wheelchair with attendant support – but one item caught her attention: a wheelchair access vehicle that would be used to take Anne out and about.

On the first day, Stasha had talked with David about the delivery of this vehicle, and it was understood that the appropriate insurance would cover all of the carers who had a suitable driving licence, enabling them to drive Anne wherever she wanted to go. So this was to be delivered in a week's time and David had arranged for a one-hour tutorial for Stasha so that she could get to know the vehicle and drive it around with the delivery driver, familiarising herself with the controls. In doing this, she had to provide her driving licence and ID documents so that everything was legal. Stasha thought it was an extravagant purchase so early in Anne's rehabilitation, but she now could see how getting out of an afternoon would be a break for both of them, and she was mentally drawing up a list of places they could visit.

There had also been discussions regarding an additional shower room, but David had been hesitant; Anne was unpredictable, and you could never be sure whether she would like new things.

The agency did not feel so hesitant, saying that Anne would benefit from proper bathing, but it was a decision that could not be reversed, so Anne was reduced to having bed baths every morning. The social services had also offered to put in a ceiling hoist so Anne could operate the hoist herself, but David had dismissed this as ridiculous.

Amy, or big Amy, as she was affectionately referred to by her colleagues, visited Anne shortly after breakfast. She found Anne busy reading the paper. Amy was one of the senior carers and went about her role in a very diligent manner. An entertaining woman in her mid thirties, Amy had a happy young family and a very modernistic mindset. The reason regarding her visit was to make sure Anne was receiving the correct medication. This was confirmed by Stasha who showed Amy the prescription medicine Anne took daily. Amy made a few notes and had a brief humorous chat with Anne before leaving.

Amy obviously knew about the difficult relationship Stasha and Anne were enduring – but she remained professional and said nothing, something Stasha was grateful for.

Anne watched her drive away, knowing Amy would not stay at the agency long; she was ambitious and capable, a good administrator with a humane touch thrown in and was clearly destined for greater opportunities.

After Amy had left, Stasha pushed Anne into the conservatory. It was a warm and sunny late spring morning; the doors to the garden were open, and the atmosphere was peaceful and relaxed. The rear garden was of an adequate size, with colourful plants and a natural pond with a waterfall and the soothing noise of trickling water. Stasha sat down across from Anne. Then came the unexpected comment.

'Did you have a good sleep?'

Stasha nodded.

'Have you settled into your room?' was another question.

'It's very nice,' Stasha replied, 'trying to keep it tidy.' There was a slight nervousness in Stasha's tone.

'I do have a cleaner. Mrs James.'

Stasha raised her eyebrows.

'She comes every Monday and Thursday.'

Stasha frowned. 'She wasn't here last week,' she said.

'It was your first few weeks, I did not want too many distractions, so David cancelled her.'

Stasha smiled. To Anne it was a warm and friendly action, and there was just – perhaps just – a very faint flicker of an understanding between them.

Stasha thought that maybe she had misjudged this woman. Maybe she was quite nice and tolerant after all. Or maybe not.

'Bring me my vitamin drink, please.'

The instruction broke through her thoughts.

Stasha went to the kitchen cupboard, retrieved what was required and then mixed a multi-vitamin drink in a glass with water. She brought it back to the conservatory and then returned to the kitchen to make herself a cup of coffee. When she returned she decided to ask Anne some questions.

'How long have you been widowed?' she asked.

There was no response from Anne, then her eyes looked up and met Stasha's.

'A long time,' Anne said.

'Do you miss … is it John?' Stasha asked and recognised immediately that it was a stupid question.

'I lived with him for forty years, so of course I miss him.'

'David works up north?'

'Yes.'

'You've got a lovely house.'

There was a pregnant pause. 'What you mean Anastazja is that I shouldn't live in a big house because I am old and alone …'

'No, I'm just saying that well …' Stasha stopped. 'It's a very nice house you have,' Stasha repeated in an attempt to smooth over the suddenly awkward talk.

'And where do you live?' Anne asked quizzically.

'Not far from here,' Stasha sighed. 'I rent.'

Anne detected a slight bitterness in the reply as she observed Stasha. She had small, delicate hands and that relaxing voice, although Anne would never say that to her.

She was an immigrant, Anne accepted, and she was going to ask a little more about her, but she decided – in a rare moment of consideration – to leave the questions for now.

There was no getting away from the fact that Stasha had not been the type of carer that Anne had anticipated, yet she had to reluctantly admit that there was potential for her to become a good companion. Nevertheless, her stiff personality and ever-increasing resentment still did not endear itself to Anne.

For Stasha, these early days with Anne had been very difficult and she was now questioning her abilities on numerous occasions. Numerous calls and texts to her mother outlined how obstructive Anne was, and how there were two words that she had yet to hear Anne mention, and how mentally she was struggling more than she had thought.

Bizarrely, Anne spoke to David every day, and not once did Stasha hear Anne mention her dissatisfaction with the care she received.

Stasha looked forward to when the other carers arrived to help her with the personal care. This gave Stasha the chance to talk to someone other than Anne, who she described as an 'irritable old woman'.

The tea and bed calls today would be done by Leigh and Cian, who were affectionally referred to by Anne as 'the models'. Two glamorous young women who always came dressed as if they were going on some exciting date. These two individuals were the flip side of being a carer, both beautiful, entertaining and good company, and despite their long fingernails and delightfully lustrous hair, they went about their tasks quickly and were calming and thorough. Anne had started to look forward to seeing these two aspirational young women and would often comment positively to Stasha about them when they left.

'Those two are lovely girls,' Anne would often say, but these comments did not make Stasha feel any better about herself or the situation.

Stasha was astute enough to realise that Anne's contract with the care company was valuable, and that any complaint or suggestion that Anne was becoming difficult would no doubt be met little enthusiasm – and if she complained too much they would probably have no hesitation in replacing her with someone else. So she kept quiet.

Stasha had no choice but to live with the permanent tense atmosphere that had refused to go away. Neither woman would accept that she was responsible for it. Apart from brief periods like that morning, when Anne had been more sociable, Stasha remained unsure if the tense atmosphere was due to Anne's dislike of her or to the resentment she felt now that her life had changed so much. In any case, verbal battles with Anne were becoming the new normal. Stasha knew her English was good enough to equal Anne's in an argument, and she would do so if needed, for she always wanted the final word. Now, more than ever, that was becoming increasingly important to Stasha.

But for now, Stasha would have to continue to hear the sighs, the tuts, even when she had not done anything wrong. It was so demoralising. Having said that, Anne sometimes showed a very generous side. Once, she had literally placed the credit card in Stasha's hand, telling her to order anything she wanted, although she had added, 'My son checks the statement every month.'

Despite Anne having offered Stasha the opportunity to sit and eat with her of an evening – something Stasha had agreed to –

there remained a crippling, uneasy tension between them, which both women contributed to. Each wanted to have their say and a battle of restraint had already started with Stasha. She had to bite her lip so often it was becoming sore.

One of the evening carers had commented that when Stasha and Anne were in the same room, 'you could cut the atmosphere with a knife.' And she wasn't wrong.

Stasha's evenings were long; she didn't follow British TV, but she watched it nonetheless on the large screen in the rear sitting room whenever Anne was asleep. She watched the nightly soaps with Anne, trying to find some common ground that they could talk about, but just as she started to translate her opinion to Anne, Anne would become unnecessarily defensive. So it was a case of two steps forward and two steps back.

Anne also tried to find some common ground on which she could communicate, but she still struggled to warm to Stasha.

Anne continued to question her regarding her native country, with Stasha replying, 'As you know, I am from Poland.' There was a pause. 'And I am proud of my country.' Anne turned her nose up but Stasha continued. 'I left my mother, my home ...' Her voice had lost the friendly, relaxed air and a clipped tone had taken its place. She sounded exasperated. '... to come and look after you.'

'Well I did not ask you to,' Anne replied and turned her attention back to the TV. Then she could not resist adding, 'You came here as a foreigner.'

There was an uncomfortable pause, for Stasha felt the remark was over the line.

'I am an EU citizen,' she said, and with that she prepared to leave the room.

'Where are you going?' Anne asked.

Stasha bit her lip, 'Leave it, otherwise we're going to have yet another argument.' She took the tray that contained Anne's empty cup and plate and went back to the kitchen. Once there, she reached for her mobile phone and contacted her mother, making a mental note to telephone the office and complain about Anne's questioning.

STASHA > STEFANIA
This woman will not give up, another bad day

Suddenly Stasha felt alone and she wondered yet again whether this move and this career were the right choices for her, but her thoughts were interrupted by the sound of the bell signalling for her to go into the lounge.

'What is the matter, Anne?'

Anne said she was not comfortable in her chair so Stasha started to rearrange the cushions and reposition Anne. But she was still not happy, which meant that Stasha had to go through the whole procedure again. Stasha tried her best to rearrange Anne and make her more supportive on one side. She heard a sigh from Anne as she was moved. 'Is that better?' she asked.

Anne nodded but did not offer any vocal reply.

Stasha went back to the kitchen to finish clearing up when the bell went again.

This time Anne wanted a new handkerchief, so one was duly given to her.

The ever-increasing animosity – which was very subtle in Anne's tone – was slowly building again. Stasha remained peeved that Anne was not offering the same friendliness towards her that she witnessed when other carers visited, and Stasha herself, much to her shame, had noticed a tetchiness in her own replies, which was not characteristic of her. She sat down at the kitchen table with a warm cup of coffee and thought about the dilemma that lay ahead – should she stay or should she go?

What was frustrating was that Stasha would've been able to enjoy this new job if it were not for Anne. Should she leave and eventually look after someone else? Someone more grateful? Anne was merely a paralysed old woman who couldn't talk very well, and who had obviously had to alter her life dramatically since her stroke. Stasha thought of her own mother and how she would cope if this same thing happened to her; a shiver ran through her body, for it didn't bear thinking about. She thought of her home and Daisy – she wanted to bring Daisy here. The office had said no, but she wondered what Anne's reaction would be if she asked whether the cat could come and stay – somehow she felt it wasn't the right time to ask that particular question.

Stasha always checked on Anne first thing after coming downstairs of a morning. This time Anne wanted a drink of water, so Stasha went to get her one, but of course the water was not warm enough, so a second attempt was made.

Stasha placed the water down on the table

next to Anne's bed and prepared the house for the day ahead.

The daily newspaper was another of Anne's peculiarities, for she got annoyed whenever Stasha picked it up to read. 'What are you doing having a sandwich and a cup of tea reading the paper?' Anne had asked Stasha one morning when she took her seat in the conservatory. Before she could answer, Anne added, 'Do you mind me reading it or would you like me to pay you to read it?'

Stasha sighed and handed the newspaper over, which Anne had already read over breakfast. Anne was nothing if not predictable with her comments.

The routine of the morning was broken when Stasha received a phone call from David saying that Anne's adapted wheelchair vehicle was being delivered that morning from a local depot. David explained again that all the legalities of the vehicle were correct and that the running costs were all taken care of, and he reiterated that any carer with a suitable driving licence could drive it under the terms of the insurance.

At eleven o'clock, the vehicle – an adapted people carrier with blacked out rear windows – arrived. This vehicle had been specially designed to allow Anne to travel in the back in her wheelchair while meeting all necessary legal regulations. It was spacious, comfortable and brand new. The demonstration was quickly and efficiently carried out; Stasha was an astute learner, so she soon mastered all the pieces of equipment and the controls. It was an automatic, with comfortable front seats and a lot of gadgets. With the other female delivery driver sitting with Anne, Stasha drove the van around for a few miles before returning. She switched it off and signed for the delivery before letting Anne know that she thought the vehicle was nice and that she would like to go out in it that afternoon.

Anne eagerly nodded.

In early afternoon, with the lunchtime care call complete and after a light lunch, Stasha prepared the van, as Anne now called it. She wanted to get this right, with no mistakes, for she could see an opening for the days to become less confined to the house, and she wanted excursions in the van to be successful.

Anne was wrapped up in a summer scarf and sweater, plus a rug on her knees. She was pushed out of the house in her manual wheelchair, which had recently developed a very stiff rear wheel, to the drive, where Stasha had prepared the van for the short journey. Anne had been allocated a blue disabled badge from the local council, and Stasha made a mental note to take this with her and then leave it in the van.

'I hope you're a good driver,' Anne said, and Stasha joked that she hadn't even passed her UK test yet.

There was a look of surprise on Anne's face, not knowing if it was an off-the-cuff remark or the truth. She allowed Stasha to attach the electric winch that pulled Anne up the ramp and into the back of the van, then Stasha secured the wheelchair into position with special clasps, put Anne's seatbelt on, pressed a switch to electrically close the large tailgate and returned to the house. Here, she put the alarm on and diligently activated the gate cameras, then she returned to the van, climbed into the driving seat and started the engine. The van edged forward, the electric gates opened and they were both out on the open road. It was a sense of freedom for Stasha.

FIVE

Anne was the sort of person to notice everything and, to her surprise, Stasha was a good driver. For someone who had not been familiar with the vehicle, she drove it well, with confidence and safely. Anne was perched in the back, monitoring all that was going on. She saw Stasha at the controls and watched as she positioned the car correctly and drove not too fast and not too slow – it was a comfortable drive with no jerking and no sudden stopping.

Anne thought back to the days when she had driven and she gave an involuntary smile, for she was the only one in the family who had been caught for speeding twice – but then Anne was always unconventional and never stuck to the rules.

'I'll take you to the garden centre,' Stasha said, breaking through her thoughts. 'Would you like me to push you around there?'

Anne agreed, and once they arrived at the local garden centre Anne watched as Stasha carefully parked the van in a disabled bay. She then helped Anne out of the van.

Once inside, Anne came across Carol, who she knew from the village. Carol crouched down to be at the same height as Anne in her wheelchair and asked how she was doing. They conversed for about five minutes, but during that time Anne did not introduce Stasha or bring her into the conversation.

Before long, Carol got up and smiled at Stasha, then she wished Anne all the best. The incident played heavily on Stasha's mind for the rest of the afternoon.

It made Stasha feel worthless that she was not even worthy of being introduced to one of Anne's friends. Perhaps Anne felt that Stasha was merely a paid help and so not worth a mention. Anne must have seen Carol glance in Stasha's direction, noticing the young woman behind the sunglasses and wondering what the situation was. It was not for her to introduce herself, so she had smiled politely, but it was another of Anne's miscalculations, and they were mounting up.

But Stasha would not let it spoil the afternoon, and she continued to push Anne around in her chair looking at the plants and the numerous small shops that were housed within the garden centre. After a slow twenty minutes of wandering round Stasha suggested a coffee in the coffee shop and pushed Anne towards a corner table overlooking a water feature.

Stasha had noticed that Anne had been having difficulty drinking liquid from a normal cup. She had spoken to her mother regarding this and Stefania had suggested buying Anne a beaker with a spout, and Stasha had done this through the internet.

Stasha had pre-empted this problem and had packed the new plastic cup in her bag. Upon returning to the table, Stasha placed the plastic beaker in front of Anne. Pouring the tea from the coffee shop cup into it, she wondered if Anne would comment on her thoughtfulness, but all she got was a faint nod of approval. Anne didn't say anything, and Stasha smiled to herself, knowing that Anne couldn't bring herself – even on this occasion – to say thank you.

So Stasha had another string to her bow now in that she was able to take Anne out in the van for an afternoon – they didn't go out every day but it did break the monotony of their daily lives. Sometimes Stasha just went for a drive with Anne positioned in the back shouting instructions and telling her where to go, and more often than not Stasha got lost and a little exasperated at the constant orders. But it was a much needed break for both of them from the house.

Stasha's initial few weeks passed and she soon found herself approaching her three-day break period, which was designed to give live-in carers a rest and a chance to return to their own homes and fulfil any personal business they might have. With Stasha living only twenty minutes away, it didn't seem such a big deal to return home to her empty house, but she was looking forward to seeing Daisy and having a break from Anne.

However, despite Anne's peculiarities, Stasha would be lonely at home. The thought of who might replace her was playing on Stasha's mind. There were a number of girls in contention but Stasha soon learned that a very slim girl with long red hair had been chosen. The other carers described her as 'rough and ready' and she was called Candy.

Stasha could not contain her delight, for Candy was loud, opinionated and at times rude. She couldn't imagine a more unsuitable match for Anne.

Candy, who only visited infrequently, had come to see Anne in the two days before Stasha had gone home. She was very much her own person, sometimes inconsiderate, selfish and full of self-pity, and she barked questions at Anne in a loud voice during their first meeting. Stasha listened in the kitchen as she made the two of them a cup of tea, smiling contentedly to herself, for Candy was truly the opposite of what Anne wanted. Candy was, however, different to Stasha; she was more confident and more streetwise, and she gave the impression of someone who was looking for the main chance. She was a divisive member of the care company – you either liked her or you didn't. She had a good figure and a lightly freckled face and was attractive in her own way; she always wore her eye-catching long red hair pulled back to reveal a carefully made-up face, and she possessed a hard-nosed attitude to life, possibly because of her past experiences of being knocked down repeatedly. But the likes of Candy always got up again and carried on, and there was a faint smirk on Stasha's face when she told Anne that Candy would be replacing her for the three days. As Candy followed Stasha round the house pointing out the various rooms and facilities, it became clear that Candy was eyeing up every possession and mentally calculating its cost. How Stasha would love to be a fly on the wall during the next few days; she was absolutely certain that Candy and Anne would have one flaming argument after another because neither would give in and both felt they were right. Candy, unlike Stasha, had a fiery temper to match the redness of her hair. So Stasha headed home on the Wednesday morning and left Candy with Anne. As she drove out of the drive she laughed to herself and said that it was poetic justice that those two had got each other, and with that satisfying thought she made her way home to Daisy and to catch up on her life.

SIX

Stasha's three days of holiday went quickly. She was due to return on the Saturday morning, but she'd asked if she could make it the Saturday afternoon and this had been agreed, so at one o'clock she packed her bags, tidied up her house, drew the curtains, dropped Daisy off with her neighbour and got back into her car to drive the twenty-minute journey to Anne. There was a sense of disillusionment as she drove down the lane knowing that it was going to be another difficult time; she simply wasn't enjoying looking after Anne. There were no highs or lows – it was just the same day repeated. But what she was really looking forward to seeing were the remnants of the catastrophic fallout of Anne and Candy's relationship, and this had secretly kept her happy and content over the past three days, as she wondered how on earth those two difficult people were surviving with each other. She had secretly wanted to ring Candy to ask, but she had refrained from doing so in case she could not hide her delight at the misery Candy would no doubt have found herself in. She could only imagine the disagreements they would have had, and she wondered if Candy had ended up throwing something at Anne.

Slowly and apprehensively Stasha approached the house. She felt a little nervous as she turned into the drive and was met with shut gates – unusual, for they were usually kept open, except at night-time. Stasha got out and entered the four-digit code on the keypad. When parking her car on the driveway, the smile vanished from her face, and again she asked herself whether this was the right job for her. How much more of Anne could she take?

After parking, she entered the house. It was quiet. She went into the lounge – it was tidy but empty. The bed was made but there was no sign of Anne. The dining room – empty. The kitchen – empty. The garden – empty. Then she heard laughter in the background so she walked through to the other sitting room. There she was confronted by Anne and Candy and two other women sitting down enjoying afternoon tea. Candy was happy and animated and Anne was laughing. There was an undeniable air of relaxation, and it was not a scene that Stasha had anticipated. It irritated her.

Candy acknowledged her presence and the

other two women smiled, but it was obvious that Stasha was the intruder. As nobody had introduced her, she quietly left them all to it. The house was tidy and clean, and Stasha wondered if Anne had missed her at all, or if she even knew she had been away. The afternoon tea continued for another half an hour before the two women, who were neighbours, left. They barely acknowledged Stasha and, with Candy clearing up after them and putting Anne back on her bed in the lounge, Stasha felt like a spare part. Not a good start.

It did not get any better for Stasha, as Anne could not wait to tell her about her time with Candy.

'We had fish and chips one night,' Anne said excitedly, 'and Candy downloaded a porn film to watch – it was fun.'

Candy gave a self-satisfied smile and collected her things.

Stasha was astounded and could not believe what she was hearing; Candy had got a Chinese takeaway on the Friday evening, and they'd had another two neighbours round on Thursday lunchtime, with Candy serving food for them all. Then they had stayed up late that evening watching an absurd blue movie.

Stasha was spitting feathers. This loud abrasive person, who usually divided opinion, had seemingly found a way to get through to Anne where she had failed. The more she thought about it, the more it irritated her.

As Candy prepared to leave, she placed her belongings down in the hall before going into the lounge, bending down and kissing Anne on the cheek.

'Come back, won't you?' Anne said, and Candy nodded.

Anne watched as Candy's car drove down the drive.

'How are you, Anne?'

Stasha made Anne jump as she came into the room after unpacking her things upstairs. She couldn't help noticing that Anne had put on a little weight and looked more contented than she had before she'd left. This did not help to lift her mood.

'What?' Anne's reply was short, then she said, 'how am I?' and she watched Stasha lower the electric window blinds to prevent some of the sun shining on to her face. 'A lot worse for seeing you,' Anne joked. She did attempt to laugh, but it fell flat. Not to be deterred, she continued to stir the pot. 'I have had a lovely three days, with proper care.'

Stasha bit her lip; she hadn't been back in the house long and the brick-bats were already being hurled at her again. She was taken aback by the sting in the reply. 'I am glad you enjoyed yourself,' she said quietly, and there was a softness in her voice which indicated a certain resignation at being second best. Or was it just that she was feeling sorry for herself?

'Why are you whispering around me?' Anne said as Stasha went to the top of the room to rearrange the cushions, 'Candy shouted at me and I understood what she said. You whisper like some dormouse creeping around.'

Stasha stared at Anne for a second and left the room. She sent a text to her mother.

STASHA > STEFANIA
Still awful. Really don't know if I can go on

Stasha stood looking out of the kitchen window, a tear forming in the corner of her eye. Anne will not get me upset, she thought to herself, then she heard Anne's bell ring so she had no choice but to return and be the obedient servant – that was what she felt like.

'Why do you walk away from me when I'm talking to you?' Anne said. 'Did anyone ever tell you it's bad mannered?' Anne's eyes were harsh and there was no compromise in them.

'You are not talking to me,' Stasha replied. 'You were criticising me again, and I don't want to hear about your marvellous time with Candy.'

'She's a lovely girl,' Anne muttered. 'Had more fun with her than I do with you – and she doesn't wear sunglasses.'

Stasha left the room, this time a little more upset.

Back in the kitchen she opened the fridge. Lots and lots of cartons had been opened, together with unfinished pints of milk. Some cold meat had been put on the top shelf and seemingly forgotten about. Stasha decided to walk around the house to give it a little check over. On the surface it looked tidy but there were things that had been put out of place. Some of the drawers had been opened and the contents scattered and shifted through. Stasha went into the bedroom where Candy had slept. It was tidy and there was still the smell of her perfume, which Stasha thought was revolting. Her own bedroom had remained untouched, as there was nothing in it to go through, but Stasha got the impression that the office had been searched thoroughly. Drawers, filing cabinets and cupboards had been opened, but there was nothing to see. Stasha went downstairs and into the dining room. Then she remembered the indoor CCTV. Surely Candy hadn't been stupid enough to do anything under the gaze of the cameras? After all, there were ten in the house.

Anne asked what she was having for a meal.

'Mac and cheese,' Stasha said but didn't elaborate.

'That's all you can think of,' Anne replied and turned her nose up before returning her gaze to the window.

'I don't know what's changed, but you had macaroni cheese before I left. And you liked it.' Stasha stood in front of Anne with her arms crossed.

'Yes,' Anne replied. 'That was before Candy came and got me Chinese takeaways and pizzas. I thoroughly enjoyed them. You're a rotten carer.'

There was a brief silence.

'You can't swallow properly and you

should not be left on your own ...' Stasha snapped. If Anne wanted an argument then she would have one.

'For goodness sake,' Anne's voice was low but snappy, 'she was gone ten minutes, it's only up the road ... and I can eat anything if I do it slowly and have the right companion, not with you hovering around the table like some possessive waitress.'

'It's against company protocol to leave the patient on their own. She should not have left you on your own and she should not have—'

'She even got a couple of bottles of wine which we both enjoyed ...' Anne interrupted.

'She shouldn't have done that either.' Even to Stasha's ears, she sounded pedantic.

'You've been back no time and you are already boring the hind legs off me.' It was another hurtful remark from Anne that made Stasha turn on her heels and head to the kitchen.

'Go off and cry!' Anne shouted after her.

For Stasha, this was too much. She was still a little upset from her early exchanges with Anne, and all she wanted was to ease back into the role of carer and not hear constant griping from her patient. It was never ending. After the three-day break she wanted her relationship with Anne to be built on something more solid, but if anything her return had caused more anguish and mental disturbance. She wondered what Candy had done to get Anne on side. They did not seem to go out in the van. Perhaps they'd watched porn all day and eaten takeaways, she thought sarcastically.

STASHA > STEFANIA
I am leaving

The bell rang again.

Stasha, ever the obedient servant, trooped back into the lounge. 'Yes Anne,' she said brightly.

'I am cold,' Anne remarked.

Stasha went back into the kitchen, retrieved the hot water bottle and filled it from the recently boiled kettle.

'What's for dinner?' Anne asked again when Stasha returned.

'Well, I don't know. You don't want macaroni cheese. How about spaghetti?'

'Out of a tin?' Anne grimaced.

'Well I haven't made it myself, Anne,' Stasha snapped. It was now her usual reply to Anne's frequent questions about the food.

Anne pulled the bedcovers up to her chin and indicated that she wanted to have a doze. 'Close the door on your way out ...'

STASHA > STEFANIA
Just a horrible day

Stasha rummaged through the freezer and found some fish cakes. Anne could have them with some chips and peas. She momentarily thought of her next three-day break; it seemed weeks away and it would only mean Candy returning to enlighten and uplift Anne's dreary life.

Stasha thought of Candy – her personality, her demeanour, her clothes, her beautifully painted fingernails which seemed at odds with the work she did, and, most importantly, the hardship she claimed. But Candy had a confidence about her and an undisguised rough-and-ready attitude that Anne perhaps liked. Stasha was not like that and would not change. She resolved not to give an inch to Anne. It would be a fight to the death.

'Did you have any alcohol with Candy?' Stasha asked later in the afternoon, knowing fine well what the answer was going to be.

'A few glasses of wine, we had it together.

It was very nice,' Anne said.

'You're not meant to be on your own or have any wine or alcohol—'

'Oh, fiddle-de-dee,' Anne replied before Stasha could finish her sentence. 'I enjoyed it, that's all that matters. Don't be such a wet blanket.'

What did matter was that Stasha had a long and growing list of things to tell the office; she was unhappy with what had happened – maybe out of resentment or irritation – but she was nevertheless unhappy. Candy had given Anne alcohol, and had had some herself; it seemed to go against all the rules and guidelines Stasha had been given. Then Anne revealed that she and Candy had spent most of their time in the back sitting room, with Anne talking about the good old days and Candy interjecting some humorous stories. Annoyingly for Stasha, they seemed to really enjoy each other's company, and Stasha wondered, not for the first time, why she couldn't capture any of the same friendly spirit that Candy had brought to the house.

But then Candy had been born in England.

Their evening meal, in the dining room, was taken in silence, with just the news for company.

Stasha served the dessert, a rice pudding, and a cup of tea.

'Candy bought me a lovely cheesecake,' Anne said. 'She went out and bought it especially for me.'

Stasha shut her eyes. She was sick and tired of hearing about this wonderful person who could seemingly do no wrong.

'All I get from you,' Anne continued, 'is the same old food over and over again,' Anne sighed, 'you've been back five hours and it seems like a lifetime.' Anne shook her head. 'You are hard work.'

'You are instigating arguments, Anne, and I'm not falling for it,' Stasha retorted, and she was pleased by the look of surprise on Anne's face.

'Pfft,' Anne sighed. 'No wonder your single – you can't cook and you're no company.'

Stasha got up from the table, gathered together the dishes and left the room without saying anything. She went to the back door and stepped outside. She allowed the fresh air to circulate round her face and blow through her hair, letting the tears form in her eyes and wander down her cheek. She was not happy, but she would not give up – not her dignity, not her self-worth, not one ounce of anything for this ungrateful woman. It was Anne who she felt sympathy for, for her regimented, paralysed life. The thought pleased her.

Stasha could walk away, go on holiday and leave Anne to it. It was she who held the power, not the other way round. Wiping the tears from her face, Stasha returned to re-commence the duel.

Anne was pushed back into the lounge for an early evening doze, while Stasha went upstairs to sort the laundry out. While she was there, she received a telephone call from one of her own neighbours who had noticed that Daisy had not settled down and was in a distressed mood. This naturally unsettled Stasha, but she had no option but to tell the neighbour to persevere and comfort the cat.

The next morning, Stasha re-examined what Candy had left in the fridge – a lot of unopened products and half-eaten things – and then checked the food cupboards, which seemed to be unusually bare. There had been seven tins of soup before she had left, but now they were all missing. She had a look again in the fridge. Cheese, cold ham and sausages all gone – odd considering they both had takeaway for two of the three nights. The food that was missing didn't tally with the food that should have been eaten. Stasha had a look in the freezer; there had been three bags of chips, but now only one bag remained, and some shepherd's pies and bags of vegetables had disappeared.

There was one area remaining. Stasha went into the dining room and opened the desk drawer, taking out the metal cash tin. She retrieved the key from the ornamental vase on the side of the window ledge and inserted it into the cash box. Before she opened it she made a mental note of how much money should be in it: four hundred pounds in ten-pound notes. When she examined the contents, she found four hundred pounds in ten-pound notes.

The money had been untouched, but there was no doubt that food had gone missing from the fridge, the cupboards and the freezer. Should she ring the office or tell Adele who was her senior, or mention it to Anne? Or should she just keep quiet?

What else was missing? Stasha went to the guest cloakroom and opened one of the cupboards. Two bottles of liquid soap had gone and two bottles of toilet disinfectant as well. It seemed that Candy had been thieving while she was in the house, for Stasha knew that she had left things in certain places, and this indicated that they had been moved – and not through dusting.

She went to see Anne but she was still asleep so she had a quick look round the lounge. Nothing was out of place or missing. The hoover was empty, so it had been used, and the rest of the domestic appliances had been cleaned, so there was nothing untoward there.

Stasha started breakfast. No doubt she would have to fend off questions from Anne as to why they couldn't have a pizza and why they couldn't have fish and chips and why she was persistent in cooking her dreary meals night in, night out, whether it be pasta, eggs, omelette or something else – all the things Anne could eat easily.

During breakfast Stasha brought up the subject of Candy seemingly helping herself to various items of food, and she couldn't resist mentioning that food items were missing from the kitchen. In the seconds after she had said it, she wished she hadn't – it felt like she was grassing on a fellow worker.

'What are you saying?' Anne's voice was laden with accusation.

'I'm saying things are missing from the

kitchen, and as you couldn't have eaten them …' Stasha stopped mid sentence.

Anne looked up from her newspaper and glanced out of the window. She took her time to reply. 'I told Candy to take those things as she was in a predicament at home which was not very pleasant, so I told her to go to the cupboards and go to the freezer and take what you want.'

The reply stunned Stasha. It was something she had not expected, and she frowned before getting up, turning on her heels and walking back to the kitchen.

Sometimes Anne's actions perplexed her.

Another difficult afternoon followed and once Stasha had pushed Anne back to the lounge and placed her on the bed, she sat on the window seat and looked directly at Anne in bed. Crossing her legs in a calm gesture, she cast her mind back to the scene she had witnessed when she arrived back at the house, with Candy, Anne and the neighbours all in the back room. The scene still irritated her and she didn't know why, but if she was being honest with herself, she reluctantly recognised the feeling within her. She was jealous of Candy and her relationship with Anne – and that surprised her.

'I want to go out tomorrow,' Anne announced. 'I want to go to the local supermarket.'

Stasha frowned. 'What do you want to go there for?' she asked perplexed because she got all the food online, but she couldn't resist adding, 'Is it to refill the cupboards after Candy?'

The remark failed to hit home.

'What did you do on your days off?' Anne asked, changing the subject, but it was a cold-hearted statement, mentioned without any warmth or interest.

'Not much, just slept,' Stasha replied.

'Your life matches your personality.' Anne paused before firing her final shot. 'Boring.'

Stasha remained silent. She looked at Anne, their eyes met and she wondered if Anne took delight in making her life such a misery. Why did this old woman dislike her so much? It surely couldn't all be because of her nationality – was Anne that petty? Was Anne resentful of Stasha's youth?

Another silence engulfed them.

'Are you gay?' Anne asked suddenly.

Stasha frowned.

'Well?' Anne said with raised eyebrows.

Stasha laughed. 'You think I am gay?'

'There is nothing wrong with being gay,' Anne persisted.

Stasha laughed at the intonation in Anne's voice.

'It's a personal question, Anne, that I refuse to answer.'

'Oh you're quite pompous, aren't you?' Anne retaliated. 'No wonder you're single.'

'You have no right to talk to me in that manner.' Stasha's voice was raised as she became battle ready.

'You're in my house,' Anne replied.

'You invited me,' Stasha retorted. 'Treat me with respect.'

'Earn it.' Anne was annoyed.

'I have always—' Stasha managed to get in, but Anne interrupted her.

'You're not wanted here or in my country,' Anne retaliated.

'You can be very cruel with your words, Anne,' Stasha replied sharply.

'Well, you have to know words to be cruel, don't you?'

'So you keep saying …' Stasha gently shook her head in despair.

'You don't know half the English dictionary, do you, Anastazja?'

Again, the way Anne said her name ignited Stasha's temper, 'Here we go again, it's all about where I come from.' Stasha paused for breath. 'Well so you keep saying it, as if it's a disease that I am not British. Why does it bother you so much?'

Anne said nothing, then she attacked, 'Because you're an immigrant taking our jobs and taking our money from the health service. Go back to where you came from.'

'You're a nasty old woman.' Stasha raised her voice further and decided to continue. 'I've done nothing to you to merit these sorts of comments other than be born outside your beloved England.' Stasha walked off to the kitchen and once there momentarily closed her eyes. She was upset.

The bell rang.

Anne had started to cough and splutter. It didn't get any worse and eventually cleared up. Once again, Stasha mulled over the reason Anne didn't like her.

Was it because Anne was a middle-class widow who had no understanding of the poverty of working-class people? She may have lived through a world war but it had seemingly given her no understanding of human nature. Stasha wanted to say all this to

Anne, but before she could Anne was suddenly sick all over the bed covers.

Speedily, Stasha placed a white plastic protective apron around her, retrieved a plastic bowl and some clean towels and removed the jumper from Anne's body. She was met with numerous cries of 'You're hurting me!' even though she was being as gentle as she could. Once the jumper was removed, Stasha bent down with some hot water in a bowl to clean Anne. Fortunately, the bed sheets had been spared.

Anne started to ask questions, but Stasha told her to be quiet until she was finished.

'You never listen to the answers anyway, Anne.'

'Well, you come in like some robotic Florence Nightingale with various implements to clean me up, but there's not a crease in your brow and there's no smile in your eyes – not that I can see them behind your glasses. You don't like the job, do you?'

Stasha didn't reply.

Stasha took the soiled clothes and bed cover to the washing machine and, on her return, she was met with, 'Why do you walk out when I'm trying to talk to you?'

'I'm busy,' Stasha said.

'Where's Candy?' Anne replied as a parting shot.

Stasha went to the kitchen.

The bell rang.

Gritting her teeth, Stasha placed the bowl and cloth on the table, went to the washing machine and set a hot wash before returning to the lounge.

'I want Candy,' cried Anne.

Stasha returned to the kitchen.

The bell rang.

'I am cold,' Anne said.

'Would you like another jumper?' Stasha asked.

'Yes.'

Stasha went upstairs to the laundry room and retrieved a fresh jumper, then she returned to the lounge and carefully slipped it over Anne's head before putting the arms through.

Anne wondered what the other carers thought of Stasha. Was she liked or disliked? It would be hard to say, for when the other carers came Stasha didn't engage them in any meaningful conversation. But Anne never heard any tittle-tattle from the girls about her.

What the other carers did know was that Anne still did not care a jot for Stasha and the feeling was probably mutual. To Anne, Stasha was too cold and not genuinely caring enough. She was not a natural carer and had no redeeming qualities to make her one. It was just a job to her.

Anne couldn't remember if she had ever seen Stasha laugh. There was no laughter, or any noise for that matter, just a couple of sighs and tuts every now and then. Candy was very noisy, loud and sometimes unconventional – already Anne was missing her.

But behind the gruff exterior, Candy was a more natural carer, and there was always laughter not far behind her. Stasha, in comparison, seemed to shift around like some ghost, miraculously appearing when you rang the bell but otherwise doing little other than look at you and ask, 'Are you alright?' There was no spontaneity. To her credit, the house was tidy and she did everything that was asked of her, but it was not enough for Anne and she was becoming increasingly unhappy with the situation.

The next morning the district nurse telephoned saying she would be round to see Anne mid morning. When the morning call was complete and the second carer had left,

Stasha pushed Anne into the dining room for her breakfast. In doing this she, once again, noted that the manual chair was becoming difficult to push.

'Looks like a nice morning,' Stasha said and placed the morning paper more directly in front of Anne. Anne glanced down at the paper signalling that she did not wish to talk over breakfast.

'I want to go out this afternoon,' Anne said as Stasha left the room.

'Where to?' came the question.

'Oh, use your imagination,' Anne snapped and Stasha retaliated.

'Well if I turn right, you'll say turn left, and if I turn left, you'll say turn right ...'

'I'm reading the paper,' Anne answered, and Stasha knew she had been dismissed.

Stasha put Anne back on the bed for the appointment to have her skin looked at. The district nurse arrived on time – which was uncharacteristic – at eleven thirty and entered the room carrying masses of paperwork.

'She wants to check out your skin and make sure everything is in order,' Stasha said to Anne as she prepared her for the nurse.

'How are things?' the district nurse asked Anne, feeling a slight tension between carer and patient.

Stasha self-consciously smiled but the atmosphere in the room was stilted; it all seemed very cold and clinical – something the district nurse had not expected.

'Stasha's lovely, isn't she?' the nurse said to Anne.

'She's hopeless,' Anne replied.

'I try my best,' Stasha cut in and caught the expression in the district nurses eyes.

'She's not good enough,' Anne interrupted.

The district nurse began to check Anne's skin on her arms and legs not wishing to be drawn on the subject.

'You know Stasha should be working in a factory where she belongs,' Anne went on, and Stasha shook her head in disgust at Anne's statement.

The district nurse was embarrassed; the comments were unnecessary and very hurtful.

'How long are you going to stand there like a soldier on parade?' The question was directed at Stasha as she stood at the foot of the bed watching the nurse go about her business.

The district nurse announced that Anne's skin was all clear, then wrote the notes. Afterwards, she stood in the hall and whispered to Stasha.

'Don't whisper in my house!' Anne said from the lounge.

The district nurse raised her eyebrows and said to Stasha, 'I'll see you again.'

Once the district nurse had left, Stasha came storming back into the lounge to confront Anne.

'How dare you treat me like that,' she said, her voice a high-pitched, irritated scream.

But Anne was quick to reply, 'I suggest that if you don't like it, you go and look for another job, and preferably go back to where you came from and don't shout at me.'

Stasha was upset. She spun on her heels and, for the first time, she grabbed the lounge door handle and slammed the door behind her. It made Anne jump.

'And don't slam my door!' came the shout, but Stasha had already gone. She was out of the back door and standing in the garden. She could not stop the tears rolling down her cheeks.

STASHA > STEFANIA
I am so upset. This horrible woman has just worn me down, I can't understand her hate of me. Just sad

STEFANIA > ANASTAZJA
If that bad leave come home and see me

But Stasha would not throw in the towel. She wanted to get the better of Anne, and – if anything – she had become more determined than ever to see this horrible task through. With so many different carers coming to the house, Stasha was able to assess their different approaches and, in doing so, she was able to figure out what – if anything – she was doing wrong. It was now no secret within the group of carers that Anne and Stasha didn't get on, and that Stasha was finding it hard work looking after such an uncompromising and difficult patient.

The following two consecutive days had seen Samantha come to the house to help Stasha with the morning calls. Samantha – or Little Sam, as she was known – had slowly become one of Anne's regulars. It was clear from Samantha's very first visit that she was the most naturally gifted carer to come to the house. A distractingly attractive young woman in her mid twenties, Samantha was experienced, sympathetic and very empathetic.

Anne soon recognised Samantha's ability

and the two women quickly developed a mutual respect for each other. Stasha just didn't have Samantha's natural ability to care for people, and she knew she occasionally came across clumsily in comparison; the likes of Samantha didn't come along every day.

While it was clear why Anne and Samantha got on, the conundrum – of course – was Candy. Try as she might, Stasha simply could not understand why Anne had struck up such a good relationship with her.

Stasha had closely observed Candy and how she went about dealing with the many questions Anne hurled at her. She was demonstrative and somewhat cheeky in how she answered, but underneath it all she was someone who knew what to do and who had seen and done it all before. Grudgingly, Stasha admitted that Candy handled Anne well.

But her friendship with Anne continued to surprise and irritate Stasha, and Candy would often come to the house, whether she was on the rota or not, just to pop in and see how Anne was. She even offered to come back late at night to help Stasha with a late night call, but Stasha had declined the offer.

Stasha could not decide whether Candy

was completely untrustworthy and out for what she could get, or a person who was simply misunderstood. Probably somewhere in between, Stasha thought.

Anne seem to take great delight in never showing any interest in who the real Stasha was. Here was someone sharing her house and her life, and she wasn't interested in finding out anything about her – except for asking if she was gay. Anne would ask numerous questions to other carers like, 'Have you had a good weekend?' or 'How is your partner?' and other banter that was easily washed over, but Anne never asked about Stasha, her life, what she had done or what she wanted to achieve. Nothing – not even when Stasha was visibly concerned regarding the health of her mother, or when she asked for a twenty-minute break so she could phone her. Anne had agreed but there was no caring interest in her voice, just a brief nod of her head.

So when the other carers came four times a day to help, Stasha just remained quiet and listened to what was being said – or what was not being said as the case may be.

Sallie, for example, related events to Anne about her life with Lucy and her numerous pets – humorous tales that showed how close Sallie and Lucy were – and they always made Anne laugh.

Leigh was still deciding whether she wanted to learn to drive or not, and this dilemma became a talking point because more often than not Leigh would attend with Cian, and she was the most accomplished driver of all the carers – or so she thought.

And Samantha – the Pocket Rocket, as Anne called her – would often talk about her fishing trips with her partner. Both Stasha and Anne were equally astonished that Samantha, with her diminutive slim figure - who had the most sensual long hair, would participate in fishing, for she seemed the least likely person to have such a hobby. However, Anne always noted her enthusiasm whenever Samantha recalled her recent adventures in the great outdoors; in fact, the more Anne learned of Samantha, the more she liked her. How this young woman had overcome the various obstacles she had already encountered in her life was a real inspiration, resulting in Anne forming a very high opinion of her.

Then there were the photographs on the carers' phones; nearly all the carers showed Anne something or other – everyone seemed to have something to say and Anne always listened and tried to retain what was said.

The sisters, Emily and Dee were both entertaining and contented individuals. Cian was another character who impinged herself on Anne – a streetwise young woman who had the potential to progress into a successful career. But Anne wondered whether Cian would fulfil her potential, or allow herself to become lost in the often shallow world of social media.

Not to forget Maggie – such a happy character with a heart of gold. All Anne's carers were wonderful, compassionate human beings, all undervalued and all underpaid, but all very much appreciated. And then there was Stasha who, to Anne, resembled a mere lightbulb; Stasha's head could be easily exchanged for another one and Anne would not really notice, or even care. On the other hand, it was sad that Anne had made her feel so inferior to some of the other girls, when in fact she wasn't.

A few nights later, Anne had a bad time being restless and uncomfortable through the night. She rang Stasha twice: the first to get a hot glass of water and the second for a complete change of bed linen. It was on the second call at four, when Stasha was a little tired and the house was not particularly warm, that she felt very much undervalued. It was a difficult call which involved hoisting Anne off the bed and changing all the soiled bed sheeting. But instead of Anne being cooperative and considerate, she was the exact opposite. It all came out then. Stasha heard that she was a poor and harsh carer, an immigrant taking other people's work, someone who should go back to their own country – preferably on the next dinghy – and someone who was simply sponging off the economy. As Stasha continued to clean Anne up, the diatribe of cruel criticism continued: Stasha was hopeless and had a stupid accent, hard hands and an uncaring attitude, complete with a total ineptitude for anything she did.

As Stasha put new sheets on the bed, she said, 'You are the most vindictive old woman I've ever come across –'

'Well I don't want you here,' Anne interrupted.

'Well I don't want to be here anymore. I'm ringing the office tomorrow,' Stasha said with clear exasperation and emotion in her voice.

'You will have to wait your turn, I'll be ringing the office about you,' Anne replied.

Stasha continued the work, placing waterproof sheeting all over the bed and hoisting a clean Anne into position.

'I don't want to see you again,' Anne said and the harshness of the statement took Stasha by surprise. 'Don't come down in the morning just go.'

Stasha shrugged. She tried to think of something fitting to say but she was too upset to battle on. 'I hate you,' was all she could muster, but before she could leave Anne had the final word.

'I can assure you, the feeling is mutual.'

Stasha collected all the things together and gathered all the laundry then went through to the laundry room, filled the washing machine and switched it on for a hot wash.

She went back to the lounge where Anne still had no bed cover sheets on and was lying in her fresh nightwear on the bed.

'I'm cold,' Anne said.

Stasha paused for a moment; it was tempting to let Anne get really cold, but that would be entirely the wrong thing to do, so Stasha went to the airing cupboard and took out two warm sheets, placing them over Anne with a secondary clean blanket. She then went back to the kitchen to fill the hot water bottle, which she then placed on Anne's legs so it would warm her up quickly. She did all this without saying anything and the two women remained in silence.

There was no flicker of appreciation or recognition in Anne's eyes. In fact, she didn't look at Stasha for the last ten minutes of the call and they both worked together without saying a word.

Stasha had been devastated by the criticism. It was too much – just too much – to be awoken early in the morning, too much to be faced with a very dirty and gruesome scene of soiled bedding, and too much of the incessant, hatred-filled criticism from Anne.

Anne did not have dementia and she did not have any mental illness. However, her stroke had affected her thinking and what she said. But even after taking that into consideration, it was still hurtful.

When Stasha was satisfied that Anne was comfortable, she went back upstairs and had a gentle cry as she sat on her bed. This whole episode was proving to be the hardest thing she had ever done. Would Anne really get the better of her? And would she let her?

So the following day passed without much communication. It was clear to Stasha that Anne remembered the incident of the previous night, but had not got the good grace to say that she had been too harsh, or that she felt the need to apologise.

Neither had telephoned the office immediately.

Prue was the other carer on the morning call. An outspoken person who like Anne said what she thought; Prue's diligent time keeping was an example for all the care staff to follow as was her conscientiousness. Anne found herself agreeing with a lot of what Prue said and enjoyed her visits.

Prue, however, soon picked up the terrible atmosphere and tried to coax Anne into talking, but it wasn't successful.

After breakfast Stasha had second thoughts. She decided to ring the office, suggesting that they perhaps find someone else to look after Anne, and this resulted in the manager coming out to visit them. She listened to Anne and Stasha without prejudice. She managed to smooth over the situation with Stasha and tell Anne that she simply would not get a better permanent carer than Stasha. Anne liked the manager, who was always ready to listen impartially to any problems.

Anne shrugged. 'She's not English,' came the reply.

So, despite the manager's best efforts, Anne and Stasha's stalemate rolled on.

Anne did refrain from full-blown criticism, although she still nit-picked that the food was cold, the tea was too hot, the bed was too cold and she was not in the correct position. Or she didn't like Stasha's clothes, and her sunglasses were worn too often. Or she didn't like her breakfast. Or she wanted to go out, or to stay in.

The incessant drip, drip, drip of criticism continued.

But, with gritted determination, Stasha forced herself to carry on. Secretly Anne had worn her down and she was becoming more and more upset.

'You never come into the room with a smile on your face,' was the latest complaint from Anne.

Stasha smiled sweetly as she showed Anne her pills before unwrapping them and placed them in Anne's mouth one by one.

'I hope your hands are clean,' Anne said, and Stasha quietly shook her head in despair, for Anne had not noticed the clear latex gloves she was wearing.

In the early stages of their relationship, Stasha had used her gloves a lot until Anne asked her to remove them. Then Stasha had used her bare hands to serve Anne her pills, only to be told to wear gloves. She could do nothing right. But now she had taken to wearing clear latex gloves to administer Anne's pills again – in fact, Stasha had tried to accommodate all of Anne's criticisms, but there was always a new one popping up every now and then, and it was hard for Stasha to remember them all, never mind act on them.

'Why do you want to be a carer?' Anne asked one morning over the coffee and chocolate she enjoyed while watching daytime television.

'I like to care for people,' Stasha replied and she sat down opposite Anne.

'You want to *care* for people?' Anne replied in astonishment and raised her eyebrows. 'You couldn't care for a budgie.'

'I try my best,' Stasha kept saying, and there was an element of resignation in her voice.

'Well you never instigate any conversation, and you continue to creep around my bed like some ghost wearing sunglasses in an attempt to shield your eyes from God knows what.'

'More personal comments, Anne.' Then Stasha took her sunglasses off and Anne looked into her eyes. They were attractive and surprisingly friendly – they held no hostility.

'Don't hide your eyes away. They are beautiful, Anastazja,' Anne said involuntarily.

Stasha was floored. It was probably the very first compliment she had received from Anne and it felt good, but she was wary of what was coming next.

'Why aren't you married?' Anne asked for the umpteenth time.

Stasha refused to comment. She got up and walked across to Anne. 'You don't know my past so don't try and guess.' Stasha battled on, determine not to skulk off this time. 'Do you want me here?' Stasha asked suddenly.

Anne shrugged, 'You're not what I wanted.'

Stasha gave a resigning smile, 'Well, I could say the same about you; you're not what I wanted for my first full-time client, an obstinate and difficult old woman.' Stasha was surprised at her own statement.

Anne smiled, in secret admiration, for Stasha was at last saying what she thought. 'Drop a plate or something so I know where you are. You creep around the place.'

'I thought you wanted peace and quiet,' Stasha said.

'There's peace and quiet, and then there's you,' Anne retorted.

'I give up with you,' Stasha said and retreated back to the kitchen.

'That's right, walk out again,' Anne busied herself with the remote control and switched the sound of the television up so she couldn't hear the noiseless Stasha in the kitchen.

Candy was the carer on at lunchtime; she arrived early and put Stasha's nose out by making Anne a cup of tea, practically ignoring Stasha in doing so. Stasha still didn't trust Candy.

'Bring me fifty pounds,' Anne instructed when Stasha entered the lounge.

Stasha frowned. 'Why?'

'Because I want fifty pounds.'

Stasha looked at Candy, who refused to meet her eyes, then went to the desk in the adjacent room and retrieved fifty pounds from the cash tin. She came into the lounge and Anne told her to hand it to Candy. Stasha's frown deepened.

'Candy hasn't got any petrol in her car,'

Anne said, by way of an explanation.

'You're not allowed to give money to carers,' Stasha said pompously and looked at Candy, 'and you shouldn't be taking it.'

Anne didn't say anything but watched as Stasha reluctantly handed the fifty pounds to Candy, who took it and placed it in her pocket. She bent down and kissed Anne on the forehead.

'Thank you, I'll pay you back you know,' Candy said.

Stasha raised her eyebrows, this merited a phone call to the office. She didn't care whether she was grassing on another carer, what had happened wasn't right. The situation only fuelled Stasha's dislike of Candy.

'Don't undermine me again, Anastazja,' Anne said once she was back in her chair and Candy had left.

Suddenly, a wave of dizziness swept over Anne. She shut her eyes and Stasha noticed she had gone quite pale.

'I feel dizzy,' Anne said.

Stasha looked at her and immediately knelt down by the chair and placed her hand over Anne's.

'It's alright,' she whispered, 'I'm here,' and

for the first time Stasha noticed there was a look of appreciation in Anne's eyes, and she laid her head back until the dizziness swept over her.

For Stasha another side of Anne presented itself. Suddenly this person who was making her life so miserable had turned into a frail and nervous old woman in need of her help. Gone was the argumentative and caustic person who seemed to take great delight in arguing every point – someone who actively disagreed with everything on purpose – and in her place was someone Stasha momentarily felt real empathy for.

'Are you alright?' Stasha asked gently.

'I would like to go to bed.'

And with that Stasha quickly and efficiently transferred Anne from her wheelchair into the bed and covered her in a clean blanket. Once back in the bed, Anne's colour soon returned and her eyes took on a battle-ready appearance once more. Predictably, there was no thank you or appreciation for Stasha's concern or care.

SEVEN

Anne did not feel particularly well the following day and spent the afternoon sitting up in bed watching television. She had not engaged with Stasha, other than to ask for some refreshments mid afternoon, and Stasha had stayed in the dining room working on some personal paperwork.

Cian arrived on her own, driving her newly purchased Audi. She was delivering boxes of latex gloves for Stasha. Stasha offered Cian a coffee and they chatted in the kitchen until Anne called them both into the lounge.

'Thought it was you,' Anne said to Cian with a smile.

Stasha listened as Cian mentioned to Anne that she was having lip filler injected the following day. 'To make my lips fuller,' Cian said when she met Anne's querying expression.

'You're gilding the lily,' Anne replied, and Cian frowned, not understanding the meaning. Anne explained, and there was general chit-chat before Cian thanked Stasha for the coffee and said her goodbyes.

'Cian,' Anne whispered to herself as she watched her drive away, 'such a vibrant young woman.'

Stasha heard it but did not reply. She still wasn't interested in engaging Anne in any meaningful conversation, for their relationship still remained non-existent beyond the basic requirements of carer and patient. Stasha was nothing more than chief cook and bottle washer to Anne.

The previous evening Stasha, like Anne, had decided to have an early night and, after finishing her paperwork, cleaning up, locking the doors, switching on the washing machine and switching on the dishwasher, she climbed the stairs, went to her bedroom and got into bed. It was twelve thirty. Relaxing in bed, she heard the bell ring.

Stasha checked the monitor.

Anne was restless and moving around in bed. Stasha quickly put on her dressing gown and went downstairs.

'I am in a mess,' Anne said.

Stasha went over to the bed and pulled back the bedclothes to reveal soiled sheets. It was like a repeat performance of the other evening when they had argued.

Stasha closed her eyes, knowing the work that was ahead; firstly she went upstairs to the laundry room for the new bed sheets, a fresh mattress sheet, another waterproof cover, a new nightie and bed socks. Wearily, she came down.

'Where have you been?' barked Anne.

'Getting your new bedding.' Stasha glanced at the clock, it was close to one o'clock. Slowly she gathered all the things required to make the best change possible. She got water and cream, but then she looked down at her own clothes. I can't change her like this, she thought, so she dashed upstairs and put on a T-shirt and a pair of tracksuit bottoms. Back downstairs, Stasha set about the task, raising the bed and removing all of the bed padding, but Anne was not happy.

'I'm cold,' Anne said.

'Well, it's the middle of the night and the heating is off,' Stasha replied.

'Well go and switch it on,' Anne instructed.

'It's summer, it should be off anyway,' Stasha stated.

'I want the heating on now,' came the reply.

Stasha closed her eyes and made her way to the hall where she overrode the central heating settings, and within seconds she heard the radiators come to life.

'In the time it took you to do that, Candy would have been able to do it all and make me a cup of tea.'

It was not what Stasha wished to hear.

'If I hear about that bloody woman one more time I will leave,' threatened Stasha. 'I'm not sure why you keep bringing her into the conversation all the time.'

'I am comparing you to her,' Anne replied. 'And why do you get my hopes up saying you're leaving when you're still here?'

The remark stung Stasha.

'She would have been finished by now,' Anne couldn't resist saying.

Stasha said nothing but continued clearing up, cleaning up and tidying up. In the end, when it was all done, Stasha asked if Anne wanted a cup of tea.

'I will save that treat till the morning,' came the sarcastic reply.

Stasha checked that Anne was comfortable before heading upstairs to get some well-earned sleep.

Stasha went back to her bed, checked the monitor to see Anne was comfortable and lay back down. Not for the first time, tears pricked the back of her eyes. She closed them and wondered if she was doing anything wrong.

Stasha was not one for stepping back from a

commitment, but Anne was pushing her to the limit. Leigh and Cian, who often came of an evening, had mentioned the tension between the two women once again; Stasha was permanently walking on eggshells and Anne sounded unhappy. Leigh realised that both Anne and Stasha had short fuses, but they also fed off each others dislike and this loop of events would no doubt continue.

Stasha wiped a tear from her eye. Again, she momentarily contemplated handing in her notice, but that would be defeatism and would let Anne win, and that wasn't going to happen. Stasha's self-worth was fuelled by feeling wanted and being thanked, and she had made a promise to herself that Anne was not going to be the one to beat her. The breakdown of her previous relationship indicated that she was stubborn and not willing to compromise.

The irresistible force was now meeting the immovable object.

Unbeknown to Anne, it had taken Stasha a great deal of courage to leave her native country and come to the UK, and the sole reason had been to earn more money, some of which would be sent back to her family. It was not that she wanted to leave her country;

it was more that she had to leave her country to make any type of progress. Anne, with her large house and money in the bank, seemed not to care one jot for what she called 'foreigners'.

One of Anne's most hurtful comments, and there had been many over the weeks, were just two stinging words: 'go home'. Stasha wondered what continued to fuel the antagonism between the two of them. Again she analysed her own feelings, but she was just going over the same ground, letting the same events filter through her mind – it was not doing her any good.

Stasha inwardly laughed as she thought about 'the models', the two young carers who came to see Anne frequently. They had gained Anne's respect quickly and she had never heard Anne criticise them about anything. Cian had brought Anne flowers one morning and another carer - a lovely Italian girl called Alessia - had given Anne chocolate cookies. Leigh had presented Anne with a new hot water bottle complete with cover and Prue had given Anne some nice cheese. They were all, Stasha admitted, thoughtful gestures. Emily could do no wrong either and Anne always liked talking to Fran.

She'd had enough of thinking and turned over in bed. She wanted to go to sleep but instinct told her to check on Anne first, so without a moment's thought she got out of bed, put on her dressing gown and went downstairs to see if Anne was asleep. She was tucked up in bed and snoring, so Stasha returned to her room.

Stasha woke from her night's sleep, and – like every morning – she checked the monitor to see Anne. She was still fast asleep but had moved position during the night, so Stasha showered, dressed and prepared herself for another day with a woman whose main goal seemed to be to make her life as difficult as possible. Methodically and calmly, Stasha brushed her long hair as she looked at herself in the mirror; she was still an attractive young woman with piercing eyes and a beautiful smile. But with one failed romance behind her and nothing in front, just a low-paid zero-hours contract as an unwanted carer, was this as good as it was going to get? Surely there was something at the end. Would the end justify her means?

She thought of Daisy again, alone and being fed by neighbours, and wondered why she hadn't felt the confidence to ask Anne if the cat could come and stay, but she knew the answer would be a resounding no before she even asked it, so there was little point in progressing that chain of thought.

Stasha looked at herself again in the mirror and her eyes told her that she was not happy with her life, and that at the present time there were no escape routes at all. She left the bedroom and went down the stairs. It was not a dark house, but the light didn't lift her mood.

The house always had a very welcoming feel. Stasha wandered into the kitchen and felt that warmth of the summer sun shining through the windows. She saw the ducks from the pond in the garden and the three blackbirds that came for their morning feed.

Stasha's routine was imprinted on her mind: preparing breakfast, getting Anne up, a little chit-chat and no doubt another argument.

Her breakfast comprised some healthy cereal that she bought from a health food shop, a cup of black tea, some toast with honey and a read of the morning paper.

The bell rang. Anne was awake.

Stasha looked at the clock. It was twenty to

eight, so she went into the lounge, opened the electric blinds and switched off various lights. She asked Anne if she'd had a good sleep and was met with a wrinkled up nose. Stasha got Anne her mouthwash and went back to the kitchen.

The bell rang again.

Anne wanted to sit up in bed.

Then Stasha's phone rang.

It was the office. There had been some sort of staffing problem and the agency asked if Stasha could get Anne up and dressed on her own.

Stasha sighed, realising her day was not going to get any better. Anne was difficult to get up – a lot of false oohs and aaahs, complaints of feeling cold, repeated requests for washing and a general sense of belittlement towards Stasha as she tried her best.

When Stasha cleaned her, Anne asked her to do it again. Then she watched as Stasha carefully dressed her. She wanted to be vocal, so she said, 'You hurt my hand,' when in reality Stasha had not touched it.

That morning, Stasha was told she had 'bony, cold hands'.

Breakfast was served as usual in the dining

room. Anne complained that the toast was too hard so Stasha had to redo it before Anne engrossed herself in the newspaper.

Mrs James, the cleaner, came on the Monday afternoon. Like Anne had always done before her, Stasha found herself tidying the house before the cleaner came, though it wasn't even her house.

Mid morning, Candy – without any notice – drove to the front of the house and parked up. Stasha watched Candy get out of her car on the hall CCTV monitor. She walked round to open the passenger door and get what looked like a cake box out from the passenger seat. Candy then proceeded to make her way to the front door. She let herself in and went straight in to see Anne in the conservatory.

'I bought you some cakes,' Candy said and touched Anne's hands in a welcoming gesture. Stasha stood watching the scene and noticed Anne's face spring into a smile. Involuntarily, Candy bent forward and kissed Anne on her cheek. 'How are you?' she asked.

'I'm fine now you're here,' Anne replied.

Stasha felt the remark as another put down.

Candy's loud voice resonated around the house, with Anne chuckling at what was being said. She came into the kitchen, ignored

Stasha and retrieved a set of plates from the cupboard. 'I'm making Anne a cup of tea,' she said.

Candy did not ask Stasha if she wanted a cup and Stasha felt frozen out.

Later, after Candy had been in the house for an hour, Stasha found her sitting on one of the easy chairs. She was talking to, not at, Anne.

Anne seemed captivated by Candy's stories and laughter, and by her general two-fingered attitude towards life. At a quarter to one Candy got up, washed the dishes and put them away. She kissed Anne goodbye and, without looking at Stasha, left the house.

During the lunch call with Lacey, Stasha once again got the sharp edge of Anne's tongue. Anne had been sick on her pullover and Stasha wanted to take it off and replace it. In doing so, she accidentally caught Anne's bad hand, which made it jolt.

Anne cried in pain.

'I haven't touched it really,' Stasha replied, and the remark was met with the usual response.

'You are a rotten carer.'

Stasha looked at Lacey, who took over the task of putting Anne in a cardigan. It was done with the minimum of fuss and without a word of complaint from Anne.

Stasha merely shrugged her shoulders.

'Anastazja is always rough with me,' Anne said to Lacey.

'That's not true,' Stasha turned to Lacey for moral support but she only got a smile back and nothing was said.

Anne had successfully made Stasha, once again, look incompetent.

Once the call had finished, Lacey asked Stasha how everything was.

'Anne is totally without compromise,' Stasha replied. 'It is difficult, she is very critical of everything I do.'

Lacey listened, for she had received the sharp edge of Anne's tongue on occasion. But Lacey was both resilient and conscientious, not to mention extremely humorous and accepting of difficult situations – the likes of Anne were always a challenge, but Lacey accepted and lived with Anne's peculiarities.

'I've been here months now and in that time I've never had a thank you or any form of compliment, just criticism after criticism, while Candy ...' Stasha rolled her eyes in despair, '... she comes in like a whirlwind of noise and the two of them talk and laugh, and it's so easy with them ...' There was a note of jealousy in Stasha's voice. But there seemed to be no solution to the dilemma in which Stasha found herself.

That afternoon, Anne had asked Stasha if she would drive her to another garden centre, ten miles away, and pick up some plants for the gardener to plant in the flowerbed outside. Stasha agreed, and so they lunched without much conversation and had a brief look at the lunchtime news before Stasha went out to the vehicle, started it up and manoeuvred it into position.

The van was very easy to use and Anne enjoyed travelling in it, although only for short distances. As it was automatic, Stasha found it relaxing to drive and was able to manoeuvre it into any space that became available, thanks to the vehicle's surround cameras. Strangely for one so critical, Anne was never overly concerned about Stasha's driving.

The garden centre was like many – a mixture of shops, textile units, building supplies and plants. It was a lovely afternoon, and Anne and Stasha alighted from the vehicle and made their way through to the main part of the garden centre. Anne was not a great shopper now, wanting only to get out of the house occasionally and have a look round the plant room. Instead, it was Stasha who picked the plants that she thought were suitable. Afterwards, she made her way to a soft furnishings shop.

Stasha was looking at some soft, brightly coloured pillows.

'Are they for your house?' Anne asked. 'They will get dirty very quickly.'

Stasha smiled. She could always rely on Anne to say the obvious. She looked at some bedding and other soft cushions before deciding to buy two light brown cushions for herself. She took pleasure in placing them on Anne's knee before making her way to the checkout. Stasha paid for the two cushions and hooked the carrier bag on the back of Anne's wheelchair before pushing Anne into the coffee shop.

They sat in the corner; Stasha preferred this position because it kept Anne away from any disturbance. Stasha had a black coffee and Anne had an orange juice, but there was a tension in the atmosphere. They sat in silence.

Finally, Anne asked Stasha if she missed her home.

'No,' Stasha said, 'I am so enjoying my time here with you.'

The sarcastic remark was not lost on Anne.

After half an hour, they left the coffee shop, and Stasha pushed Anne around the garden centre's various departments before getting back to the van. The gardener had fixed Anne's stiff manual chair and it was now so much easier to use.

'Take the long way home,' Anne said and Stasha duly obliged.

Once home, Stasha placed Anne back on the bed, tucked her in, and made sure she was comfortable before leaving her alone. The room was warm from the sunshine so she switched on one of the cooling fans. As she left the lounge she saw Anne's eyes close and she nodded off. It had been a reasonably pleasant afternoon, although she still had not heard the words she yearned for: a simple thank you.

It was one of those evenings when Stasha had prepared the dinner for Anne and was waiting on the carers to arrive, when she received a phone call from the office to inform her that the carers had been delayed. Once again, they asked if Stasha could do the call herself.

Stasha sighed and placed the phone down, then she went in to tell Anne, who was half asleep and didn't realise what was being said.

There was always a certain reluctance when Stasha did Anne on her own. This time was no different and as soon as she had got together everything that was required the criticism started in earnest, but this time Stasha momentarily and uncharacteristically snapped.

'Will you stop complaining at me when I'm trying my best.'

'Well your best isn't good enough,' came the now standard reply.

'You're an ungrateful old woman,' Stasha shouted and this time Anne did not reply. For a moment Stasha felt ashamed of her behaviour. Stasha closed her eyes and counted to ten. What she really wanted to do was pick up a pillow and place it over this woman's head and get her out of her life once and for all. But she could not do that, so she carried on with the task at hand.

'You really are a moaning old woman,' Stasha continued as she turned Anne over to wash her back.

'A moaning old woman?' Anne replied. 'Who's paying your wages.'

'You are the most hateful person I've ever met,' Stasha snarled back.

'Just leave me alone,' Anne instructed. Stasha snapped and slammed the towel down on the side of the bed, before walking out of the room.

The call had not been completed but the criticism had finally made Stasha walk away from the patient – never a good thing. She stood in the hall listening to the grandfather's clock ticking her life away.

She turned on her heels and went back to look at the helpless figure lying on her bed with virtually no clothes on. Stasha realised she could walk out of the house and leave Anne like that forever – but that would be cruel and abusive behaviour. So, slowly, she walked back and started the procedure again. They did not speak. Anne realised that Stasha did not want to communicate. The personal care was finished in silence. Stasha put Anne in the hoist jacket, placed it correctly round her shoulders and hoisted her back into her wheelchair. She pushed Anne into the dining room and positioned her at the head of the table. She placed a napkin round her neck, switched the television on, placed a fresh beaker of water next to her, then brought the food in and placed it in front of Anne, an action that was met with a large sigh.

Stasha decided to sit in the kitchen on her own.

'Where are you?' Anne asked, and Stasha knew she had to go into the dining room for her meal.

She sat down in the usual place but they still didn't make eye contact. Anne picked at her food with little enjoyment.

'What's for afterwards?' Anne asked.

'Whatever you want,' Stasha said and refused to meet Anne's eyes. 'Ice cream, cheesecake, trifle, anything.' She tried to make her voice sound friendly.

With her usual sarcasm, Anne replied by saying that she sounded like a waitress.

The remark fell flat.

Anne settled for another trifle and Stasha retrieved it from the fridge. She cleared the dishes away and sat down at the table to watch the early evening news. There was a feature about the number of migrants entering the country.

Anne turned to Stasha, 'Well, I suppose you're not illegal, are you? Although God knows why they let you in.'

Stasha suddenly felt tears prick at the back

of her eyes, for this woman would simply not give up; she was incessantly cruel, without any compassion and relentless in her personal attacks. 'How dare you say that. Take it back, Anne,' Stasha demanded and removed her glasses. Her moist eyes met Anne's with unconcealed hostility.

Anne would not back down. 'Stop crying,' she said and the remark hit home.

'I have never hated anyone like I hate you,' Stasha lashed out.

'And, as I have said before, the feeling is mutual, Anastazja,' Anne replied.

Silence engulfed the rest of the evening.

As irony would have it, Candy came round to assist with the late call. Suddenly Anne was talkative, pleasant and friendly.

This bloody woman, Stasha thought, can cut through all of Anne's nastiness and make her laugh. Anne seemed a different person. Now it wasn't just Anne who Stasha disliked; Candy was also near the top of her list.

Candy and Anne chatted together and Anne asked Stasha to go to the fridge and get Candy a bar of chocolate.

Stasha paused, knowing that the chocolate had been bought for Anne's morning coffee and that there was one bar left until the delivery came the following afternoon. 'But there's only one left,' she explained. 'You won't have any for the morning.'

'I want you to give it to Candy,' Anne repeated.

Reluctantly, Stasha went to the kitchen, opened the fridge and retrieved the chocolate bar. She came back and handed it to Candy who bent down and kissed Anne on the cheek.

'See you soon,' Candy said and left, pointedly ignoring Stasha again.

As Stasha predicted, Anne castigated her the following morning for allowing them to run out of chocolate.

'You know how much I enjoy my chocolate of a morning,' Anne said to Stasha when she was served her morning tea. 'You can't get anything right, can you? Just hopeless.'

Stasha left the room without saying a thing.

EIGHT

And so it came around again – Stasha's three-day break.

This time Stasha couldn't wait to get away from Anne's abrasive character. She would spend some of her time cycling, and she needed some long walks with her own thoughts; she had a craving to be by herself. Her mind wandered to her future and rested a little on her past – the broken engagement, the broken dreams of the life she had planned and the uncertain journey that lay ahead. And then there was Anne. She had never met anyone like her, and she never wanted to again.

She missed home. She missed her parents, especially her mother, but most of all she missed being in a job that valued her. She was irritated that she still had not found such a position.

There were plenty of jobs available in the city for factory work, shop work, even warehouse work, but it wasn't what she had envisaged for herself. She was also beginning to hate Anne's beloved Britain. Despite what Anne had said to her many times, its pavements were indeed littered with gold –

although she soon realised that the gold was only for certain people. It was true that Poland offered limited opportunities, but Britain also offered surprisingly few opportunities if you took career progression and the cost of living into account. It was definitely an us and them society.

Stasha felt that her care work should be fulfilling – she was helping people, assisting the elderly and making a difference – but the coolness between her and Anne showed no signs of thawing.

If Stasha was honest, although she did not care much for Anne as a person, she remained irritated that Anne had little or no understanding of poorly paid people, and that she did not consider her circumstances.

Reluctantly, she thought about Candy spending a few days with Anne. There was a tinge of envy, for she knew that the two of them would no doubt have some entertaining times.

Stasha's break passed without much happening. Then, on the day of her return, she packed her bags, loaded her car, placed Daisy with a neighbour and set off for Anne's. She wondered how much money Candy would have been able to take from Anne and how much food would have disappeared from the house. She dreaded returning because of the unpleasant atmosphere; it was emotionally draining, since she was not an argumentative person, but Anne had a knack of bringing out the worst in her. Anne had got firmly under her skin and Stasha was annoyed with herself for allowing it to happen. She could see no way back.

It was erosive to her soul getting out of bed each morning just to receive criticism after criticism, with not much backup from the office. In fact, there was no backup from the office because Anne paid the bills, and this type of care was expensive, although this was certainly not reflected in Stasha's pay.

She drove the twenty minutes to Anne's house and turned in to the drive. The gates were closed so she opened them with the key fob and drove in. Other than Candy's car, there was no other vehicle in the drive, so it was obvious that Candy had taken Anne out in the van.

Stasha entered the house, half expecting it to be untidy and messy, but she was surprised when she walked from room to room – it was tidy and clean and looked like it had been freshly polished. It was almost too clean. She went upstairs to her own room and unpacked. She then went to the room Candy used. There was a suitcase on the bed, some clothes over a chair and sandals on the floor. She went to the office and had a look at her little traps that she had set, for she knew Candy was nosey and she wanted to convince herself she was right. Stasha noticed that the traps had been moved so that the desk drawers could be opened. She then went to the secondary office. Again, the traps had been moved and the drawers had been opened. Candy must have known there was nothing of any value – just files that would be meaningless to her. But she had opened them nevertheless.

Stasha walked downstairs into the dining room and went to the desk, opening the drawer where she knew there should be five hundred pounds in the cash tin. Stasha opened the tin and counted out the money. There was five hundred pounds. Nothing was missing.

Almost disappointed, Stasha walked back to lounge and had a look round. It was tidy. There was no newspaper for Anne and no mat for her cup. The bed was too well made with neat hospital corners, but there was nothing to point to anything untoward.

Stasha felt a little deflated. She looked at the clock. It was four o'clock in the afternoon – she wondered how long Candy had gone out for. She went back to the office and checked the CCTV by replaying it in fast forward mode from lunchtime. She saw that both Anne and Candy had left at one thirty, but there was somebody else with them, somebody had got into the passenger seat of the van and – try as she might – Stasha did not know who it was.

It wasn't until four thirty that the van returned. Candy helped Anne to exit the vehicle and they came in through the front door.

Once inside, and with Anne more settled, Candy explained that they had gone to a local U3A meeting at the village hall, and that they'd also taken a neighbour. It was this neighbour who had suggested Anne come along.

The U3A talk had been interesting. It was about the Lancastrian region. Candy had sat next to Anne during the whole talk, and then she'd gone to get Anne a cup of tea and a piece of cake, and had chatted to other members of the group. They seemed to have had a nice afternoon. It was another incident that made Stasha increasingly irritable.

Stasha was, not for the first time, spitting feathers. Was there nothing Candy couldn't do?

Anne had gone back to bed and was now tired, since the afternoon had taken a lot out of her. The meeting with all those people, all the noise in the hall and no doubt Candy's booming voice would have tired anyone. Stasha and Candy had nothing to say to each other, and so Candy left.

Anne was now fast asleep. When the tea time call came, it was missed, since Stasha did not want to wake her. She made a light chicken salad sandwich and waited patiently for Anne to wake, which she did around seven thirty.

Stasha decided to give herself a freshen up before placing Anne in her chair and sitting with her for her light supper.

'Did you enjoy the afternoon?' Stasha asked

Anne nodded. 'It was noisy.' She frowned, then smiled, and Stasha involuntarily smiled back at her.

'Did you enjoy your time off?' Anne asked. The question was stilted and hung in the air. Without wishing to be drawn, Stasha nodded.

'I won't ask if you missed me,' Stasha said as an afterthought and looked across at Anne, whose face gave nothing away. The remark was not answered.

'How is Candy?' Stasha asked, determined to get an opinion on the past few days.

'You don't like her, do you, Anastazja?'

Stasha did not answer.

'I understand her,' Anne replied. 'Someone who has not had it easy.'

'We have all not had it easy,' Stasha interrupted, 'not just Candy.'

'Not like Candy,' Anne retorted.

'You won't have a bad word said against her,' Stasha snapped.

Anne did not respond and Stasha gave up. Discussing Candy was like wading through treacle: hard going, and you would never get anywhere.

Stasha decided to clear up and left Anne to no doubt reminisce over her time with her beloved Candy. Anne called her back.

'Yes, I did, as strange as it may seem,' Anne said.

Stasha frowned.

'Miss you,' Anne said.

Stasha came back into the room and knelt down next to Anne's chair. 'I have a favour to ask you,' she said, and Anne raised her eyebrows in expectation. There was a pause and Stasha wondered how she would frame the question. It was a test. 'Would you mind if I brought my cat here to stay with me?'

Anne was surprised at the question. 'Is this an indoor or outdoor cat?' she eventually asked.

Stasha nodded, 'Indoor.'

'What's its name?' Anne asked.

'She's called Daisy.'

'It's a nice name,' Anne said and paused. 'But I don't want animals in my house.'

Disappointed, Stasha got up from the side of the chair. She said nothing and went to the kitchen to make herself a cup of tea. One step forward and two steps back, she thought to herself.

For Stasha, it was Groundhog Day. There was not much uplift in the rapport she had with Anne; it was still difficult, even after all the time they'd had together, as neither of them seemed to be able to relax in the presence of the other. It was tiring constantly being on guard.

Candy was the opposite of Stasha. She didn't care what people thought; she was her own person – not perfect, but with her it was a question of like it or lump it. Anne responded to that. Stasha tiptoed around, not wanting to make any waves. She was silent as she moved around the house, which Anne still thought was quite creepy; she had little presence and would appear at the side of Anne's bed, often waking her up with a start.

Candy was the opposite: loud and proud.

On the Tuesday morning, the manager briefly stopped by with an envelope addressed to Anne. Anne was unable to open it so, as usual, Stasha offered to help her. She retrieved the three-page letter and handed it to Anne to read. It was a customer satisfaction survey from the agency office. Stasha immediately frowned, for she could sense trouble ahead.

Stasha decided to get it over with quickly. So, after their morning coffee, when Anne had had her drink and chocolate, Stasha sat down opposite her and started going through the questions. They had to be answered using a score of one to ten, with ten being the most satisfied. There were a few easy-to-answer questions, then came the ones that related to Stasha.

'Are you satisfied with the time-keeping of your carer?'

Anne answered ten.

'How satisfied are you with the care you receive?'

There was a pause as Stasha hovered the pen over the list of numbers, and Anne thought for some time. She answered seven.

It was the next question that was the real test.

'How happy are you with your live-in carer?'

Stasha smiled across at Anne, wishing to break the ice, but Anne ignored the gesture. She answered three.

Stasha would have liked it to have been eight or maybe seven, and she knew that anything below five would mean questions from the office. One last question remained.

'Do you have any further comments?'

Anne answered and made Stasha write that she wished Candy was her permanent carer. She looked across the room and said with a deadpan expression, 'I don't like you, Anastazja, I wish you would do as you have often promised and leave.'

Stasha rose from her chair feeling upset and angry. She would now telephone the office and hand in her notice. There was no point in getting annoyed about the questionnaire, so they moved on to lunch, and Anne had her afternoon nap and more carers' visits. Then dinner. Then bed.

It was normal practice for Stasha to drive Anne to the village cashpoint every Monday or Tuesday afternoon, so that she could withdraw three hundred pounds in cash from her account, whether this was required or not. This money would then be placed into the cash tin in the desk drawer in the dining room, and Stasha would have free access to the money to pay the likes of window cleaners, chiropodists, physiotherapists, Mrs James and other people who came to the house. Because most of the shopping was done on David's credit card, the amount of ready cash could build up. Stasha knew that every single penny she'd spent was accounted for, and she kept receipts for everything. Nothing was ever spent without Anne's or David's knowledge, and if it was a big purchase – like the recent washing machine – then David would give authorisation for it. After these cashpoint visits, Anne liked to be driven around the countryside for perhaps half an hour, and they would visit small market towns, garden centres and farm food shops, and Stasha would dutifully push Anne around until she wished to go home.

Stasha had mentioned that she was saving up for a new car, but Anne offered no encouragement or advice regarding her savings plan.

The questionnaire was handed to the office the next day and, as expected, the office called Stasha the next morning and asked why her personal score was so low. Stasha suggested that Candy should take over the live-in care. Stasha still harboured a grudge for the dramatically low score Anne had given her on the feedback form. Even the office thought it was harsh, and they informed Stasha – after speaking with David – that they had her backing.

Indeed, David had telephoned Stasha and had said he was more than happy for her to continue – it had been a thoughtful and most welcome call from David, who always considered both sides of a story before making a judgement. He had never once complained to the office regarding Stasha, even though she had a feeling that he had seen and heard some of the altercations via the cameras.

Stasha stopped on the way home at a cake

shop and bought some lemon cake. Anne thought it was a case of anything Candy could do Stasha could do better …

When Cian and Leigh arrived for the evening call, Stasha had to dash off in her car to the shops for some items she had missed off the home delivery. As she was returning, she accidentally clipped her car wheel on one of the curbs on the narrow lane, bursting her tyre and damaging the wheel. She managed to drive back to Anne's house with the tyre shredded and flapping off the wheel, and when she arrived back Leigh asked what was the matter. Stasha relayed the incident to both Anne and the carers – it would probably be a few hundred pounds to repair – an amount that Stasha could not really afford, with her rent due and other bills needing to be paid.

'You should drive more carefully,' Anne said.

Cian looked at Leigh with an expression that seemed to say, 'That's not what Stasha wants to hear!'

Stasha left the room, annoyed not so much at the incident but at Anne's insensitive remarks. She was a person without any perceptible tact at all.

Stasha emailed the local garage asking them

to collect her car and take it to their premises where they could repair the tyre, replace the wheel and give the vehicle a new MOT. All in all it was a very expensive afternoon for Stasha – something that was not welcome at all.

The following day was a day of domestic chores around the house. They had Mrs James for the inside and Ray for the garden, and then later on in the week the grass cutters would come and cut the grass. They had all worked for Anne and the family for years.

Stasha had been surprised that Anne employed a cleaner, for it was within her remit to keep the house clean, but she wasn't complaining. It gave her time to relax in the conservatory over her morning coffee while keeping a watchful eye on Anne.

On the Thursday of that week, Candy drove up unannounced and helped Stasha with the lunchtime call.

As per usual, Candy had some calamity going on in her life; this time she needed shoes for her young children, for they were growing fast and scuffing them at every opportunity, and she said she simply could not afford to replace them.

Stasha had sighed and looked at Anne, who she knew was going to offer to pay for them because Anne was a soft touch with Candy.

'You have to save up, Candy,' Stasha said and noticed the frown on Anne's brow.

Anne listened to the exchange between the two carers.

'How?' Candy said in a grumpy manner.

'Spend less,' Stasha said.

'You have no children, so you don't know what it's like.'

'How much do you need?' Anne asked, and Stasha's mood sank.

'No Anne,' Stasha complained.

'A hundred pounds,' Candy said.

'I am telling the office,' Stasha stepped in.

'Nobody tells me how to spend my money,' Anne ignored Stasha's shake of the head. 'Go to the desk and get a hundred pounds.'

Stasha had no option but to oblige. Anne could hear her fumbling around in the drawer.

Stasha came back. 'There was nothing in the cash tin,' she said.

Anne propelled herself in her electric wheelchair to the dining room and examined the cash tin. There was no money. She turned around to Candy. 'I'll get David to transfer some money to you.'

'Anne, just stop giving her money,' Stasha said.

Anne frowned, for there was an odd expression in Stasha's eyes. Anne wondered if it was guilt.

Stasha, who had been in the house all morning, couldn't remember when she last saw the money, but she felt it was recently, as she had paid Ray, Mrs James and the window cleaner in the past few days.

'Where is the money, Stasha?' Anne asked with clear suspicion in her voice.

Candy excused herself.

'Have you taken it, Stasha, for your car repair?'

The question remained in the air.

Candy now said her goodbyes and left the house.

Stasha walked out of the dining room up the stairs and into her room. She opened the built-in wardrobe, extracted her suitcase and placed it angrily on the bed. Then she went back to the wardrobe and started to fill the suitcase with clothes.

She ignored the ringing of Anne's bell.

Stasha threw all her belongings into the suitcase. Then she phoned the office to inform them that she was resigning.

The office were concerned and the manager immediately came out to Anne's house to see exactly what was going on. When she arrived, Anne was upset and Stasha was in the kitchen refusing to continue the care. The atmosphere had finally boiled over and there seemed no way back for either of them.

What puzzled Stasha was that the money was indeed missing and she knew she hadn't taken it. But there hadn't been anybody else in the house except for the regular carers. As Stasha glanced around the dining room for inspiration her eyes rested on the CCTV camera in the corner of the room. She remembered David's explanation as to why they were installed; this was surely the perfect time to use them. She rang David to explain the situation and he said he would ring back once he had looked at the relevant footage. Within ten minutes David did indeed ring and informed Stasha of exactly what had happened.

Triumphantly Stasha walked back into the lounge where Anne was discussing the situation with the manager.

'Here.' Stasha placed the money down on Anne's lap. 'Mrs James had inadvertently placed the money in the vase. Presumably I had accidentally left it on the desk after paying the window cleaner.'

Anne remained silent.

The manager looked at Stasha and shrugged. 'Mistakes can happen,' she said, but Stasha stood firm and shook her head.

The manager always had a difficult job; on the one hand, she had to keep the carers on side, while on the other she had to please the service users. It was never an easy task, but she seemed to have the knack of getting the best out of people, which was probably why the agency was so successful.

'I'm out,' Stasha said and went to climb the stairs to her room and collect her things.

Anne remained defiantly silent until she glanced at the manager. 'I'm sorry,' she said by way of an explanation, but it really did sound hollow and did nothing to alleviate the difficult situation.

Stasha came down the stairs with her suitcase and a selection of jackets thrown over her arm. She opened the front door and went to pack her car. The manager went outside to try and coax her into reconsidering, and to see if there was any way forward for these two obstinate women.

The manager went back into the lounge and said, 'You have lost a wonderful person, Anne.'

But even now, at this crucial moment, Anne would not capitulate.

'You can send Candy instead,' Anne volunteered, but the manager shook her head.

'We cannot. She will not do full-time living care as she has a family and responsibilities,' explained the manager.

Anne shrugged.

Stasha returned to the lounge. 'That's all my things,' she said to the manager, ignoring Anne.

Anne refused to look into Stasha's eyes; instead she pressed the controller on her wheelchair and spun the machine round so she could look out of the window. It was a cold and hurtful gesture.

'Let me ring David,' the manager temporised, and with that she called a number on her phone.

Both David and the manager had spoken to Stasha in an attempt to change her mind, but Stasha was adamant that she had had enough and started to gather her final few things together. She went into the lounge and across to Anne who was sitting in the wheelchair looking out of the window. She was not oblivious to the situation, but she preferred not to engage anyone. Stasha placed a hand on her shoulder and said simply, 'Goodbye, Anne.'

The manager witnessed the scene but did not interfere, for even she recognised that the animosity between Stasha and Anne had gone too far and felt that there was no way back for the two of them.

Stasha glanced up at the manager. 'I'll be in touch,' she said and went to leave the room.

As she reached the door she gave one last glance at Anne who, still facing away from them, suddenly said, 'Why don't you bring your cat here, Stasha?'

The remark made Stasha stop in her tracks, for it was the first time Anne had addressed her by her preferred name, and she realised the significance of this.

'Pardon?' Stasha said and she looked at the manager.

'Why don't you bring Daisy to live with you here?' Anne said again. 'And let's put all this behind us.' She spun the chair round to face Stasha and paused before saying, 'Please continue to look after me.' There was a feeble, almost begging tone in Anne's voice.

Stasha faced a dilemma.

Anne continued. 'I am sorry for the atmosphere. I suppose I'm not used to people looking after me.'

It was an olive branch from Anne. Stasha was unsure of how to proceed. She looked across at Anne, who was now upset with the whole situation.

'I know you didn't take the money. I'm sorry for accusing you. Please reconsider about leaving me.'

The manager observed but said nothing.

'I can bring Daisy here?' Stasha asked.

'She can have the run of the house. I look forward to meeting her,' Anne said.

The manager looked at Stasha and shrugged. It was an overture and she hoped that Stasha was not so stubborn as to ignore it, but before she could say anything Anne interrupted the silence once again.

'Don't go,' Anne said quietly, and there was emotion in her tone that was not lost on the other two women. Anne used her paper handkerchief to wipe away the tears from her eyes.

There was a pause and Stasha considered her answer. She liked living in the house and didn't really want to go through the process

of getting to know somebody new – even
though Anne could be a pain. Stasha balanced
the scales of her indecision. The atmosphere
was charged with unsaid emotion. Stasha had
proved she was no pushover, but she did not
want to seem as if she was milking the
situation, so she shrugged.

'If it happens again, I go,' Stasha finally
said, and the manager nodded.

For Anne, it was a compromise, but for the
manager it was a weight off her shoulders;
trying to find a replacement for Stasha at such
short notice would have been difficult to say
the least.

So the argument was smoothed over and
the manager left. Stasha returned her things to
the upstairs room. Once she was finished,
Anne called her into the lounge.

'I'm sorry,' she repeated, 'I have been unfair
and unnecessarily harsh in my talking to you.
I feel ashamed of what I said.'

Stasha nodded. She became quite emotional
and surreptitiously wiped a tear from her eye.
'It's all new to me as well Anne.' There was a
pause. 'I know I'm not perfect, but I'm trying.'

'Come here Stasha,' Anne instructed.

Dutifully, Stasha went across to Anne's
wheelchair and knelt down. On impulse Anne

stretched her hand out to Stasha, who took it. 'Let's start again,' Anne said simply. Her voice was persuasive and Stasha smiled. 'Do you ever wish you had a second chance to meet someone for the first time?'

The remark was lovely and it was not lost on Stasha. Anne squeezed her hand. The action took Stasha by surprise, for it was Anne's first demonstrative act and, despite all her misgivings, Stasha felt the gesture came from Anne's heart.

After an easy afternoon, Anne was put back to bed at three. She immediately closed her eyes and appeared to fall asleep, giving Stasha a chance to collect her thoughts and think about the best course of action.

STASHA > STEFANIA
Something's changed, progress perhaps!

STEFANIA > ANASTAZJA
I told you, she will come round
See you for the lovely person you are

STASHA > STEFANIA
Maybe

Anne didn't feel like a snooze, and she suddenly felt muddled in her thinking. She waited for Stasha to leave the room. She thought of Stasha and considered the unfair preconceptions she had formed regarding her.

The fact that Stasha was young and attractive was no excuse for the comments Anne had made to her, and she knew that. But part of the reason for the comments, Anne summarised to herself, was that she had underestimated the shock and fear she would feel when leaving the safe - if noisy - environment of the hospital to return home and be confronted by someone who was the exact opposite of what she thought a carer would - or should - be. She was, initially, apprehensive regarding Stasha and the complete control she would have over her life.

Anne's self-defence mechanism had been immediately activated when her eyes had flickered over Stasha's youthful composure on that very first day, with her immediate thoughts being 'Can this girl really look after me?'

Anne reasoned that, for her own well-being, she had to be hard on Stasha, and her pride and self-belief had not allowed her to back down. Anne would never admit it to Stasha, but the first time Stasha had become visibly upset Anne had gained a renewed confidence about her abilities – you rarely cried if you didn't care. But Anne's stubborn pride had prevented her from backing down – it had become a type of Russian roulette to see how far she could push Stasha before she broke. But Stasha, not for the first time, had surprised her, and she had become a worthy, clever and capable adversary.

It then became a game; Anne knew she had taken a little pleasure in aiming her frustration at Stasha, but she also realised it was shameful behaviour, despite the fact that it made her – at the time – feel superficially better about herself.

It almost backfired. Stasha could have walked away, but she hadn't, and to her credit that said an awful lot about her.

It was all very complicated, was Anne just trying to justify it all to herself, was her relationship with Stasha on a firmer footing or was it just a temporary respite until hostilities reared their ugly head again?

Thinking like this made Anne tired. She was confused and closed her eyes. Now she slept.

The following day Anne was true to her word. After breakfast she instructed Stasha to get the van ready, get her in it and drive to Stasha's house to retrieve Daisy from the neighbour and bring her back home. This took Stasha by surprise; in the space of a few hours Anne seemed to be a different woman and she wondered how long this truce would last. But for the time being she was not going to look a gift horse in the mouth. Stasha got the van ready, put Anne securely inside and drove the two of them to her house. She was interested in how Anne would react to where she lived.

It was a city street with no off-road parking. There were bins lining the road and cars dotted about that looked like they hadn't moved for ages. Stasha's house was in the middle of a terrace with no front garden and one window next to the front door. There was a curtain that had been drawn across the window and a black front door. Stasha parked the van carefully three doors away and made her way to her own house before coming out with the cat carrier. She signalled to Anne that she was going next door. She was next door for ten minutes, then she came out with the cat carrier and what looked like a black cat inside. Her other carrier bag held cat food, a few dishes and a litter tray. She placed the cat carrier on the front seat and carefully put the seat belt round it.

'This is Daisy, Anne,' Stasha said before opening the rear sliding door and placing all the rest of the paraphernalia next to Anne.

'Hello Daisy,' Anne said and smiled as the cat looked at her. 'She's beautiful!' Anne remarked.

So Daisy integrated herself into the house and soon made herself at home, comforted by Stasha's presence and the warmth of the conservatory, which soon became her favourite spot. Like all cats, she was discerning as to whom she became friends with and it took a little while for her to approach Anne and her wheelchair. But, when she did, Anne spoke softly to her, and Daisy would often return to her once or twice a day.

Stasha and Anne were still walking on eggshells, neither wanting to disturb the truce that existed between them. Stasha had telephoned her mother, saying that Anne was more amenable and certainly not as frosty.

A turning point came when Anne suggested to Stasha that she accompany her to another U3A meeting in the village hall. Whereas it had been Candy last time, now it was Stasha's turn to integrate herself with the aged membership. She wondered if this was a test for her, as apparently Candy had been well received and became talkative with the other members very quickly.

It turned out to be a pleasant afternoon. The members of the village group were friendly and kind to Anne, reserving her a space at the front of the hall with Stasha next to her. Stasha enjoyed the talk and reflected on Anne's change of attitude; there was the start of a genuine understanding now between them, and although their relationship was far better than before, the term 'friendship' still couldn't be used.

Suddenly, halfway through the talk, Stasha received a notification on her phone. It was a new rota. A cloud formed on the horizon. The two evening calls had been changed, and it was now Candy who was the sole second carer. Stasha wondered how all this would now play out. How long could Anne keep up this pretence of being nice, especially when Candy would be present? Which side would Anne come down on? It was something Stasha was interested in witnessing.

Despite the news, Stasha continued to enjoy the talk, and afterwards she was helped by a male member to get Anne back in her van.

Annette De Burgh

NINE

Candy arrived ten minutes early. As usual, she let herself into the house and went straight to Anne's bedside without acknowledging Stasha. She had brought with her a small bag from the bakery and in it was a cheese scone, which she knew Anne would like. She placed it on Anne's side table and kissed her on the forehead. 'For your sweet,' Candy said.

Stasha rolled her eyes at the gesture.

'How are you?' Candy asked and Anne nodded.

'I am okay, thank you,' Anne smiled,' I wasn't expecting you tonight.'

'There was a change of plan. Are you pleased to see me?' Candy asked.

'I'm always pleased to see you, Candy.'

This soothing reply was overhead by Stasha as she re-entered the room. She removed her glasses and the two carers barely acknowledged each other. Stasha got together what was required to do the personal care.

'I'll do it tonight,' Candy said, meaning she would take charge of the call.

Stasha waited for a response from Anne but none came. She dutifully took up her position and Candy once again took charge. Stasha stared down at Anne as the personal care was started.

Anne caught Stasha's expression and the look in her eyes, and she suddenly said, 'I want Stasha to do this.'

There was instant surprise, and Candy stopped and gave a disingenuous shrug. Anne finished off her request with a 'please'. Candy raised her eyebrows and walked round to the other side of the bed. She was not pleased, for she always liked to take charge, even when Stasha was present. Stasha found the whole episode quite amusing, particularly because Candy was so perplexed, but she made sure there was no self-satisfied expression on her face.

'I thought you were pleased to see me,' Candy asked in a loud voice as Stasha continued with the personal care. Stasha said nothing, but Candy kept asking questions that really had no answers. Stasha knew she was rattled.

'Have I done something wrong?' Candy asked, and Anne merely shrugged, saying that she wished Stasha to be in charge from now on. There was a crestfallen look on Candy's face, for she couldn't understand the change of attitude.

Reading Candy's expression, Anne suggested that Stasha – as her main carer – must remain in charge.

When the call was over, Anne asked Stasha if she could speak to Candy on her own, so Stasha gathered all the things together and left the room. Candy shut the door. Looking through the glass in the door, Stasha could see them both in conversation, but she couldn't decipher what was being said. Anne was seemingly doing all the talking and Candy was standing in front of her with her arms crossed in a defiant manner. Then Candy slowly nodded her head, walked across to Anne and kissed her on the forehead before saying she would see her later.

Stasha did not know what had been said.

The following day, Stasha had placed Anne in the conservatory for the afternoon. It was a pleasant day with warm sunshine and it wasn't too hot. The conservatory was reasonably comfortable; it had the sun at the start of the day but by mid afternoon it was in shade. The room remained warm and comfortable during these summer months.

The atmosphere in the house was different

now and the two women were starting to explore each other's opinions. Both found the other to be of interest and worth listening to. Stasha had made afternoon tea for them and now they sat together in the conservatory enjoying the late afternoon warmth.

Both wanted to talk.

'What can you see yourself doing in five years' time?' Anne asked, and Stasha knew it was a question that merited a thoughtful answer.

Stasha thought about her response. 'I want to be happy,' she said, 'because if you're not happy, nothing else matters.'

Anne considered Stasha's response, saying, 'Will you stay in care?'

'I would like to get into adult nursing,' Stasha replied, 'try and make a difference ...' She tailed off.

Anne noticed the pensive expression on Stasha's face. 'What are you thinking?' she said.

Stasha fought a smile. 'My life as it could have been,' she said.

Anne was nothing if not observant. 'Tell me about it?'

Stasha shrugged, 'Where to start?'

'The beginning is always the best place,'

Anne laughed as she took a sip of tea from her beaker.

'I grew up in a small, impoverished Polish town that had little going for it and the inhabitants were all known to each other. It was not easy to meet new people, we did not have a car and the transport system was poor, so you lived within a half-mile radius of your house. That radius was your shops and your school and your friends, so it was a case of making do. For a young woman it was terribly restrictive compared to the West – very hard to meet someone suitable to be a partner, and the thought of staying in that small community all my life was quite oppressive. Meeting someone was difficult. I also had no money, something that must be alien to you, Anne, but as a family we were poor.'

It was faint rebuke, but Anne allowed the comment to dissolve and said, 'Bit like the war years here. Very restrictive, a life lived in containment.' Anne's tone signalled her sorrow.

Stasha went on. 'But I could see another life, a life where there was uplift and where it looked like the sun shone every day.'

Anne nodded.

'I did find my Prince Charming, Anne. He was a neighbour, the son of people who lived very close to where I was. My parents had … have a shop, and he would often come in and out, dark hair and polite … my mother always joked that I should marry him. We became engaged, but little did I realise the joke would eventually be on me.'

Anne listened.

'We fell in love, as you do, but I didn't have an abundance of suitable men to choose from, so I suppose I took the first opportunity that came along, and it was good because we both got on well. There was an immediate connection and all seemed good. I wanted to come to your England, Anne, because I believed there was a better life over here for us.' Stasha paused. 'Is there anything wrong in that? I guess you would call me greedy, for I wanted it all … what was it you said? I wanted the benefits of living in the West without all the hard work.'

Anne said nothing but realised her earlier remark had been remembered.

'It was clear my partner and I didn't want the same things. He was content to stay in the small village and the small town. We argued. I suppose it was lucky that we realised we were different before we got married, or we would have been worse off, so the engagement was broken and I stayed in the small bedsit above my parents' shop before making the decision to come to England. I'd heard about the separation from Europe that the Britons wanted, but I was not prepared for some of the comments I received when I finally got here.'

'You argued with your fiancée?' Anne smiled before taking a swipe at Stasha to redress the balance, 'Who would have thought that?'

It was now Stasha's turn to let the remark dissolve.

'You were not prepared for the comments from the likes of me, a white, middle-class, English woman, as you called me,' Anne could not resist saying.

Stasha did not answer, but she continued to describe her work in the factory. 'It was not what I wanted,' she said. 'I wanted to work in a smart outfit every day, drive a good car, be well presented. That was my dream, as there seemed little point in coming to this country to do similar work I could have gotten in Poland. My dream resulted in me standing on the factory floor working shifts with other east Europeans who had suffered the same broken dreams – or promises – as I had. So I wanted to change my career, do something, and that's how I became your carer, Anne.'

'And the welcome you had was not the warmest, was it?' Anne took a sip of her tea, knowing Stasha would not pass up the opportunity to bite back.

'What hurt the most was that you judged me on where I came from and not the person I am,' Stasha continued. 'You seemed more interested in the place I was born than the care I could give you, and that really grated on my nerves. You were the most unwelcoming you could be to me.'

Anne nodded, 'I suppose I was, but remember it was and still is an enormous life change for me as well.'

Stasha ignored the statement. 'If we started again and I came through the door for the first time, would you still judge me on my accent or how good a carer I could become?'

Anne thought for a second or so. 'I would like to think that I'd learned a lesson.' There was a peevish note in her voice. Stasha was not convinced, so Anne continued, 'You only have to see how I react to Candy to know that I never judge a book by its cover, but I always feel there's a connection that is established immediately between two people, and we failed to do that. We got off on the wrong foot and our animosity and irritation grew, with neither wanting to back down. Although I did say some hurtful things which I apologise for once again.'

Stasha smiled and knew she had been successful in having her say.

'My stroke came out of the blue and my life changed literally overnight from chairing meetings, travelling and communicating with people to severe disablement, muddled thinking and an almost permanently bedridden existence. So initially my concern for carers and their feelings was not at the top of my list.'

This time Stasha listened.

'From becoming an independent widow to someone who's dependent on a stranger to do the most intimate care possible was hard, and sometimes I feel that carers don't always appreciate the huge change in their patient's lifestyle. Sometimes it felt like they were changing tyres on a car.'

'But it was you who invited me into the house, Anne, I did not ask to come,' Stasha said.

Anne paused, 'But it was you who applied for the job, Stasha.'

There was a slight undercurrent in the exchanges. Neither woman wished to be put down by the other, so Anne continued.

'I was a war child so I know about being brought up in a restrictive way. We had no luxuries – what with food rationing – and only a small circle of friends, not to mention the German bombers overhead wanting to kill us at every given opportunity. Then family members going to the front and the devastation that war brings to your community. So I do recognise the predicament you were in. It's not unique, here in Britain we suffered as well, although I admit it was different.'

Anne placed a small slice of cake in her mouth.

'My father went to work one morning and waved goodbye to my mother at the garden gate only for him to die at his office. And I never saw him again. Like you, my pathway was severely disrupted. You lost the love of your life through choice, just like my life changed for the first time overnight. My mother and I had to cope running the house and paying the bills. This current "woke generation", as you're sometimes referred to, has to acknowledge that different times bring different hardships, so when the young say that my generation have had it too good, they should consider everything before they speak. The very reason that you could travel from Poland to Britain is due to my generation and the sacrifices they made.'

Stasha acknowledged the remark.

'I met a salesman who had a car and wore a suit, and I watched him climb the corporate ladder while I played the housewife. I kept the house going and looked after the children. I was restricted during those years. I couldn't travel and I couldn't leave the house for longer than a half a day.'

'But you were comfortable and you didn't have to look for work, did you?' Stasha interrupted.

'You're making out that I didn't want to work.'

'You didn't need to work.' Stasha wanted the final say. 'There's a difference. I have to work. If I don't work, nobody is going to pay my bills and nobody will pay my rent. I have no rich husband.'

Anne allowed the remark to pass, but then she compromised, 'We had different problems in those days. Nobody is right or wrong.'

'You have a very nice house, Anne, you're comfortable,' Stasha remarked.

'Don't make me feel guilty, Stasha,' Anne raised her hand to make a point. 'I lived in Glasgow for twenty-five years, and let me tell you I know all about the poor, deprived areas of a city; you can't say you've known poverty unless you've seen Glasgow's social housing of the sixties and seventies.'

'Very much like Poland,' Stasha interrupted. She leant forward to the coffee table and helped herself to another small slice of cake.

Anne ignored the remark. 'I served on the children's court and I saw the young offenders stand before me – twelve years, fourteen years of age – and the hopelessness and consequences of their lives as well as the sheer inhumane living conditions they came from. So yes, I have seen poverty and I know what it's all about. You can't tell me anything about deprivation that I don't already know.'

'If that is true, I would have thought you would have shown more compassion for me.' Stasha revelled in the competence of her answer as it stung Anne.

Anne bit back, 'I was expecting a middle-aged woman who'd had children, perhaps an ex-nurse, and I was confronted with a young, attractive Polish woman wearing sunglasses who stood over my bed and looked down on me without even smiling. You didn't do anything to make me feel at ease or dispel my embarrassment.'

'I was new in the job, Anne, and didn't want to make any mistakes. You gave no consideration to how nervous I was.' Then, after saying this, Stasha cooled off, recognising that a huge, destructive row could be coming. 'Why don't you tell me about the Anne before your stroke? I have known you for a few months and I still know nothing about you. I imagine you had a fulfilled life.' Stasha's voice was soothing.

Anne glanced out of the conservatory window and cast her mind back over the decades. 'I originate from Liverpool. I worked for a shipping company in some very posh offices in the city centre. There was a group of us and, as young women, we had a wonderful time working. Our offices were opposite the Martins Bank Building in Liverpool and we faced the same clock tower they always show whenever Liverpool is on the television. Every night at four thirty we would all studiously watch the hands make their way to five o'clock, and then we would be free. I would get the bus home and would spend the rest of the evening with my mother doing various things.'

Stasha gave a voluntary smile, surprised that Anne could remember so clearly.

'I met John through his sister. He was older than me and wore a suit and a Crombie coat, which was a long, well-made coat that you wore over your suit. He also had a car. But most of all John, an ex-army officer, gave the impression that he was going places. We moved to Scotland shortly after our marriage to a small town near Loch Lomond and lived in a tiny company house. I had moved my mother to live with me, and John, who worked for an American company, travelled extensively. Initially he travelled in the UK. But what I didn't know at the time was that John would spend half his life away from home on business.

'John's career progressed rapidly and we had two children, David and Michael. As the years progressed we moved from the small town to a suburb of Glasgow, which was … how can I call it …? Well to do. John rose through the ranks of the American company and became its vice-president. He wanted to move us to Arizona, but I wished to stay in Britain, so he continued to travel, but it was now mainly overseas and for long periods. I have met some very interesting people, and some very famous people, through his work.'

'Astronauts, Prime Ministers, the Queen, Philip ... yes, I have seen the photographs upstairs,' Stasha gushed.

'John had an amazing career.' It was all Anne would say.

'Two sons?' Stasha asked. 'I only know David.'

There was a long silence before Anne said, 'Michael, my eldest son, died from complications of alcoholism.'

Stasha was shocked and surprised; she had seen a framed photograph of what she assumed was another son in the house, but she hadn't asked about him. Now she realised that even Anne's gilded cage was not immune to the harsh realities of life. Stasha thought of Anne's description of Michael's death. 'Complications of alcoholism' meant a long-term heavy drinker. She allowed the thought to rotate into her mind.

'It must have been hard,' Stasha said.

Anne merely nodded.

'And David?'

There was another pause. 'When they were growing up I never gave the same attention to him as I did to Michael.' There was another lengthy pause. 'I often think about that and regret it. David always acquired friends of both sexes very easily, John said of David, "if he fell into the River Clyde he'd come out dry," I think it was sometimes hard for Michael to live alongside that type of character. Maybe that was the basis of the continued resentment, but their brotherly infighting is a story for another day.'

'Why did you come to England after that marvellous life in Scotland?' Stasha asked, for there seemed much more to Anne than met the eye.

'For John's retirement.'

Both Anne and Stasha continue to talk and explore each other's differences and boundaries; Stasha was not keen on talking about her broken engagement, while Anne shied away from discussing Michael. But overall it had been an interesting afternoon, and a lot of the resentment had faded away. Both women had suffered, and they each had a story to tell.

'Why did I not like you?' Anne asked as

Stasha prepared to put her back on the bed.

Stasha thought about her answer, wanting it to have the maximum impact, so Anne would not forget it. 'You pre-judged me,' she eventually said.

Anne did not reply but allowed the answer to absorb into her mind.

Once Anne was settled, Stasha asked. 'What did you talk to Candy about when the door was shut the other day?' She'd been struggling to contain her curiosity since the incident.

Anne could not remember the exact gist of the conversation but said, 'I told her you are my main carer and that you're in charge, and that it doesn't mean I have taken a dislike to her or think any the less of her.'

'And what did Candy say when she heard that?' Stasha took great delight in asking.

'Candy understood. I don't think she wanted any trouble. She knows I like her, and that I don't want to lose the friendship that we've built.'

'An odd match, you and Candy?' Stasha straightened Anne's bed sheets and made her more comfortable.

'I liked her from the moment I met her,' Anne said simply.

'Unlike me,' Stasha could not resist saying. Anne chose not to reply but Stasha was like a dog with a bone. 'Why Candy?'

Anne thought for a few seconds about Candy and a brief smile hovered on her lips. 'I could see my young self in her.' She laughed at the absurdity of the remark. 'Loud, unconventional, headstrong. That was me, and that is Candy.' There was a brief silence. 'I got lucky. I hope Candy finds the same luck.'

Stasha said nothing.

So a mutually respectful truce had settled on the house, and consequently the atmosphere had changed. Anne could still be awkward, but her stinging criticism was gone and on more than one occasion she had held Stasha's hand and said thank you for the care she'd provided.

Stasha, in turn, had relaxed and become more talkative and confident. As a result, the two women now had a better understanding of each other, though their relationship was still not completely without difficulties. Colin – one of the agency's few male carers, who was known for his diligence and willingness to help – had noted the positive change in the atmosphere in the house. Candy, however, still had not returned to the house since her conversation with Anne.

It was a beautiful Tuesday afternoon – a perfect day for an invigorating summer walk in Stratford along the river Avon. Anne had asked to go, since she had often gone there with John and wanted to return. So in the early afternoon the van was loaded and off they both headed to Stratford.

Stratford-upon-Avon was as chaotic and busy as ever. Stasha had been lucky and managed to find a suitable disabled parking spot, and – with a sense of accomplishment – she helped Anne out of the van. She then proceeded to guide her along in her electric wheelchair to the canal area where they looked at the long canal boats and then had a brief stroll along the towpath of the river Avon.

'Are you okay, Anne?' Stasha asked, and Anne nodded.

The weather was turning warmer and it was a particularly pleasant afternoon. Numerous people passed them by, nodding to Anne and smiling at Stasha. Stasha wondered what people thought of their relationship, for she was never in any uniform. Perhaps they see me as Anne's granddaughter, she thought.

'I will treat you to afternoon tea,' Anne said and guided Stasha to the rear entrance of the Shakespeare Hotel in Chapel Street.

The hotel, situated in the centre of the town, featured oak beams and an old-world atmosphere; it was a luxurious and comfortable hotel which Anne knew well, for she had stayed there many times with John on trips from Scotland. The hotel welcomed them, and one of the porters helped Stasha to put Anne in a nice position by the bay window. There were other guests in the lounge, including American tourists, who were revelling in the traditional English atmosphere. Anne and Stasha ordered afternoon tea, with scones and clotted cream. The service was prompt and courteous, and Stasha noticed the ease with which Anne adapted to her surroundings.

The waitress treated both of them with the utmost courtesy.

'When you said afternoon tea, I thought you meant a cafe,' Stasha laughed. 'This is absolutely beautiful.'

'I stayed here with John when we lived in Scotland. It has remained quite a good hotel.

I'm glad you like it.'

'Like it?' Stasha said. 'It's how the other half live, isn't it, Anne?'

Anne merely smiled.

'You must have stayed in some nice hotels, Anne?' Stasha asked as she spread the cream and jam over her scone. On tasting the scone, her facial expression revealed how divine she found it.

'I have,' Anne replied. 'Where would you like to go in the world, if you had the choice?' Anne asked.

'I know exactly where I'd like to go, but it's not choice I am lacking, it's the funds and the time.' There was a matter-of-fact tone in Stasha's voice.

'So tell me where you'd like to go?'

'I'd like to take a year off and see America. The big cities. Experience the vibe of the affluent American life. New York, Los Angeles, San Francisco, Chicago, Florida, and then on to Asia, the Philippines, Australia and New Zealand. The whole world is waiting for me, Anne.' Stasha sighed. 'That's my dream, I wonder if I will ever see it.'

Anne gave a whimsical nod of her head, saying, 'My mother used to say "do not chase your dreams, for they will find you" ... you'll get there, Stasha.'

Stasha liked the remark, and she pondered on it.

'Would you travel on your own or would you look for a partner?' Anne asked.

There was a pause. 'I thought Filip and I would be travelling together before having children to see the world, to gain some sort of perspective on our own lives. But as you know, that wasn't to be. But, yes I would like to have a companion. But even more than that, I would like to have a partner.'

'Are you looking?' Anne asked as she sipped her tea. 'I always see the men looking at you.'

Stasha blushed, 'Thank you, but with this job you don't get much time to go out.'

'Well, give it time. You'll find someone, you'll settle down and you will have children.'

But Stasha remained unconvinced.

It had been a relaxing few hours; their conversation had been interesting and stimulating, and when they'd finished their afternoon tea Stasha asked the hotel reception if she could leave Anne in the lounge under their supervision while she went to get the van. She walked briskly to the car park and returned, reversing the vehicle into the hotel's side entrance to load Anne into it. Anne was getting tired, but Stasha had prevented her the hassle from being manoeuvred along the busy streets and the general melee of taking her to collect the van. She wanted now, more than anything, to get Anne back home.

The return journey on the busy roads was slow and hot. She was thankful that the air conditioning cooled the interior of the van quickly and efficiently. The drive lasted forty minutes through heavy traffic and Stasha had to telephone the office to say that she was running late for the tea time call. They arrived home and Stasha safely extracted Anne from the van. Once inside, she placed Anne on the bed, took her outdoor cardigan off and watched her doze off.

STASHA > STEFANIA
Surprise! Had a lovely afternoon with Anne

Anne was zonked out for the rest of the evening. When Gail came at eight o'clock, she and Stasha woke Anne for her personal care. Gail was another of Anne's favourites – heavily tattooed with a hairstyle of mixed colours and styles which Anne always commented on. She was an interesting and very caring person who Anne liked.

When Gail had left, Stasha gave Anne a slice of toast and a cup of tea, but Anne was soon off to sleep again. This left Stasha to go into the sitting room, have a snack, watch TV and phone her mother.

'There has been such a change,' Stasha told her mother.

'I told you to give it time, you have to have sympathy and patience,' Stasha's mother said and this echoed a remark that Anne had also made. It hit home. Despite Stasha feeling hurt and demoralised from Anne's constant put-downs, she hadn't flipped the scenario and put herself in Anne's shoes. She hadn't imagined what it would be like for a stranger to come to live with her, basically take over her house and carry out the most personal tasks. It was something that her training had glossed over: the psychological effect of the humiliation and helplessness experienced by the patient. Life was never black and white – the colour grey intermingled with both.

'There's an easy truce,' Stasha said to her mother. 'I hope it lasts, but we have had a frank talk. I see her point and she sees mine, so there was no point in carrying on something that has no ending. We are good at the moment ...'

Stasha's voice tailed off and her mother interjected, saying that perhaps she came across as too serious. She felt that this might have been part of the problem, for she knew Anastazja took things to heart and pondered on everything that was said instead of brushing things aside and carrying on with life.

Stasha disagreed.

They talked about Stasha coming home for a weekend in the next few months to see everyone; she missed her family – especially her mother – and she missed her native country like never before. Then the two of them caught up on more news before Stasha ended the call.

Once the phone call was over Stasha checked her social media and browsed her phone, but she was tired from the afternoon and decided to have an early bath and then perhaps an early night. She didn't think it was likely that Anne would wake up again that evening.

Anne had been unusually tired since the

trip to Stratford and Stasha realised, perhaps for the first time, that Anne was not as robust as she'd thought. Anne had asked Stasha to take her to the water gardens, which were around twenty minutes away. The gardens consisted of two large man-made lakes; people went there to sail boats, water ski, have picnics, walk their dogs and generally have a nice, refreshing time in the open air with the lakes as the backdrop. There was a good path around both lakes, and Anne and John used to visit frequently with their border collie – a walk around the lake and then refreshments in the outdoor cafe was a usual jaunt of a summer weekend.

Stasha had wanted Anne to recover from visiting Stratford, so during the next few days she had perused the website for the water gardens, wanting to know exactly where they would be going. It looked very pleasant, so the following Monday Stasha decided to have an early lunch before putting Anne once more into the back of the van, programming the vehicle satnav and then driving the short distance to their destination.

Anne became a great talker when Stasha drove, although neither could hear the other clearly, so it was a bit of a mismatched conversation. Humour was also starting to emerge between the two women.

It was half term week, so the lake and its surroundings were busy with children, dogs, babies, mothers and grandparents. As usual, Stasha managed to find a parking space in one of the disabled bays, extracted Anne from the van and began to push her along the footpath which ran adjacent to the lake. There was a faint breeze, but it was very relaxing and reminded Anne of days gone by when she would walk around the municipal waterworks near her home in Glasgow. This was a large reservoir set in the beautiful countryside of Strathclyde, with the Campsie Hills in the background and the refreshing Scottish air invigorating her lungs. Today was somewhat noisier, with the children playing and the dogs barking, and the air wasn't quite as fresh, but it was enjoyable and they both allowed silence to engulf them as they made their way around the lake, each occupied by their thoughts.

Stasha found it amusing that members of the public would step aside and make way for Anne in her wheelchair, as if she were some sort of royalty. It had also happened in Stratford, when members of the public had stepped out of the way as if Anne was Moses parting the seas. Anne ignored everyone, so Stasha was the one left to say thank you.

Stasha's walk lasted approximately forty minutes and, with no hills or gradient, it was quite an easy push with Anne, although Stasha did momentarily wonder why she had elected to put Anne in her manual chair rather than the electric. And then she remembered Stratford again. If the public hadn't made way for Anne on the pavement, Anne would have simply run them all down. She did not wish for a repeat of that.

They finally reached the outdoor cafe, which was relatively busy, and Stasha managed to find a table that had been cleared of dishes. She ordered a coffee for herself and an orange juice for Anne and sat back and absorbed the scene with the children, dogs and happy families.

'You said you brought John here?' Stasha asked, and Anne nodded.

'Many times with our dog,' Anne replied.

There was an air of reminiscence in her voice that was not lost on Stasha, and Stasha wondered momentarily what thoughts were going through Anne's mind.

It had been established early on that Stasha

would pay for everything using another of David's credit cards, and she was authorised to use it whenever she took Anne out for petrol, food, clothes and other things. When suggesting the arrangement, David didn't have any doubts about Stasha's honesty.

The two women were starting to find a tentative common ground, but the foundations on which this was built were not solid. Frequently they pushed each other's boundaries, but neither of them wanted to cross those boundaries, and so an easier understanding had developed between them. For her part, Anne had changed her attitude slightly, and she now said things like 'thank you' and 'have a good sleep' at the end of the day, which went some way towards making Stasha feel more appreciated.

Stasha was herself beginning to overlook some of Anne's involuntary remarks, and because of this new attitude there was very little friction between them. They had decided to go out in the van twice a week to visit various different places, but they both agreed the Anne should be back home by four thirty, otherwise she would be very tired the next day.

Anne had also kept her promise regarding Daisy; she had welcomed the cat into the house and she had full run of the inside and the garden. Stasha became a little miffed when Daisy decided to make the foot of Anne's bed one of her favourite spots, but Anne was quite content to share the mattress with Daisy, as she was comforted by her gentle purring. With Anne's permission, a cat climbing frame had been purchased, and Daisy enjoyed sitting on it and observing what was going on. Anne enjoyed a little play with Daisy when Stasha was busy. It was an arrangement that suited everyone.

But there was a cloud on the horizon looming ahead, written clearly on the kitchen calendar: Stasha had three days off and Candy was coming back. These breaks came round quickly, and Stasha had a suspicion that Candy would try and poison Anne's mind and set back all the progress she had made.

It wasn't that Stasha disliked Candy, for underneath the brash exterior was a good carer who would sometimes show her new ways of doing things. It was that she did not trust her and she knew Anne had a soft spot for her; Candy, being Candy, would exploit the situation.

On the following Saturday, Stasha and Anne went out to the fresh food market at a local town. It was a popular event, and the main road was closed so that local traders, farmers and food producers could sell their products. Stasha guided Anne's wheelchair through the crowds and bought the odd item from the various stalls.

'Let's have a coffee,' Anne suggested, and Stasha pushed her into one of the numerous coffee shops dotted along the high street. This time they sat outside enjoying the warm weather. Stasha ordered a latte while Anne stuck with a traditional white tea. They were observed by onlookers; it was not the first time their relationship had caused curiosity. Stasha poured Anne's tea into the special beaker that she always carried with her and helped Anne to sip it. The onlookers observed with interest.

As they sipped their drinks, Stasha asked Anne about her life. 'I still really don't know much about you,' Stasha said.

Anne paused for a minute, 'Well you know I came from Liverpool, I was an only child, I lived through the Second World War, my father died when I was young and I had to look after my mother and run the house.'

Stasha realised that Anne was repeating a few things but listened anyway.

'It must have been hard for you,' Stasha said. 'Life can turn so quickly.'

Anne nodded. 'One morning we were a normal family, then the following day my mother was a widow and our income dropped dramatically. My mother was vulnerable and took a long time to recover from my father's death, if she ever did. She died at ninety-seven.'

'How old was your mother when your father died?' Stasha asked.

It was obvious that Anne could not remember.

'In her forties?' Stasha suggested, and Anne nodded.

'I worked five days a week and travelled to work on the number seventy-three bus into Liverpool. I had tried my hand at nursing but that was a disaster, I left after one day.'

'One day?' Stasha said. 'And you criticised me!'

Anne placed her hand over Stasha's. 'I know,' she said. 'I resigned from a career that undoubtedly had prospects, but I couldn't handle the sight of blood or the unpredictability of the job. My father was very understanding about my situation. I am ashamed I did not show you the same compassion.'

'And you met John?' Stasha smiled.

'I met John through his sister,' Anne repeated. 'We played badminton together and she introduced us.'

'Was he rich?' Stasha asked with a wink that took the sting out of the question.

Anne smiled, 'When I met him, he wasn't rich but his prospects were very good.' She paused, searching her memory. 'He was a measured man, fifteen years older than myself and very assured - served eight years in India during the war – the Burma Campaign.'

Stasha momentarily reflected on what Anne had remembered, before saying, 'I noticed the framed D.F.C. medal upstairs and those magnificent swords on the wall.'

'The medal was awarded to Leslie, John's brother for a mission over France,' Anne involuntarily smiled remembering Leslie. She added, 'John was given those two combat swords from the Japanese capitulation ceremony in Rangoon ...' Anne slowly shook her head.

There was a pause and silence engulfed them.

'Tell me more about your life, Anne.' Stasha gave a gentle reassuring smile.

Anne gave a reflective pause.

'I had to move from Liverpool to a small village on the outskirts of Loch Lomond, which was around ten miles from the American manufacturing plant where John worked. It was a major employer in the area – people from nearby villages and towns depended on it. John joined as a salesman but quickly rose up the ranks to finally take charge of the factory and numerous other operations around the world. He escorted the Queen round the Scottish plant and other dignitaries often visited. John went everywhere first class, and on Concorde. He stayed at some amazing places. Someone told me he had a gilded life and it was true, although he had tremendous responsibility. The Americans loved the British army officer angle – John was someone you listened to. We moved to another house near Glasgow, which was bigger and more spacious, my mother was with us and life was good.'

Stasha raised her eyebrows. 'Quite a journey,' she said.

'Having my mother to stay with me was a great help. John was away most of the time and I would get telephone calls and Telex messages from the most far-flung, exotic-sounding places that I couldn't even find on the map! He would tell me how hot the weather was, when I was looking out of the window at the Scottish rain.'

Stasha laughed.

'We had a good life, plenty of holidays, and initially a happy, healthy family.'

Stasha smiled as Anne continued.

'John knew a lot of financial people in London. He was advised very well and he took that advice. I am now reaping those benefits.' Anne momentarily looked skywards, as if to say thank you.

Stasha raised her eyebrows and nodded in an understanding way.

'I did volunteer work with the children's court and then became a magistrate. Then I took some time out to be a Samaritan, and I heard the most heart-rending stories from helpless people, then I would drive home in my Jaguar thinking how fortunate I was.' Anne paused. 'But John was taxed very heavily on his earnings here in Britain, at one point ninety-eight pence for every pound he earned went on tax, so we did our bit.'

Stasha mentally did the sums.

'When his working life was over we downsized our lives, left Scotland and went to live in what we called "our retirement house", the house I have now.'

'Downsized?' Stasha said in surprise.

'Yes,' Anne replied. 'We no longer needed a large, opulent house.' Anne took a sip of her tea. 'You must think I am a spoiled bitch in the way that I treated you. And perhaps I am.'

Stasha did not reply.

'It was hard to adjust and, like I said, you are not what I expected, but I'm so glad we have overcome our problems.'

'So am I,' Stasha replied.

'John was not as impetuous as me, and he would have told me to hold my tongue in those instances when I was particularly sharp with my words.' Once again Anne placed her hand over Stasha's and squeezed it.

'It's in the past,' Stasha soothed. 'I enjoy your company.'

The day had gone well and Stasha had more insight into Anne's previous life and what made her tick. She had been an independent, successful woman, but she now found herself dependent, not only on other people, but also on complete strangers, some of whom she had no choice but to accept.

Stasha wondered if she would ever meet someone who would give her the same opportunities as John had given Anne. The whole family seemed to have been built on a settled, established foundation – and yes, she envied that.

Stasha drove home and the usual routine was followed. Anne was back in her bed by four thirty, tired from talking and tired from exertion; she dozed off and Stasha had the rest of the afternoon to herself.

The evening was spent, once again, watching television. Then Anne had an early night, and Stasha had a long phone call with her mother, during which she related everything Anne had told her.

The next few days saw Anne and Stasha in the rear garden enjoying the fine weather. It was at this stage that Anne pointed out that one of the fences looked tatty and needing painting. To her surprise, Stasha volunteered to do it, so the afternoon was taken up with Anne watching a determined Stasha paint the fence with paint she had found in the shed. It was therapeutic for both of them, with chit-chat thrown in and Daisy watching on. Anne would joke that Stasha had missed a bit and there was a relaxed atmosphere.

Once finished, they had refreshments on the patio, and it was Anne's turn to ask Stasha questions.

'Are you on one of those dating apps?' Anne asked.

Stasha could not help but laugh. 'Are you saying I need a man, Anne?'

'Somebody like you ...' Anne tailed off and smiled, she noticed a shy expression sweep across Stasha's face. 'I'm sure there are plenty of men wanting to take you out.'

Anne's tone indicated that the remark was meant with sincerity and Stasha knew it was said in a kind-hearted way.

'But am I waiting for them, Anne?'

Anne gave a knowing smile and said, 'Always wait for *the one*, Stasha, but never wait for someone to be the one.' They both laughed and Anne asked what it was she was looking for in a future partner.

Stasha took a sip of her coffee; it was a question that she had asked herself a few times – what was it that would attract her to someone? She thought of Filip, who was a tall, good-looking man, but who lacked ambition and did not necessarily connect with her own ideas of what the future should hold. Stasha shrugged before saying, 'I think stability, first and foremost.'

Anne raised her eyebrows, 'You would put stability above appearance and personality?'

The question hung in the air and momentarily threw Stasha; a measured answer was called for. 'I guess I want the dream relationship.'

'You mean everything?' Anne smiled.

'House, money, cars, everything,' Stasha joked. 'But I don't want some knobhead, a lot of rich guys can be super arrogant.'

'Just a lovely, rich man,' Anne said and added, 'a rich man is nothing but a poor man with money.'

Stasha acknowledged another one of Anne's sayings, but before she had time to reply Anne added another saying, 'Men, coffee and chocolate are all better rich, Stasha.'

Stasha threw her head back and laughed, 'Oh Anne where do you learn this from?'

'Life,' Anne replied and she gave a sage nod of her head. 'You are discerning.'

Stasha frowned, 'Now, what does that mean?'

'It means that you've probably learned the lessons of the past and you will not jump at the first man who gives you attention. A very wise thing to do.'

'Did you jump at John, Anne?' Stasha raised her eyebrows.

'He was a good man. It's a woman's instinct to know if a man is good or not.'

The afternoon passed with more light-hearted banter between them; it was as if the months preceding had been forgotten as the young lady and the elderly woman laughed and joked like they were old friends.

Stasha had started to enjoy Anne's company, as she was not unintelligent and was someone she could learn from, despite some of the things she'd said which were not to her liking. And for Anne, there was so much more to Stasha than she had first thought. Here was a thoughtful, ambitious, beautiful young woman who, in today's society, was only trying to keep her head above water – her predicament seemed unfair.

Anne was thankful that she was not at Stasha's life stage, for the world today was harsh, cruel, and at times downright horrid. She looked across the table at Stasha and realised the difficult journey she had in front of her. For every young woman, security was the key and Anne wondered if she could help

Stasha become more secure and have a head start; it was something she would mention to David to get his advice. Or was she just trying to ease her conscience about those terrible early weeks with Stasha? Anne wasn't sure.

The Thursday morning had arrived and Stasha had packed her bag and was waiting in the lounge with Anne for Candy to arrive. It was the three-day break for both of them and this time it had come round at an inopportune moment, for they were getting on so much better and a mutual respect had developed. The daily routine had changed. Stasha no longer sat alone in the kitchen with her coffee – it was now morning coffee with Anne and a lively chat. They would watch morning TV together and, if it was fine and warm, they would go in the garden, or Stasha would test Anne's brain and do some crosswords. Afternoons were taken up by short excursions in the van, sometimes more than twice a week, or by watching films downloaded from the internet. But, over the next few days, their relationship was to be tested to its limit.

Candy arrived like a sandstorm in the desert. She swept into the house with noise, bustle and bags, pointedly ignoring Stasha in the hall. She went straight into the lounge, knelt down next to Anne's chair and asked how she was.

Anne gave a welcoming smile. 'I'm fine,' she said.

Stasha witnessed the interplay between them. There was still this invisible bond; Candy was so demonstrative towards Anne, and it still irritated Stasha. Candy quickly engaged in small talk, deliberately excluding Stasha from the conversation.

Stasha realised again that these coming days were to be a real test of her relationship with Anne. She went across to Anne saying, 'I am off now.'

Candy offered a smile, but there was a look off sadness in Anne's eyes.

'How long will you be gone for?' she asked.

'I'll be back on Sunday,' Stasha said quietly and knelt down and kissed Anne on her forehead.

'I will miss you,' Anne said, and the remark was not lost on Candy who knew there was a change of attitude between the two women. 'Come back, won't you?' Anne added.

'See you later,' Candy said dismissively to Stasha as she and Anne watched her pick up Daisy's cage and leave the house.

TEN

Stasha drove back to her house, parked on her cramped road, got out of the car and walked with the cat carrier to her front door. She unlocked the door and entered. The lounge was cold and dark as the curtains had been closed. She let Daisy out of her cage and she quickly familiarised herself with her surroundings and went upstairs to have a snooze. Stasha checked the fridge. There was little or no food in the house and she felt irritated. Truth was, she was just feeling low. Stasha was usually good with her own company but this time she wished to be anywhere but here. Flashbacks of conversations she'd had with Anne played like a video inside her mind. What was she going to do with her life? Who was she going to meet? What did the future have in store for her? Surely it would not just be coming back to this small, cramped house day in day out with no one to greet her. She knew she deserved more.

The longer she thought about her dilemma the more determined she was to pick herself up. She opened the curtains, tidied round the house, went back to her car and headed to the supermarket. She bought sufficient food for the next few days, but it was a hassle compared with the online ordering she did at Anne's. In the evening she went to the gym and exercised thoroughly. She tried not to think of what Anne was doing with Candy or whether they had had another takeaway or pizza – or porn film. She found it peculiar that she was thinking about them; perhaps she had become slightly protective of Anne and hoped Candy didn't overtire her – or overfeed her.

On the Saturday morning, Stasha decided to have a long, well-earned lie-in with Daisy next to her on the bed. She would not get up till midday and would have an easy afternoon around the house, but her morning was disturbed by a phone call. She didn't wish to answer it, but when she picked up her iPhone she saw that the call was from Anne's phone number. Curiosity made her answer it; it was Candy who immediately handed the phone to Anne.

There was a muffled and muted voice on the other end of the line. It was Anne asking if a she was alright and if she was enjoying her time off. It was a short call but it really set Stasha back, as it was absolutely not expected but very much welcome nevertheless.

The rest of her weekend was spent pottering about her house and doing some general housework. She had telephoned her mother and then one of her friends from Poland, and they'd discussed the possibility of her flying out to see them. The end of her break was approaching and this time she had found it difficult to get into a routine. She was at a loss as to how to spend her time, and this surprised her. Anne's words had been going over and over in her head during these last few days. Everything looked a little bleak and there was a niggle at the back of her mind as to where she was heading. Ideally, she wanted to travel the world then become more settled, perhaps put a deposit down on a house, invite her mother over to stay for periods, some type of progress, but it was all a pipe dream. A zero-hours contract was all there was and a deposit for a house was unobtainable.

On the Sunday afternoon Stasha drew the curtains, switched off the hot water, locked all the doors, placed Daisy in her cage, then went to the car and loaded it with all her personal belongings. She wondered what Anne and Candy had been up to. Had Candy been successful in setting Anne back to her old ways, or had Anne been resolute? Time would tell.

Stasha approached Anne's house and turned in to the drive. She opened the gates and noticed the lounge blinds had been closed. It wasn't that sunny, so she wondered what was going on.

Stasha entered the house carrying Daisy's cage. It was quiet and she immediately went into the lounge to see Anne lying on her bed, asleep. Candy came out from the kitchen and offered a short smile towards Stasha, who did not smile back but placed Daisy's cage down and let her out. She walked back into the lounge to see Anne still asleep. She looked peaceful; the room was tidy, the bed was well made – everything seemed fine. She immediately went across to the hand-held thermometer on the mantlepiece and placed it in front of Anne's forehead to give a reading – the temperature was slightly high but nothing to be concerned about. It was then that Anne opened her eyes and noticed Stasha looking at her.

'Stasha,' Anne said in a quiet voice. She held her hand out so Stasha could hold it.

'How are you, Anne?'

'All the better for seeing you.'

The remark made Candy, who had been hovering around, frown.

'You want rid of me, do you, Anne?' Candy said, her laughter taking the sting out of her comments.

Anne shook her head. 'I love both of you,' she said.

'Has the doctor been round?' Stasha asked, and Candy said it had just been the district nurse. Anne had been under the weather and wanted the afternoon in bed.

'What have you done since I have been away?' Stasha asked.

'We went to the park yesterday. I was pushed around in my chair. It was a very nice afternoon – we had ice cream,' enthused Anne.

'Was she wrapped up?' Stasha asked.

Candy frowned, irritated at Stasha's line of questioning. 'Absolutely she was wrapped up; had a scarf on as well, it was a nice afternoon.'

Stasha left the lounge and went upstairs to unpack. She then returned downstairs to give Daisy some food and water just as Candy was preparing to leave.

'I'll pop in in the week to see you,' Candy said and waved goodbye to Anne.

Stasha went back into the lounge and asked Anne if she was really all right.

'A little cold,' Anne replied, and with that Stasha went to the kitchen, retrieved the hot water bottle, filled it from the kettle and gave it to Anne.

The following day saw no improvement, so Stasha asked for the doctor to make a home visit to make sure everything was okay. Anne had developed a nasty cough and the doctor prescribed antibiotics and told her to have plenty of fluids and bed rest, and this is what Anne did for the next three days. It gave Stasha a lot of time to herself, so she did a bit of gardening, caught up on some personal paperwork and generally relaxed around the house with Daisy as Anne slept.

The second night Anne had a particularly difficult time. She rang the bell four times, and then asked Stasha to sit with her for an hour. So, in the early hours of the morning, they both shared a cup of tea together and had little chat about what was going to happen to Anne in the future.

'Will I go in a home?' Anne asked.

'I don't think David will put you in a home.'

'I want to stay in my own house,' Anne had

said frequently, and from what Stasha could determine from David, that was what was going to happen. But Stasha realised that things could change so quickly, and Anne could become quite unwell and require hospital treatment or maybe a placement in some kind of hospice.

It was all very depressing.

By the fourth day Anne had improved and had got up for her breakfast. She ate only sparingly – her appetite had not returned – and she went back to bed mid morning and slept for the rest of the day. It was a concerning time for Stasha, for this was a dramatic change in Anne's behaviour and mental state, and there was concern among the other staff that she was on a downward spiral.

On the sixth day Anne got up and spent most of the day in her chair. Her appetite had returned and the glint in her eye had come back. Stasha had missed the more mischievous Anne over the past few days.

The antibiotics had started to take effect. The doctor had extended the dose for another ten days to clear the nasty chest infection that Anne had mysteriously picked up.

Candy had popped in to see if Anne was

okay and had reassured Stasha that Anne had been wrapped up on her trip round the park, but Stasha remained unconvinced, although she was thankful that Anne was getting back to her normal self.

'I have been quite worried about you,' Stasha said softly when she had made Anne a cup of tea in the afternoon.

'I felt quite unwell,' Anne replied. 'Got cold going round the park.'

Stasha gave a concerning smile. She knew Candy had not wrapped Anne up enough when she went out on the Saturday.

'It got me thinking these past few days,' Anne said and looked into Stasha's eyes. 'Let's do something different,' she announced over dinner one evening. 'Let's live a little.'

'Do something different?' Stasha frowned.

'Let's go to London, see a show, have afternoon tea at a nice hotel,' Anne suddenly suggested.

Stasha's eyes widened. 'Really?' It was all she could say. 'It sounds absolutely lovely but it's a little far fetched don't you think, Anne?'

'We can have a two-night stay in London. See the sights,' Anne babbled on as she ate her trifle.

The idea appealed to Stasha but she knew

Anne was talking in the abstract, for it had no bearing on what could be achieved.

'You look sceptical,' Anne said as she sipped her tea in the late evening warmth of the conservatory.

'How can we do that?' Stasha asked.

There was a pause before Anne said, 'That's what David is for, to arrange things!'

Over the last few weeks there had been a new carer accompanying some of the more experienced carers coming to see Anne. Jasmine had just turned thirty. She was of small slim build and had the most attractive eyes. She came from a job in retail.

If Samantha was the most natural carer, then Jasmine, initially at least, had the most natural manner. Jasmine seemed to have a very gentle and considerate way of communicating with Anne, but this had, for whatever reason known only to Jasmine, started to recede and had been replaced with a more superficial attitude.

In return Anne had started to pick up on what she felt was a pseudo-friendly tone that Jasmine had adopted, and Anne was no longer buying into the ability, or personality, of this young woman. As such, her opinion of

Jasmine briefly changed, and she told Stasha, 'I am not sure about her ...'

This resulted in a tetchiness from Anne whenever Jasmine visited and Stasha recognised the signs only too well. Anne was starting to nit-pick Jasmine for various reasons that were, to Stasha, unjustified. Jasmine responded with a willingness to learn, but although she became a little over-sensitive – she did remain scrupulously polite and had a wish to please.

Sometimes Jasmine would attend with Colin. Anne affectionately referred to them both as *Dastardly and Muttley.*

Anne remained stubbornly unconvinced regarding Jasmine and a love–hate relationship developed between them. On one occasion Stasha had said to Anne that she was being unfair to Jasmine and had told her to scale back the criticism.

'You mean I'm treating her like I treated you?' came Anne's reply.

Stasha raised her eyebrows but her eyes answered the question.

To Jasmine's absolute credit, she persevered and within a short period started to win Anne over – and far quicker than Stasha had managed. They soon developed an easy rapport. But like Stasha before her, Anne had got Jasmine completely wrong, for in the end she turned out to be a genuinely lovely, caring individual – headstrong yet, bizarrely, easily influenced by others – but a very appealing person nevertheless.

Jasmine soon found another position at one of the airport's hospitality lounges and left the agency just as she was getting into her stride.

Although Jasmine and Anne parted on good terms, with no hard feelings on either side, both Anne and Stasha felt they had not got the best out of her – and that was very much regretted.

So the idea of Stasha and Anne visiting London hung in the air over the next few days and was talked about repeatedly by Anne, with Stasha doing all the listening.

'I still think it is too much for you, Anne,' Stasha said and there was a note of caution in her voice.

'I feel fine. David is sorting it,' Anne would reply.

'But you get tired so easily,' Stasha would signal a note of caution.

Another week had passed and nothing had happened. Stasha had the impression that

Anne was merely talking about what she would like to do in London, rather than what she could do.

On the Wednesday morning David had telephoned Stasha and informed her that plans were being made for a two-day trip to London later in the month for herself and Anne.

Stasha was astonished but agreed to the proposition.

So David confirmed that they would have a private wheelchair taxi to travel down in to London to stay at a hotel, visit Harrods, have afternoon tea and take in a London show. Everything was being organised.

It was not long before the rest of the care staff knew about Stasha's trip to London and there were a few envious comments, especially since they knew of Anne and Stasha's tumultuous start and how quickly their icy relationship had thawed.

Candy was struck by the ironic situation, and immediately after hearing the news came round to see Anne for a supposed chat.

'You're not taking me with you?' Candy asked.

'Just Stasha,' was Anne's reply, and Candy give a loud sigh as she shot a glance in

Stasha's direction.

Candy persisted but Anne noted that she had children and commitments at home. The reply did not satisfy Candy and she shrugged and walked to the kitchen to make herself a cup of tea.

Stasha looked on and raised her eyebrows, knowing that Candy would try and persuade Anne to change her mind. Candy returned with cups of tea for her and Anne, but nothing for Stasha.

'I'm disappointed in you,' Candy said straight out of nowhere.

Stasha smiled. Perhaps Anne would now see the real Candy.

'Stasha is my main carer,' Anne said but it sounded hollow.

Stasha felt a sudden sense of victory. It was rare for Anne to disagree with anything Candy said, but on this occasion Anne was standing firm and Candy did not like it. She pursed her lips, smoothed her hair, picked up her phone and went into the kitchen to wash out her mug. Afterwards she returned to the lounge, still engrossed in her phone.

'What will you be doing in London?' Candy asked, looking up momentarily from her phone and taking a seat.

'Harrods, afternoon tea and a show,' Stasha said and savoured the moment.

'I thought we were friends, Anne?' Candy said.

'It will be Anastazja and me,' Anne replied.

With that, Candy shrugged her shoulders, got up from the chair and left the house, this time without a kiss or a hug for Anne.

And so the stories swept round the other carers.

It was decided that the trip would be taken in three weeks' time, just before Stasha's two-day break. The specially adapted taxi would drive Anne and Stasha down to London, where they would stay at the Ritz Hotel in Piccadilly, and the hotel would obtain tickets for them to attend a theatre show of their choice. David informed the hotel of Anne's requirements. As a surprise, Stasha would not be told that they would be staying at the Ritz until they arrived there. They could either have their evening meal in their two-bedroom suite or in one of the restaurants. On the first afternoon they would have the world-famous afternoon tea at the Ritz, and the following day they would have the morning at Harrods and a show in the evening. All transfers would be arranged by the hotel.

But today was merely a visit to yet another garden centre. The area in which they lived had many gardening enthusiasts and consequently there were many garden centres, all selling and offering similar things.

'Are you looking forward to our trip?' Anne asked as she took a bite of a small slice of carrot cake in the garden centre coffee shop.

'I am,' came the short reply.

'Do you know London?' Anne asked.

Stasha shook her head. 'I suppose you know it, been there many times, have you?'

'I know parts of it. To be frank, it was so dirty, but I think it's improved now. John used to like going to London. He was a great one for the museums and would spend afternoons looking through them when he'd retired.'

'Where are we staying?' Stasha asked again.

'It's a surprise for you.'

Stasha raised her eyebrows, 'Surprise? What does that mean?'

'Bring your best clothes with you,' Anne laughed.

'So it's not bed and breakfast?' Stasha replied jokingly.

Back-stabbing comments, gossip, jealousy,

resentment and good old-fashioned annoyance from some of the care staff were beginning to surface. Since the trip to London had been arranged, Stasha had been the subject of petty digs and pointed remarks. It troubled her, so she phoned her mother one evening to vent her frustration. David had also been told of some of the comments being made about his mother. His philosophy was that other people's comments were none of his business. He did, however, give his support to Stasha over the phone, and this was welcomed by her.

Candy had come midweek in another attempt to try and persuade Anne that she should take her to London as well, saying that if she came, her kids would be looked after by her parents.

But Anne was resolute in her decision. 'I love both of you,' Anne said, 'I won't forget you, Candy.'

The remarked soothed a little of Candy's irritation.

The distinct chill from some of the carers continued during the week as they learned more of Anne and Stasha's extravagant trip. There had been numerous loud sighs and mutterings of, 'We don't get anything like that, do we?' And, of course, the estimated cost of the trip was being bandied about. Everyone seemed to be an expert on prices and they all agreed that it must be thousands of pounds. All of them held the same opinion that it 'seemed unfair to single out one carer for such an occasion.' This bad feeling did not affect the care that Anne received, for they were all very professional, but the general consensus was that David was trying to buy back Stasha's good favour after the months of harsh treatment his mother had dished out to her. David just dismissed the comments.

While Anne had not changed her mind on immigration, and she still felt that there was too much of it to the UK, she now recognised that people like Stasha had something to offer, a different way of doing things and a different method of going about their daily business. In an odd sort of way, the whole episode with Stasha had taught her not to be so impetuous in her judgements – her assumptions about Stasha had been unfair, but Anne would never admit to this.

If truth be known, Anne wished she had been less judgemental and allowed Stasha to become her caring self far quicker, for Anne now liked her immensely. A case in point was Anne's ridiculous insistence on calling Stasha by her full Christian name, despite it being quite a mouthful for Anne to say at times, while knowing full well she wished to be referred to as Stasha. Anne had never considered Stasha's feelings, and it had turned into a laborious point-proving exercise that had been ill considered. It was only when Anne asked Stasha why she preferred her nickname that Anne finally understood the reason for the initial request.

'My mother is the only person who frequently calls me by that name,' Stasha had replied and there was a note of tetchiness in her voice that was not lost on Anne.

'I am sorry I did not realise, but Anastazja is a lovely name.'

Stasha grabbed this opportunity to redress the balance, for she had suffered weeks of Anne's insistence on calling her a different name, and she said, 'Perhaps if you had asked me ...'

Anne allowed Stasha the final say on the matter and decided she would not reply, preferring instead to let sleepings dogs lie.

ELEVEN

A hospital appointment for an X-ray on Anne's knees had been pencilled in on the calendar a few weeks ago, and it was due to take place the following day.

The hospital, part of a large NHS hospital trust, was situated in the next town, around twenty minutes' drive away, and Stasha had convinced David that she was able to handle the appointment with Anne on her own. And so, the evening before, she prepared Anne for the appointment, which was scheduled for ten o'clock.

'Is this for my knees?' Anne asked, and Stasha nodded. 'But they feel okay, now?' Anne muttered under her breath.

'You still have to go, your doctor wants the X-ray,' Stasha replied and then sighed, for she secretly thought the doctor's request was an overreaction to knee pain that was probably just age-related arthritis.

'We will be leaving at nine fifteen,' Stasha said. She touched Anne's shoulder and smirked before saying, 'I don't want anything to postpone the departure time or any last-minute situations to deal with.' It was a playful warning from Stasha, and Anne nodded her head in acknowledgement.

It was the morning of Anne's X-Ray and Fran came with Leigh to get Anne up. Fran, being an older member of the care team, was an experienced carer who had seen the joys of the job as well as the downsides. Fran was someone you could learn from, ever the diplomat in her manner and unquestionably a valued member of Anne's care team.

Leigh, one of the infamous 'models', was always vivacious, cheerful, talkative and friendly. Leigh had air stewardess written all over her, for she was poised and always beautifully presented. Leigh always displayed a decorous attitude whenever she dealt with Anne, her manners were impeccable, and she was not only a glamourous individual but one who was also tremendously good-natured and amiable. Anne never uttered a negative remark regarding this engaging young woman.

Both carers got Anne up on time with the minimum of fuss.

Stasha and Anne left for the hospital on time at nine fifteen. The weather was not ideal, a light summer drizzle, so Stasha remembered to take an umbrella as well as a bottle of water for Anne. The drive was complicated by numerous roadworks and portable traffic lights dotted along the route, and Stasha felt unusually stressed as she tried to get Anne to the hospital on time. She did not speak to Anne during the journey, nor did Anne speak to her – instead, they both listened to Radio 2. When Stasha arrived at the hospital she was met with a huge queue to the car park; she then realised she should have brought someone else with her and she began to constantly check the time on the van's clock. Her thoughts turned to the forthcoming trip to London. If a hospital appointment generated so much anxiety, how would she cope in the capital city? It was something that was praying on her mind, but since Anne was looking forward to it so much she didn't have the courage to mention that the trip could be problematic. Maybe, just maybe, she should ask to take another carer with her. It was something to think about. But did she really want Candy with her all week?

The queue to the car park cleared fairly quickly, but then Stasha could not find a disabled parking space, so she had to queue again for the overflow car park. Because of this, the time she had allowed quickly ran out.

Eventually it was her turn to enter the car park and search for a suitable space. This took a further five minutes and then she had to wait patiently for an elderly lady to reverse her small car out of a space before she could park the van in the vacant area. It was a tight squeeze but she managed to do it. Then came the ordeal of getting Anne out of the back of the van in a busy car park in the rain. She had to be careful, as it was not easy; there was quite a strong wind and a light drizzle, so she hovered the umbrella over Anne and placed a waterproof hat on her head. Stasha was now feeling even more stressed, but Anne was oblivious as she sat in her wheelchair complaining that they were late.

Anne waited for Stasha to lock and secure the van before proceeding to the hospital entrance. Once inside the hospital they were directed to the X-ray department, and as soon as Stasha arrived she closed her eyes and gave an inward sigh, for the waiting room was full, even at ten o'clock. Stasha checked Anne in for her appointment and was advised that there would be a lengthy wait. As Stasha surveyed the cramped waiting room she silently cursed Anne's doctor for insisting on what she felt was a totally unnecessary appointment.

Anne also noticed the number of people in the waiting room and asked, 'How long is the wait?'

Stasha ignored the question. She was busy trying to find a suitable space for Anne's wheelchair so as not to cause any obstruction. Stasha managed to sit next to her; she knew it was not going to be an enjoyable experience and this was confirmed when Anne turned to her, saying in a loud voice, 'I should have gone private.'

For once, Stasha agreed.

They were soon joined by the inevitable screaming and out-of-control child, whose mother's excuse was 'he's only young', as he screamed his way from one side of the hospital corridor to the other. Stasha glanced round the waiting room. Patients of all ages, engrossed in their magazines, phones or newspapers were trying to ignore the badly behaved child and the long wait.

'I do wish someone would shut him up,' Anne said and the mother looked across at them.

Stasha soothed the situation with a disarming smile. She knew the woman had mistaken her for the granddaughter. The unexpected stress of the morning was starting to get to Stasha, but she had to keep calm for the sake of Anne. Again she thought of the trip to London and all that it would entail. She would telephone David and voice her concerns.

'Can we go home?' Anne asked and Stasha shook her head. 'I want to go home,' Anne repeated.

'It won't be too long now,' Stasha lied, but it fell on deaf ears anyway as Anne made an attempt to move her chair by searching for the controller, forgetting that she was in the manual chair.

'Take me to the window,' Anne instructed and Stasha replied that they could not leave the waiting area.

'I want to go home,' Anne repeated and then added, 'my knee's alright now – I want to go home.'

Stasha closed her eyes and quickly considered how to deal with the increasingly tense situation. For the first time she wished Candy, with her bombastic attitude, was there to help.

There was a few minute's respite before Anne raised her voice a little.

'I want to go home,' she demanded.

Stasha had to think on her feet, for Anne was becoming stressed. She looked round the waiting room. There were other elderly people there and she knew she had no right to push her way to the front, but she had to make Anne more relaxed and comfortable. She got up, walked to the reception desk and asked how long the wait would be. The answer did not reassure her – six people were in front of them.

Stasha glanced at her phone. It was now twenty to eleven; they had been sitting there for almost forty-five minutes but it felt like an eternity. Ironically, the screaming child and her mother got up and were seen quickly, and Stasha was thankful that a semblance of peace and quiet had returned to the waiting room. But Anne was getting stressed, repeatedly asking to go home, and Stasha was having to soothe and comfort her all the time. Stasha started to talk about inconsequential things to try and take Anne's mind off the wait and it worked for a short time, with Anne's attention momentarily distracted. And then there was the inevitable question.

'When are we going home?'

Eventually, after a further fifteen minutes, Anne was called in and Stasha pushed her wheelchair into the X-ray room. But their relief at being seen was short lived, for the radiographer said that Anne had to be put on the examination table. This meant that a hoist and suitably trained staff would be required to help with the transfer from the wheelchair to the X-ray machine. Stasha said she could hoist Anne on her own, but the radiographer pointed out that there was no hoist available in the department, so they had to return to the waiting room until a suitable hoist was found. Stasha closed her eyes, wishing she was anywhere but there.

Another forty minutes passed before Stasha saw a hospital porter pushing a hoist down the corridor. She gave a sigh of relief, but it was now twelve thirty and there had been no morning tea for Anne and no chocolate. Anne was snappy and sleepy and the whole thing had turned out to be an absolutely horrible experience.

The X-ray of Anne's knees was efficiently done, but further time was taken up by hoisting Anne on and off the examination table and making sure she was okay. Once done, Stasha pushed Anne to the hospital exit and then, to cap her morning off, she noticed that it was now deluging with rain and there was no way she could push Anne to the van in such wet weather. Stasha saw a hospital porter and asked if they could keep an eye on Anne while she braved the elements and retrieved the van. Ten minutes later, after paying the exorbitant parking charge and then queuing to get out of the car park, Stasha returned with the van looking somewhat bedraggled. Her dark glasses had splashes of rain on them, her hair was damp and she had a general demeanour of 'will this ever end?'

'You took your time,' Anne said, as only Anne could.

Stasha bent down and kissed Anne on her forehead saying, 'I love you Anne,' before pushing her to the van. And finally their morning from hell at the hospital was over.

They had spent a more relaxed afternoon sitting in the conservatory enjoying tea and cakes with little conversation and Anne dozing on and off. Stasha was busy on her phone and laptop.

'I'll put you back on the bed now,' Stasha suggested, and Anne nodded as she was being pushed back into the lounge.

Then Anne said, quite unexpectantly, 'Thank you for this morning, Stasha. I know it was stressful but you coped.'

There was a moment's pause as Stasha absorbed Anne's words. They were very welcome.

'Thank you, Anne,' she replied.

TWELVE

Stasha had telephoned David voicing her concerns about the forthcoming trip to London and Anne's ability to cope with such a hectic couple of days. David said he would think about what Stasha had said and telephone her back. Within an hour he confirmed that the hotel would provide any help that was required. Which hotel it was, David still wasn't saying.

'It is to be a surprise for you, Stasha. Something to show how much Anne and I think of you.'

It was a nice gesture, but Stasha would have preferred to know where she was going so that she could mentally prepare for what was ahead and, more importantly, decide what to wear.

David also mentioned something quite disconcerting and unusual; there was going to be a visit in the week from Anne's solicitor. Anne, the solicitor and David would all attend a virtual meeting, possibly held in the dining room for around an hour, and he asked if Stasha could leave the house during that time. It was an odd request, and Stasha wondered what the reason behind it was.

After all, Stasha was supposed to be with Anne at all times. She informed the office of this request.

Curiosity got the better of Stasha when she served Anne a glass of hot water later in the afternoon, and she asked about the forthcoming visit from the solicitor. Anne merely nodded, saying, 'It's just something I have to do.'

'Do you want me to leave the house when they are here?' Stasha asked with a frown, and Anne didn't immediately catch on to the significance of the question. 'David has asked me to leave the house while the solicitor is here.' Stasha was hoping that Anne would inadvertently divulge something, but she said nothing, merely nodding and saying that if that's what David had said then that's what he'd said. She gave nothing away.

The chiropodist arrived the following morning to attend to Anne's feet and hands. Andrew was a jovial chap with lots of gossip who went round many care homes and elderly people's houses. He was polite, well presented and had obviously been caring for Anne for a long time, even before her stroke. Stasha offered him a cup of tea then duly made one for him before he and Anne set about putting the world to rights. He stayed for about forty-five minutes and, during that time, they covered all the topics, from politics to the weather and what was in the news. Stasha busied herself in the hall and kitchen, listening to what was being said, and then – by chance – she heard Anne comment on her.

'I would be lost without her,' Anne said.

'She seems a nice girl,' Andrew replied.

'She's wonderful. I haven't been that kind to her but I'm hoping to make amends.'

Andrew laughed, for he knew Anne only too well.

Stasha smiled to herself. There was a definite change in Anne and the more time she spent with her the more she got to like her. Would wonders never cease? she thought to herself.

It had been on Anne's mind ever since she and Stasha had reconciled their differences. Anne felt that she had pushed Candy out unfairly in favour of Stasha and that concerned her, for Candy had done nothing wrong. And with this trip to London being talked about repeatedly by various staff members, Anne felt it was time to smooth things over with Candy, who had recently been a little tetchy whenever she came round.

She had asked Stasha if she would mind if Candy came round for a cup of tea and a chat. She thought perhaps that Stasha could join them and any differences between the two women could be temporarily set aside for Anne's sake.

Stasha gave a reluctant nod, but it was not convincing because Candy was not the sort of person she could ever get on with. Candy was brusque and loud, Stasha was quiet and calm.

Afternoon tea. How civilised it all sounded, but how long would the peace remain before Stasha and Candy, in the same room, would be fighting for Anne's affection?

Anne had asked Stasha which one of the London shows she would like to go and see, and after some consideration and consulting her phone she mentioned Mamma Mia.

Somewhat cunningly, Stasha asked Anne how she could get tickets so quickly for a London show that was presumably fully booked, and Anne replied that David was handling all the arrangements.

Stasha had telephoned her mother on repeated occasions, excitedly telling her of her forthcoming trip to London, and her mother had listened in astonishment to the complete turnaround of Anne and Stasha's friendship. Stasha also mentioned the forthcoming visit from Candy where they were all supposed to sit down and 'be friends'. Her mother gave her some sage advice that she should accept the situation with Candy and take deep breaths. Then Stasha brought up the proposed visit of the solicitor and the fact that they wanted her to leave while the meeting was in progress.

'It's their business,' Stefania said. 'Don't interfere.'

Stasha persisted, 'Why would they want me out of the house?'

'It doesn't concern you, Anastazja.'

Stasha noticed the emphasis her mother used on her name, and she knew to let the topic subside before her mother had the final word.

'Let it be and do as they say.'

The day of the afternoon tea arrived. It wasn't an ideal situation for Stasha, but she'd agreed to it to please Anne. Deep down, Stasha thought it was a preposterous idea, and she knew that Candy would rinse the occasion for all it was worth.

And so it was. Candy arrived at the house at two, her long red hair flowing over her face. In a box, she was carrying two beautifully decorated cakes covered with strawberries and cream. She managed a very weak smile at Stasha as she passed her in the hall before her usual gushing greeting to Anne.

'I bought you these, Anne,' Candy said and she bent down and showed Anne the two cakes through the clear plastic lid. 'I thought you and I could enjoy them together.'

Anne nodded.

Stasha noted that there were only two cakes, not three. Clearly Candy was putting down a marker before she'd even sat down.

'Would you like me to make you a cup of my strong tea?' Candy asked Anne.

Anne agreed.

Stasha, as usual when she was with Candy, felt like a spare part and she looked for reassurance from Anne, who smiled at her before saying quietly, 'Just go with it, Stasha.'

Stasha smiled back and went to rearrange the chairs in the conservatory so they could all sit together in a circle.

Stasha reviewed her opinion of Candy. She was a manipulative bitch, and she felt incensed that Anne, for all her faults, could not see what was going on, but she ignored those feelings and went into the kitchen to help.

She was met by Candy's faint, unfriendly voice saying, 'I can do it.'

Both women returned with plates and the tray of tea. Stasha positioned Anne's wheelchair and they sat around the glass coffee table like three acquaintances – not friends. Candy again took the initiative and poured Anne her cup of tea, cut her cake in half and presented her with a napkin. Stasha sat back and watched how she was able to successfully pull the wool over Anne's eyes.

But was Anne really so stupid that she couldn't see what was happening?

'It's nice having you both here,' Anne said and smiled, before adding, 'I wish you two would talk to each other.'

It was Candy who turned to Stasha and placed her hand on her arm, saying directly to Anne, 'We're friends.'

Stasha raised her eyebrows and Anne gave an inward laugh. 'I might be old, Candy, but I'm not stupid – yet.'

They all laughed together and there was a feeling of a temporary warming between them.

Anne asked Candy about her children.

'They don't do what they are told,' she said.

'Do you find it difficult coping on your own?' Stasha asked, and she couldn't resist ending with, 'Especially since you have no reliable partner.'

'Like you,' Candy replied.

'I have no children.' Stasha spat the reply.

Anne witnessed the interplay; these two women were totally at odds with each other and neither would allow the other to have an edge.

Candy went on to explain about various incidents she had encountered while doing care and some of the stories were eye-wateringly funny. Others were quite sad and, although she described them in detail, neither women could detect a sense of mocking from Candy. The tone changed as Candy, who had once worked in a care home, told of the numerous incidents of helpless old people locked in bedrooms.

'It's terrible what goes on. You're very lucky to have a son who looks after everything,' Stasha said.

Anne tried to eat her cream cake in a dignified manner but failed. The girls watched as Anne got cream and strawberries all over her fingers and down the front of her napkin – they laughed as they got up to clear the cream away. Anne laughed as well and for a brief moment there was genuine camaraderie between the three women. It was a nice atmosphere.

'You know, I shouldn't say this ...' Anne paused. 'You two are my favourites.'

The remark was not lost on the two women, and Candy asked if there were other carers she liked.

Anne hesitated and the girls laughed. 'Some,' was all she said. 'I like the manager,' added Anne, 'And her daughter and her partner, nice girls.' Anne paused to think of another name, 'Emily,' she finally said, 'Is lovely.'

'What about Marie?' Stasha suggested and Anne nodded.

Candy threw down the gauntlet. 'But which one of us is your favourite, Anne?'

Anne suddenly became diplomatic as she sipped her tea. 'I said, I love you both equally.' Stasha and Candy laughed before Anne continued. 'Stasha and I got off on the wrong foot, but I would be lost without her now.'

Candy turned to Stasha and smiled. Stasha raised her eyebrows.

Anne added, 'And Candy is welcome here any time.'

'Tell me about your trip to London?' Candy asked and there was a faint note of irritation in her voice.

'A two-day trip for myself and Stasha,' came the reply from Anne.

Candy raised her eyebrows. 'Very nice.' She turned to Stasha. 'Are you looking forward to it?' She managed to get the words out without showing too much resentment.

Stasha nodded. 'They still won't tell me where we're staying.' She looked at Anne for an answer, but none came.

Candy turn back to Anne. 'Where are you staying?' Her question was more of an accusation with a hint of 'How much are you actually spending?'

'It's a surprise for Stasha,' Anne replied. Looking across, she met Stasha's eyes. She could see in them a look off appreciation. 'It's my way of saying sorry to her.'

'Sorry?' Candy asked as she sipped her tea. 'What on earth have you got to be sorry about, Anne?'

'I treated Stasha badly,' Anne said.

'I wish you'd treated me badly; then I could have gone to London.' Candy gave an involuntary laugh.

'I can't take you Candy, you know that.' Anne's voice was soft.

Candy did not answer but looked to the ground in disappointment.

'You've got your children, got responsibilities, it's midweek ...' Anne tailed off.

Candy did not answer but secretly acknowledged that Anne was right. Through gritted teeth she turned to Stasha and said, 'I hope you have a nice time.'

Stasha replied that she hoped she would and was very much looking forward to it.

Anne then pursed her lips and thought about what she was going to say, and more importantly how she was going to phrase it. 'I am an old woman,' she said to both of them, 'and it will come as no surprise to you both that I like you.' Anne gave a crooked smile. 'Equally ...' she said as an afterthought.

Stasha frowned, not fully understanding, but Candy knew what Anne was referring to.

'Are you going to leave me all your millions?' Candy joked and winked at Anne, who gave an involuntary laugh.

But the answer did not materialise and the question hung in the air, with Anne merely giving a indiscernible nod of her head.

Stasha wanted to change the subject. 'Do you miss going on holidays?'

It was a safe question, but Candy was irritated at the subject being changed, for she wanted to know how much was she going to get.

Stasha continued, 'Anne showed me some photographs of where she has been ...'

Anne smiled. 'John came into contact with all sorts of people. One of his business acquaintances, an Australian millionaire, used to take us to expensive restaurants in London and insisted on ordering *everything* on the menu.'

The girls' eyes widened in disbelief.

'And he rarely ate anything, just wanted it brought to the table and then asked for it to be returned to the kitchen,' Anne went on.

'Wouldn't like to have paid his bill,' Candy joked.

'Well, he had a huge yacht complete with crew, so I guess he could afford it,' Anne laughed. 'A real character.'

'You must miss all the travel?' Stasha remarked, and Anne gave a shrug of her shoulders.

'When you've seen one hotel room, you've very much seen them all, and I'd had enough of airports and being away from home. But John would travel all the time. He was really a married bachelor.'

'I've been to Margate,' Candy joked and the other two women laughed.

The afternoon tea was drawing to a close. Anne was starting to get a little tired but it had been an enjoyable time for all three; the women had accepted each other as tentative friends. There was still an edge to Candy in her relationship with Stasha, but Anne realised they were getting on solely for her benefit and that it would probably be like that whenever they met, for neither girl wished to upset her.

Then there was the race to see which carer would clear the dishes away first; this time it was Stasha who won, and she confidently cleared the trays away and stacked the dishwasher. This left Anne with Candy, who showed her some pictures on her phone. Stasha could hear them both laughing but she didn't mind. She returned to the conservatory just as Candy bent down to kiss Anne on her cheek, saying, 'Thank you for a lovely afternoon.' Candy turned to Stasha saying she would see her later.

THIRTEEN

The following morning Anne's GP made a visit to take her blood pressure and inform her of the results of the X-ray on her knees.

The GP told Anne that she had severe degenerative arthritis in both knees and that there was very little that could be done other than a steroid injection and copious amounts of pain relief cream, which should be spread over her knees of a morning and evening. Anne agreed to the steroid injections, which the GP had brought with him.

I could have told her that, Stasha thought to herself as she positioned Anne in her chair and rolled up her trouser legs so both knees were visible. As she was doing this the GP prepared the injection and informed Anne that the benefits would last around two to three months.

Stasha held Anne's hand and stroked her forehead as the GP inserted the needle into Anne's left knee.

'Ooh, that's sore!' Anne yelled.

'Be brave,' Stasha said in her soothing voice, which Anne had come to appreciate.

Anne glanced up and met Stasha's eyes. The GP was oblivious to the silent message that passed between them.

'All done,' the GP said as he got to his feet and repeated his advice to rub the cream in every night and every morning.

Stasha saw the GP out and returned to Anne who was sitting in her chair feeling drowsy. It had taken a lot out of her and Stasha knew only too well that a change of routine always exhausted Anne. She momentarily wondered just how Anne would be able to manage the adventurous trip to London.

The lunchtime call was undertaken by two women who Anne referred to as 'the model sisters'. These were not 'the models' (Leigh and Cian) but Maggie and Marie – two sisters who looked similar despite being a few years apart in age. These were two particularly kind-hearted and polite young women who, judging from what they said, came from a happy, stable home environment, and this shone through in their respective personalities.

'Those two are so, so nice,' Anne remarked when they had left, and Stasha agreed.

Stasha had always been coy about her own mother. She had only recently revealed her name to Anne and explained where she lived. Anne was in no doubt that Stasha enjoyed a close relationship with Stefania who, Anne realised, often gave her daughter sound advice, as only a mother could.

Stasha spoke warmly of her relationship with her mother, and she wondered whether her difficult start with Anne might have been partly due to her feelings of guilt – she wondered if she was betraying her own mother by looking after somebody else's mother instead. All very complicated, she knew.

Anne also began to realise how difficult it must have been for Stasha to go from factory worker to carer. It must have been a steep mental hurdle, and Anne was aware that she had given little consideration to Stasha's feelings in those early days. Anne asked again about her mother's birthday, for Stasha had said it was soon. Stefania would be sixty-four and would probably spend the day in the general store serving people.

'Why don't we brighten her day and send some flowers,' Anne said as they sat in the conservatory having their morning tea.

Stasha frowned. 'There's no need for that, Anne,' she replied, but Anne was not deterred.

'I'd like to do it, Stasha,' Anne said, and there was a slight silence as Stasha toyed with the dilemma. Anne's voice was persuasive and Stasha quickly weighed up the pros and cons of such a gesture. She agreed and Anne asked Stasha to get David on the phone. She did this and then passed the phone to Anne, listening to the somewhat muddled instructions she gave David. David asked Stasha to text him her mother's details. She did this and David said he would sort the rest out.

Stasha had experienced very odd days in Anne's house, but this particular day felt even stranger with the peculiar business of Anne's solicitor coming to the house at ten-thirty and the unusual request for Stasha to leave the house for around one hour.

It was Louise's turn to help Stasha out this morning. Louise, Samantha's sister, was a self-assured and a positive member of Anne's team; she was rarely late, very capable, and had a happy and contented disposition. She also possessed, at times, one of the most seductive voices Stasha had heard – she pointed this out to Anne who agreed with the observation. Louise handled Anne well and, with Stasha's help, washed and dressed Anne and placed her into the chair, then propelled her into the dining room for breakfast.

A phone call from David interrupted them. He reiterated to Stasha that they would prefer her to leave the house for a short period in the morning or busy herself in the garden, maybe walk to the shops for a coffee. There was no hint of an abrasive tone – David was friendly and not at all confrontational. Stasha decided she would quickly return to her own home to check on the house and pick up some clothes to wear in London. She would leave Daisy at the house to listen in on what was going on, but obviously she wouldn't be able to tell her what she'd heard.

Once she'd had breakfast Anne remained in the dining room, and at ten-thirty, almost on the dot, a large luxury four-by-four vehicle came up the drive and stopped outside. Out of the vehicle came a very competent looking, smartly dressed young female. She opened the back door of the vehicle and extracted her laptop case before securing the vehicle and walking to the front door. Stasha opened it and was met with a friendly smile from the young woman standing opposite her.

'It's Anastazja, isn't it?' the woman said. 'I've come to see Anne. My name is Lorraine.'

Stasha was surprised that the woman knew her name. She invited Lorraine into the house and escorted her to the dining room where she said a familiar hello to Anne, who nodded her welcome.

'You look well, Anne,' Lorraine said.

It was obvious that Anne knew Lorraine. She sat down confidently at the dining room table, took a folder out of her bag and placed it on the table before extracting her large laptop and placing it on the table as well.

Lorraine asked Stasha for two coffees.

Stasha – now feeling like a servant – smiled, though she knew she was being dismissed. Dutifully, she went to the kitchen and prepared the coffee. She returned to the dining room and served it before saying, 'I will be out for an hour or so.' She bent down and asked Anne if she would be all right. Anne nodded and touched Stasha's hand in a reassuring manner. This gesture did not go unnoticed by Lorraine; her eyes also rested on the plastic beaker Anne used to drink from.

Stasha gave Lorraine her phone number in case of an emergency and then went upstairs, gathered her things and went out to her car.

Anne and Lorraine watched as Stasha drove out of the drive. Lorraine turned to Anne, met her eyes and said, 'Tell me about Stasha, Anne.'

'She is my carer and she lives here with me,' Anne replied simply and watched as Lorraine took a sip from her coffee.

Lorraine placed the cup gently back down on the table saying, 'Anything else?'

Anne shrugged.

For Lorraine, the meeting was delicate. She wanted Anne to open up and talk to her, but Anne was on her guard.

'How do you find her?' Lorraine asked. It was a pointed question and she waited patiently for Anne to conjure up an answer.

'Initially hard,' Anne answered. 'We didn't get off to the best of starts.'

Lorraine frowned. 'Why?'

Anne looked around the room, she wanted to be honest in her reply, for she felt she owed Stasha that. 'I pre-judged her from the moment she walked into the house.' She paused. 'And she pre-judged me from the moment she cast eyes on me.'

'Why did you pre-judge her?' The question was almost an accusation.

Anne thought about her answer. 'To my

shame, I was put off by her nationality and her overall youthful appearance.' Anne gave an inward laugh. 'She looks more like a glamourous actress than a carer.'

Lorraine acknowledged the observation, 'What did you want from a carer?'

'A Miss Marple-like figure.'

Lorraine laughed; she could empathise with Anne's initial dilemma.

Anne continued, 'From then on it was a battle of words, but mainly from my side, I know she was often upset, but she kept it hidden.'

Lorraine pencilled a few notes. 'And how do you think she pre-judged you?'

'Wealthy, selfish, rude old woman.' Anne paused. 'Stasha has a chip on her shoulder. She is a lovely person but feels part of this job is beneath her.'

Lorraine raised her eyebrows and glanced at her laptop screen. 'Explain.'

'She wants to better herself.' Anne paused to think of Stasha and her peculiarities but ended up saying, 'Nobody deserves a chance more than her ...'

'A change of attitude from you?' Lorraine sounded surprised. 'After all the disagreements, it's quite a turnaround—'

'I was wrong, but then I got to know her. I like her,' Anne interrupted.

'And does she like you?' Lorraine fired the question back.

'She's caring, that's all I know.'

'If you were so unhappy with her at the start, why did you not change her?' Lorraine knew it was a difficult question for Anne to answer.

Anne shrugged and took another careful sip of her coffee, placing the beaker back on the small mat Stasha had put on the table. 'I felt superior to her, and believe you me, in this condition it's a nice feeling to feel superior to anyone.'

Lorraine frowned.

'Stasha resembled a battered wife, she kept coming back for more insults.' There was a pause. 'And I treated her like an abusive husband would, and for that I have deep regrets.' Anne's eyes were beginning to well up. 'Stasha is such a lovely, gentle person but I could not initially see that.'

It was not the answer Lorraine had expected. 'Did you like arguing with her?'

Anne shook her head. 'I wanted to put my point across to her, however biased it was, about people like her coming over here, taking jobs off our own, sponging off the NHS, a lot of hurtful stereotypical remarks ...' Anne paused. 'Now I say it, I can see that it sounds unfair to treat someone like that, but at the time I couldn't understand why an immigrant was looking after me, and I couldn't accept it.'

Lorraine made a note of the terminology Anne used on her piece of paper, but Anne was in full flow.

'I suppose it went on from there, my irritation with her lack of patience —'

'Lack of patience?' Lorraine interrupted. 'Was she aggressive?'

Anne shook her head. 'Absolutely not,' her tone was firm, 'but she was ...' Anne stopped and thought, '... just trying to do her job.'

'Has she ever pleaded hardship to you?' The question hung in the air, but before Anne could answer Daisy jumped up on the table and wanted Lorraine to stroke her.

'She is Stasha's,' Anne said.

Lorraine dutifully stroked Daisy, who then sat at the top of the table next to Anne.

'Has Stasha pleaded hardship?' Lorraine asked again.

Anne frowned. She thought about her answer. 'She's a carer, Lorraine,' Anne said,

'She's not paid well …'

Lorraine made notes.

'But no is the answer to your question,' Anne added.

Lorraine wrote down a few remarks. 'And tell me how are you two today?'

A smile crept over Anne's face. 'We have resolved our differences.'

Lorraine shrugged. 'From her being an immigrant over here taking jobs to someone you now like?'

Anne thought about her answer. 'I had misconceptions about immigrants. I thought they were untrustworthy, disloyal, incompetent. I soon found out that, in Stasha's case at least, it was the complete opposite.'

'What does she do for you, Anne?'

Anne felt slightly embarrassed as she told Lorraine of the personal care she received from Stasha, the running of the house, the ordering of the food, the security, looking after the garden, looking after Mrs James. Most importantly, Anne noted, Stasha looked after her and took her out in the van, and generally entertained her day to day.

'You sound like you now get on quite well, yes?' Lorraine said.

Anne replied that she would be lost without

Stasha, adding, 'She's a stable, likeable, honest young woman who, like many, needs some luck in her life.' Anne hesitated before saying, 'I wish to give her some luck.'

Lorraine noted the remark.

'David told me about Candy. What is she like?'

'We hit it off straight away.'

The terminology made Lorraine smile.

'She's very loud, boisterous, noisily spoken, sometimes rude, sometimes ill mannered and sometimes a pain in the arse ...'

Lorraine laughed and noted the different inflection in Anne's voice when speaking about Candy.

All this time, David was listening in on the video call.

'You like her better than Stasha?'

Anne shook her head. 'Candy tries to influence me, but she knows how far she can push me. I like her differently to Stasha.'

Lorraine drained the remainder of her coffee from the cup.

Anne continued. 'I suppose I could see a little of my younger self in Candy and that's why I initially got on with her. When Candy stomps round the house, you know exactly where she is and probably what she's doing as well. Stasha is quiet and appears from nowhere. They are two different people. Consequently, I like them both for different reasons.'

'Do you know why I'm here today?' Lorraine asked. It was a direct question and she wanted to see how much awareness this ninety-one-year-old lady had.

'You've come to see if I have lost my marbles, haven't you?' Anne laughed.

Lorraine laughed as well. She asked, 'Who's the Prime Minister?'

'Some little girl called Liz – don't know her second name.'

'What happened a month so ago that was such a shock to the nation?' Lorraine saw the flash of uncertainty grow across Anne's face and she knew she was struggling to remember or perhaps comprehend the question.

'We lost our Queen,' Anne replied simply. 'I remember meeting her with John when she toured the Scottish plant and also at Holyrood.'

Lorraine continue to ask a few more questions before she went to her laptop and pressed a few buttons.

Lorraine had not told Anne she had been

video recording the entire conversation, with David on a virtual meeting. David now suddenly appeared on Lorraine's computer screen, as if by magic. He asked how Anne was.

'I'm fine,' Anne shouted at the screen.

David asked Lorraine how she felt his mother was. There was a brief conversation about recent events and then Lorraine said to David, 'I'm satisfied Anne knows what she's doing, so I'm quite happy to go ahead with those requests ... shall we do the videos now?'

FOURTEEN

It was like packing for a summer holiday. Stasha had retrieved one of Anne's suitcases from the storage area in the loft and, once downstairs, had hoovered it out before placing it on Anne's bed and asking her if there was anything she particularly wanted to be dressed in during her trip to London.

'Smart but casual,' Anne replied, 'and something to keep me warm.'

It was primarily up to Stasha to decide which clothes Anne should wear. She had gone upstairs to one of the bedroom wardrobes where Anne's clothes remained. She retrieved three blouses, a cashmere cardigan, six pairs of trousers, two pairs of shoes and some warm comfortable socks, then she took them all downstairs and showed them to Anne.

'How's this?' she asked.

Anne nodded her agreement. 'What are you going to wear?' she asked pointedly.

Stasha turned to Anne with a smile and said, 'It all depends where we're staying, doesn't it?' Stasha sighed for Anne had still not told her which London hotel they would be visiting, and Stasha was becoming more and more curious. 'Can't you give me a clue?' she asked, but Anne shook her head.

'I said it was a surprise for you. Pretend you're going to church.'

It was all Anne would say and it didn't release any of Stasha's anxiety, but she could see she was going to get no further with the questioning so she continued to pack the suitcase and make sure everything was in place before moving it into the dining room.

'Let's have a cup of tea,' Stasha suggested and she pushed Anne into the conservatory, and they sat down and enjoyed a discussion about what was going on in the world. Suddenly there was the ping of a notification on Stasha's phone – she had received a message from her mother, along with a few photographs. Stasha got up, went across and bent down next to Anne's chair.

'These are pictures of my mother, taken today with the lovely flowers you sent her,' she said.

Anne studied the pictures on Stasha's phone. Her mother was a distinctive-looking woman who dressed well and had a warm, wide, welcoming smile. She had Stasha's beautiful eyes. There was another photograph of her mother standing in front of their shop.

'You've got her eyes and smile, Stasha,' Anne remarked.

Stasha smiled, for everyone said that and she knew it was true. Stasha went back to her chair. 'You never showed me pictures of your family,' she said, 'only the ones on the walls upstairs.'

Anne screwed her nose up. 'It's in the past, and what happened in the past stays in the past. I don't like looking – they bring back some good memories and some sad times as well. The farther backward you can look, the farther forward you can see ...' Anne tailed off.

Stasha raised her eyebrows. 'That's nice, who said that?'

'Winston Churchill,' Anne replied.

'You always come out with these lovely sayings,' Stasha said.

Anne nodded. 'It comes from a lifetime of reading, Stasha.' She smiled. 'Reading is the greatest thing you can do. Every page you read, you learn more.'

'You don't write any more, Anne?' Stasha asked. 'I purchased one of your e-books even before I came here.'

'Did you like it?' Anne raised her eyebrows.

Stasha was non-committal. 'I wanted to see

the types of book you wrote.'

'And what was your conclusion?' Anne asked and waited for the answer, which she knew Stasha would take time over.

'The writer was not the person I first encountered.' It was all Stasha said.

Anne frowned. 'Explain.'

'You sometimes write about marginalised people, people who are compartmentalised in our society, rightly or wrongly. Yet at the same time you never afforded me the benefit of the doubt, you acted on your preconceptions ...'

Friction returned and hung in the air. Stasha wondered if she had gone too far.

'I must have disappointed you, Stasha,' Anne eventually said.

The atmosphere had changed and suddenly it seemed cold. There was hesitation in Stasha's eyes. Stasha wondered whether to pursue this or let it go, but she was always like a dog with a bone and she was still hurt by her early experiences with Anne. But, more than anything, Stasha felt she was owed another say.

She lowered her voice, 'You were the opposite of the person I thought you would be. Your books were well constructed, well written and at times thought provoking. But as a person, and the one I met initially, you were one-dimensional and blinkered.'

Anne allowed the criticism to wash over her. 'I was wrong, and you are right.' Suddenly Anne became a little upset and Stasha quickly got up from her chair. She walked across to Anne and knelt down next to her, placing her hands over Anne's.

Anne realised the scars of those initial encounters had turned into wounds that ran deep within Stasha. Anne thought Stasha had put them to one side but they were obviously still lurking under the surface. She wondered if Stasha was a genuine friend or merely an imposter. She could not resist saying, 'How do you feel today? Do you still feel the same way towards me?'

Anne had to wait a few seconds for the answer because Stasha was weighing up what to say. 'We're good,' she finally said with a smile.

Anne frowned not knowing the meaning of this modern terminology.

'Good friends,' Stasha said and she kissed Anne on the cheek.

Annette De Burgh

FIFTEEN

So Monday arrived, the day of their trip to London. It was arranged that the taxi would be at the house by eleven o'clock. Stasha had got up at the usual time and, with the help of Louise, had got Anne up and ready. Louise asked what they would be up to in the next few days and Stasha answered as honestly as possible. Louise said she hoped they had a nice time, and there was no discord in her tone. It was a genuine statement, very much like the previous evening when Pollie had helped Stasha put Anne to bed. Pollie always had a story to tell and had been at the agency for a few years; there was no negative side to her and she wished Anne and Stasha a nice break.

The manager had arranged for Leigh and Colin to come to the house and feed Daisy while they were away. It was a good choice.

Anne had her usual breakfast, which consisted of warm porridge and a cup of tea, and after freshening her up Stasha wrapped her in a cashmere cardigan. A thick rug was placed over her knees and they both waited in the lounge for the taxi to arrive. Stasha was dressed in blue slacks and a waist-length coat.

The weather was warm but not hot.

'You look smart,' Anne remarked and Stasha smiled nervously.

The taxi entered the drive at precisely eleven. It was a luxury vehicle, and Anne entered via a side entrance and her wheelchair was positioned to enable good visibility of the road ahead. Stasha sat in a comfortable chair that swivelled round.

The ride was smooth and quiet, and there was faint music playing in the background. The driver wore a tie and was professional and courteous; he didn't speak unless he was spoken to. Stasha asked him which hotel they were staying at, but he merely said that he was under instruction not to comment on the destination.

'I wish you'd tell me the hotel,' Stasha said as the driver joined the busy A45 road to head south towards the M1.

'Be patient.'

It was all Anne said.

Stasha enquired as to why they weren't travelling down the M40. The driver replied that it was due to extensive road works around Bicester. Then Stasha tried to trick the driver by asking what part of London they were heading for, but the driver remained non-committal.

Since it was the start of the week, the M1 was busy with lots of slow, stop-and-start traffic. Anne remembered how she used to drive down this route herself in her own car, and she reflected on the days when she wouldn't have batted an eyelid at driving two hundred miles. How times changed. Now she could only watch others drive their nice cars and break the speed limit just like she had done.

Stasha was quiet. She checked her phone and sent a text and selfie of her and Anne to her mother, explaining that they were on their way and that she hoped Anne would have enough strength to survive the strenuous few days ahead. If truth be known, Stasha still felt it was too much for Anne. She thought about the carers' comments when they'd learned of the trip to London.

'I thought they hated each other,' a few of them had remarked.

'It's not what you know ...' another had said.

'Money talks ...' was another comment.

There were a few other comments that were biting and a little bitchy, but Stasha had remained silent. Anne was oblivious to them.

The M1 was as chaotic and busy as ever, and the driver positioned the vehicle in the middle lane doing a good, average speed. Stasha chatted to Anne. She would have felt better if she had known where she was going, for this was a tremendous responsibility and she would have liked to have been a bit more informed. She felt anxiety sweep over her – and not for the first time.

The taxi stopped for a comfort break halfway through the journey, and this enabled Stasha to get out and treat herself to a takeaway coffee. She had brought Anne's special cup with her and she let her have a sweet drink to keep her energy up. There had been no time for Anne's vitamin drink but she would get it once they arrived at this hotel, Stasha thought to herself. The joke, if you could call it that, would be on her and she laughed inwardly – it could well be a bed and breakfast somewhere in London, but somehow she didn't think Anne would fit into any type of bed and breakfast accommodation.

With the help of the driver, Stasha extracted Anne from the taxi in the large service area car park to give her a breath of fresh air; she ensured she was wrapped up with her cashmere scarf and double rug on her knees, then she pushed Anne to a seating area. Overhead, the September sun was getting stronger. They enjoyed ten minutes in the fresh air drinking their refreshments while their driver remained in the vehicle.

'Please, Anne, tell me where we're going,' pleaded Stasha.

'I want it to be a surprise for you; something that you will remember.' Anne was infuriatingly non-committal.

Stasha didn't want to push it, and eventually they got back into the taxi and their journey resumed. This time the London traffic was heavier, slower and more tedious, with multiple stops and starts, until they finally reached the end of the M1 and they turned and headed towards St Johns Wood. The roads were busy, the traffic was slow and it was crowded with people – traffic light after traffic light came and went until signage for the West End came into sight and, after more traffic lights, they were soon adjacent to the Lord's cricket ground at the top end of Baker Street.

Baker Street was as chaotic as always – the traffic was bumper to bumper – and eventually they made their way down to cross the Marylebone Road. Stasha was still not aware of where they were going and she wasn't familiar enough with London to start guessing hotels. She looked out of the window; to her mind they were heading into central London, and then the taxi took a right and she read the road sign: Green Street. Then they travelled along the road for a few minutes before turning left to enter Park Lane. It looked wealthy and ostentatious. The taxi headed down to Hyde Park corner where the traffic was crazy, with cars coming at you from all directions, but they turned left and headed towards Piccadilly. Stasha was puzzled, but then in the distance, above all the traffic and congestion, she saw a sign illuminated with white lights – it read 'Ritz Hotel'.

'Surely not?' Stasha turned and met the smile on Anne's face.

'I said it would be a surprise,' Anne said. 'Two nights at the Ritz Hotel, Stasha.'

'Oh, Anne!' Stasha said in astonishment and placed her hand over her mouth. Then she took out her mobile phone and filmed the last part of the journey as the taxi approached the hotel. She then sent the video and a text to her mother.

STASHA > STEFANIA
Guess?

STEFANIA > ANASTAZJA
Wow!

Suddenly other considerations ran through Stasha's mind. Had she got the appropriate clothes? Did she know the appropriate etiquette? And how would Anne cope with a busy international hotel full of people? More importantly, how would she?

The taxi drew up outside the imposing building. Immediately two doormen stepped forward and waited for the taxi's electric side door to open. With Stasha's guidance, they assisted Anne out of the vehicle. Their baggage was taken separately.

For Stasha, this was one of the most opulent buildings she had been in, with beautiful furnishings, high ceilings and elaborate woodwork – it was light, bright and spacious with an air of well-trodden affluence. There were beautiful rugs and magnificent tables and chairs. Exotic plants, colourful flowers, glistening mirrors, large pictures and obsequious staff.

Stasha was shaking with self-conscious

nerves as she observed the magnificent staircase. Anne was not affected. The check in was quick and effortless.

'There has been a private nurse arranged for you during your stay,' the receptionist had said, and Stasha was taken aback at the statement.

'A private nurse?'

The receptionist nodded, 'She will be on hand to assist with any help you need.'

They travelled up in the elevator to their room and were shown a two-bedroom suite with views over Green Park and a sitting room overlooking Piccadilly. The whole area was larger than Stasha's house, and it was far beyond what she'd expected. There was a complimentary bottle of champagne, colourful flowers filled the vases, up-to-date magazines and newspapers were on a side table in the sitting room, and there were beautiful towels in the large bathroom. Everything looked affluently pristine. Then Stasha noticed that one bedroom had an adjustable hospital bed, an electric hoist and other medical equipment to make Anne's stay as enjoyable and as easy as possible.

Stasha raised her eyebrows; it was something she had not expected. But then she hadn't expected to be at the Ritz. While she was excited, she was also a little anxious.

It was, perhaps, a little too much.

Stasha had been introduced to the hotel nurse shortly after they'd arrived. Her name was Belinda and she was from the Caribbean. She was friendly and accommodating. Since Anne was tired after the journey, Belinda and Stasha hoisted her on to the bed and freshened her up, and it was not long before she was enjoying an afternoon snooze. Stasha decided not to wake her, so she unpacked a few things, got the medication sorted and freshened up. The afternoon tea had been booked for four thirty, and she needed to get Anne up and ready well before then. She gave herself until four when Belinda would return to help get Anne out of bed and back in her chair.

Stasha took selfie after selfie of herself in the Ritz suite and sent them to her mother. Then she texted.

STASHA > STEFANIA
Can't believe this, hotel is out of this world

STEFANIA > ANASTAZJA
Nothing more than you deserve after what happened

STASHA > STEFANIA
Anne has been so generous, see pictures of our suite

STEFANIA > ANASTAZJA
Looks beautiful!

STASHA > STEFANIA
Anne coping well with the travel

STEFANIA > ANASTAZJA
Look after her, she's old!!!

STASHA > STEFANIA
I do like her but …

STEFANIA > ANASTAZJA
??

STASHA > STEFANIA
Is she not buying me?

STEFANIA > ANASTAZJA
No, she likes your company

STASHA > STEFANIA
Really?

STEFANIA > ANASTAZJA
They would not be doing this

STASHA > STEFANIA
Maybe

STEFANIA > ANASTAZJA
She has seen the beautiful person you are

STASHA > STEFANIA
Awww Mum!

STEFANIA > ANASTAZJA
Where is Anne?

STASHA > STEFANIA
Asleep, afternoon tea is next!

STEFANIA > ANASTAZJA
Jealous!

STASHA > STEFANIA
Going to wake Anne up now, speak later

Then, somewhat mischievously, Stasha posted a few images of their suite on the care agency's WhatsApp group – it was bound to cause some reaction!

Stasha was still concerned about whether Anne would have the energy to get through all that was planned, and just as she was thinking those thoughts Anne opened her eyes and became fully awake. It was three thirty.

Stasha sat on Anne's bed and they had a brief chat, with Stasha asking Anne if she knew where she was.

Anne raised her eyebrows, annoyed at the silly question. 'We are in London at the Ritz Hotel, and you and the other nurse are going to get me up. We are going for this world-famous afternoon tea,' Anne said, adding, 'I hope I don't clear the dining room with my table manners.'

Stasha laughed.

It was four o'clock on the dot when Belinda arrived back at the room. The hotel had a strict smart dress code, even for their guests, but David had spoken to the management in relation to Anne and subsequently this had been waived, in respect of Anne's circumstances. Stasha and Belinda put another cardigan over her blouse and placed a rug over her knees.

Stasha, however, had to change. Gone were her usual jeans and trainers and in their place was a pale blue jacket and matching skirt – it was not too short and not too long. She glanced at herself in her bedroom mirror, pleased with what she saw.

As she came out of the bedroom Anne surveyed her up and down. She nodded her head in admiration, 'You look beautiful, Stasha.'

Feeling reassured, Stasha moved Anne into the corridor and towards the elevator, en-route to afternoon tea. Belinda said she would be back of the room around five thirty or six o'clock.

Travelling down in the mirror-adorned elevator, Anne told Stasha of the afternoon teas she had previously enjoyed, name-dropping hotels: Raffles in Singapore, the Peninsula in Hong Kong and Reid's in Madeira. 'So it will be interesting to see how this compares,' Anne added with an air of scepticism.

'I wouldn't know Anne,' Stasha joked as the elevator opened its doors at their designated floor, 'I've only had takeaway coffee.'

They made their way to the hotel's former ballroom on the lower ground floor. The room was exquisite – a huge and imposing chandelier dominated the room, the ceilings were adorned in pastel-coloured frescoes, mirrors were everywhere and the tables were covered in acres of snowy-white linen and the carpets were so plush you felt you dared not walk on them. Stasha was speechless in admiration of all the decadence; Anne merely sat in her wheelchair enjoying the experience.

An over-polite waiter showed them to their table and fussed around them as they settled down.

'Oh, Anne this is magnificent,' Stasha said, enthralled. 'I've never been anywhere like this.'

'It's nice, isn't it?' Anne replied.

Afternoon tea at the Ritz had been served since 1906 and it was well regarded the world over, especially with the well-heeled American tourists who loved the opulent surroundings.

Stasha perused the menu saying, 'You can apparently have sandwiches made with every bread imaginable and every ingredient.' She raised her eyebrows as she continued to read. There was no limit on how much you could eat, but it was rare to ask for second helpings. 'Eighteen different types of tea,' Stasha said in amusement.

'You can have a glass of champagne if you like,' Anne said as she also read the menu, but Stasha politely declined. 'Could you live like this Stasha?' Anne asked, and Stasha shrugged.

'You bet.'

'You would fit in.'

'Oh, thank you, Anne,' Stasha gushed.

There was a pause as Anne looked around. Suddenly she said, 'You have an admirer.' Anne laughed and pointed her gaze at one of the young male waiters.

Stasha turned round and accidentally met the eyes of the young man. They both laughed in unison before Stasha turned away, her face slightly flushed.

The tea was served, it started with a selection of sandwiches and dainty side dishes.

Stasha had decided not to use Anne's bib, for it seemed inappropriate for such an occasion, but she did tuck the large pristine white napkin into Anne's chin and, in doing so, caught the look of the woman on the next table. Stasha knew that she was trying to work out how she was related to Anne, but Stasha remained unmoved – it wasn't the first time someone had wondered about this. Suddenly Anne sneezed loudly, causing other diners in the room to look around with curiosity. Stasha kept her composure and handed Anne a paper handkerchief from her pocket before sitting back down to resume her tea. When she was finished, more waiters suddenly appeared with multiple plates of warm scones, fresh from the oven. They smelt lovely and Stasha could not resist them, consuming not one but two. Anne laughed as the cream framed Stasha's mouth but neither were embarrassed, for they were enjoying each other's company.

Anne had a mouthful of scone and suddenly she felt the urge to sneeze again. The sneezing was noisy and disturbed the restaurant's ambience. One more heavy sneeze and Stasha saw bits of chewed scone splatter over the beautiful table cloth. Stasha stared at Anne and mouthed the word 'behave!' Now some saliva was dribbling down Anne's chin, so Stasha got up to wipe it clean. The look of the woman on the next table had gone from a sympathetic understanding to veiled irritation as she commented to the other diners at her table.

Anne and Stasha both finished their scones

and were basking in the overall ambience of the restaurant. It was beautiful, but Stasha found herself, like Anne, not taking it too seriously. The tension and apprehension she'd felt had been broken by Anne's self-deprecating attitude, and she was thankful for this. Only Anne would be completely unaffected by these surroundings, and she laughed and there was a genuine meeting of minds across the table.

Suddenly Stasha recognised the expression on Anne's face. Was she now going to be sick? Stasha raised her eyebrows and mouthed silently to Anne 'Not here!' but Anne continued to heave.

Stasha quickly and without fuss called the waiter over. 'Have you got a bowl?' she asked.

'A bowl, madam?' the waiter said in astonishment.

'Yes,' Stasha said, 'I'm afraid my friend is going to be sick.'

There was a look of horror and dismay on the waiter's face as he rushed to one of the side cupboards and retrieved a porcelain white bowl with 'Ritz' written on it.

By the time the waiter had returned, Anne had composed herself and said to Stasha,

'False alarm.' Without hesitation, she continued to devour another cake and sip her tea. It was as if the past five minutes had not happened.

Both Stasha and Anne continued to meet each other's eyes across the table. There was a mutual, empathetic understanding and a silent message passed between them. The eyes spoke of a genuine affection for each other and the whole episode made their afternoon tea far more memorable than it otherwise would have been.

Before returning to her suite after their afternoon tea, Anne wanted to have a quick look around the interior of the plush hotel. Once in the elevator, both Anne and Stasha allowed themselves one more quick laugh about what had happened at tea before returning to their suite and meeting up with Belinda, who helped Stasha put Anne on her bed for a rest.

It was decided that in the evening they would have a light meal delivered to their suite before venturing out in a taxi to see the sights of London. This luxury disabled taxi was outside the hotel promptly at seven o'clock. David had arranged for them to have an hour's drive.

They set off from Piccadilly towards Piccadilly Circus, then turned left on to Regent Street, which was adorned with lights and fanciful shop windows – Hamley's toy shop, Liberty's department store and more. Then across Oxford Circus, around Cavendish Square – where Anne said she used to park when visiting London – and on to Harley Street. Then they headed to Portman Square and into Park Street before joining Park Lane. They passed more famous hotels in Mayfair, then went on to Wellington Arch and Knightsbridge, then Brompton Road and Harrods, where they would be going the following day. The taxi went through an intricate network of roads to end up in Victoria, then to Buckingham Palace, Westminster Abbey and Downing Street before heading down Constitution Hill and back to Wellington Arch. Finally, they went around Hyde Park and back to Piccadilly.

Once back in their suite, Stasha and Anne reflected on their day.

'Eventful, wasn't it?' Anne said, and Stasha nodded.

'I won't forget that afternoon tea in a hurry. Anne, you made it all the more memorable.'

There was a brief pause.

'It's such an exciting place, London, isn't it?' Stasha said.

Anne nodded and she sipped a cup of tea Stasha had made for her in her special beaker.

'The city never seems to sleep, does it, Anne?'

'Do you know the saying about London?' Anne asked.

Stasha shook her head. 'No ...' Stasha's eyes were friendly but her voice was pinched, for at times she felt a little insecure. She never had a suitable response to Anne's infamous sayings – Anne was so well read and knowledgeable, it sometimes got to her that she lacked the same qualities.

Anne had picked up the peevish note in Stasha's voice, saying, 'I won't bother telling you.'

With that, Stasha went across to Anne's chair and placed her arm round her neck in a comforting gesture, saying, 'Please, tell me.'

'Samuel Johnson said,' and Anne paused for effect, '... when a man is tired of London he is tired of life.'

Stasha raised her eyebrows. 'And are you tired of London?' she asked.

Anne shook her head. 'No. I always liked to

travel, and with hotel's like this, how can you get tired of anything?' Anne paused. 'But I am too old now.'

Stasha smiled. Then there was a knock on the door. It was nine o'clock. It would be Belinda arriving to help put Anne to bed.

Once in bed, Anne fell asleep quite quickly; it had been a hectic day and there was an even more hectic day coming, but Anne was coping quite well.

Ironically, it was Stasha who felt tired tonight. She retired to her bedroom and had a nice hot shower then dressed herself in the warm fluffy Ritz bath robe and relaxed in front of the television in the sitting room with a hot cup of coffee. She felt peaceful as she reflected on the day and checked her phone; a few of the carers had sent responses to Stasha's earlier images of the hotel suite posted on WhatsApp – most were positive.

She soon retired to bed. Despite being in central London, Stasha couldn't hear anything from her room, although she was subconsciously aware of the busy atmosphere around her. She texted her mother.

Both Anne and Stasha had a good night's sleep; Anne always slept well and it was rare for her to wake in the night. Unlike at home,

Stasha could hear Anne's gentle snoring from the next-door bedroom.

Stasha got up at seven o'clock the following day; she toyed with the idea of going for an early morning stroll but decided it would be inadvisable to leave Anne on her own, so she had another hot, invigorating shower. She knew another busy day lay ahead. They would breakfast in their suite before a taxi would take them to Harrods, where they would be escorted around the store by a personal shopper. They were due back at the hotel at one o'clock, after which they would have a restful afternoon before going to the Novello Theatre in the evening to watch their production of Mamma Mia – it would be a tiring, if entertaining, evening for Anne.

Anne was wide awake by seven thirty, and at seven forty-five she rang the bell that Stasha had brought with her. Stasha entered the bedroom and made sure Anne was comfortable – she opened the curtains and sat Anne up in bed before straightening the bed sheets. London was already fully awake.

'Do you remember what we're doing this morning?' Stasha asked.

Anne paused for a moment and Stasha

could almost see the memories shifting around in her mind until she found the right one. 'I think we're going to Harrods,' Anne said with a smile.

'Never been there,' Stasha remarked.

'I always consider it one large, expensive junk shop, selling everything under the sun,' Anne remarked.

At eight thirty on the dot there was a knock at the door. It was Belinda, who was ready to help get Anne up and dressed.

Their breakfast was served on two delicate trolleys that were wheeled into their suite at nine o'clock prompt. Everything in the hotel was done to excess. Their table was beautifully laid with a crisp white table cloth, the cutlery glistened under the lights and beautiful silverware accompanied everything. Not only did they have brown toast, they also had white toast with five different types of marmalade. There were beautiful morning croissants and delicious orange juice. They were also two different types of morning tea. The night before, Stasha had ordered a muesli made especially by the chef as well as an omelette. Anne had her porridge and toast with marmalade. All the plates were covered in a silver cloche with the waiter revealing their splendour in an exaggerated manoeuvre. The waiter laid their breakfast table for them, getting in Stasha's way – she just wanted to let Anne eat and start her day without too much stress.

Then two more hotel staff came in and quickly and efficiently took away the three vases of flowers and replaced them with fresh ones. Not that there was anything wrong with the old ones, Stasha thought. Yesterday's newspapers were removed from the side table to be replaced with the most recent ones.

'I think we can manage from now on, thank you,' Stasha said.

Anne was relieved that she had taken the initiative.

'Please ring the bell if you want anything madam,' the waiter said in an unctuous tone and left.

'Porridge from Scotland, Anne,' Stasha remarked.

'Proper porridge,' Anne said as she watched Stasha arrange the cutlery for her before sitting down and starting her own breakfast.

'Do you miss living there, Anne?' Stasha asked as she devoured her healthy cereal, which tasted lovely.

'Very much so,' Anne replied, 'we had a good life.'

They continued to eat their breakfast, Stasha pouring the tea and buttering Anne's wholemeal toast. 'Where was it you lived again?'

Anne gave a wistful look. 'A suburb outside Glasgow, but we were located near to Loch Lomond, the Trossachs ...'

'The Trossachs?' Stasha frowned.

Anne tried to remember what they were. 'A range of mountains that you can drive through, very dramatic, like the Rest and Be Thankful ...'

Stasha screwed her face up. 'Rest and be thankful?'

'Another range of mountains ...'

'Some nice names,' Stasha replied, 'I must go to Scotland.'

'We used to go to Gleneagles for Christmas,' Anne remarked as she looked around the hotel suite. 'Very much like this hotel.'

'Never heard of it,' Stasha replied, 'Glen-what?'

'Gleneagles,' Anne finished. 'Up in Perthshire.'

Stasha screwed her nose up, 'You are so used to these sorts of places, aren't you, Anne?'

Anne laughed, she had come to like Stasha's direct and sometimes indiscreet talk. She knew there was a little resentment in there, but Stasha was never one to put the knife in too far, especially now. But it was always near the surface. 'Afraid so,' Anne cajoled, and Stasha smiled.

'Lovely butter,' Stasha remarked. 'I could put on weight here.'

'You're look beautiful, Stasha,' Anne said involuntarily.

Stasha paused and gave Anne a questioning look.

'You're beautiful, Stasha, a real beautiful person in every way possible.'

Stasha felt the tears prick at the back of her eyes, for the sentiment in Anne's voice was genuine and she knew the remark had been said with sincerity. 'Thank you, Anne.' It was all she could say before Anne moved the subject on.

SIXTEEN

David had arranged the Harrods personal shopper experience. It was quite easy to organise – a mere phone call and an exchange of information and the personal shopper was booked for Stasha and Anne.

'What will you treat yourself to, Anne?' Stasha asked as she placed a cashmere scarf around Anne's neck and made sure that her woollen cardigan was on properly, and that the travel rug was placed carefully over her knees.

'I won't be treating myself, Stasha, but I might treat you,' came the reply.

It was not the answer that Stasha had expected and she quickly said, 'I do not need anything like that from you, Anne, it is just a joy to be here with you.'

Anne took no notice of what Stasha said. 'I want to get you something to remember this by Stasha,' and there was a pause as she said almost coldly, 'please accept something.'

Stasha was tempted to ask Anne whether she wanted to ease her conscience by giving her a gift, but she decided against it. At that moment, it suddenly struck Stasha just how similar they both had become. Here was an elderly lady with a sharp tongue who would enjoy point-scoring in any conversation, even with her disability, and sometimes could be quite cruel and heartless in her comments. And then there was Stasha, who fought hard not to be put down by Anne's remarks. Stasha's belief was that she was a person in her own right; she had her own opinion and she would not be afraid to voice it. Anne, at times, brought out the worst in her and she wondered why. Stasha could only refer back to her original thoughts on the matter. When she had come to care for Anne she'd been feeling unfulfilled in her life. Anne was at the end of her life, but her life had been fulfilling, and so Stasha's sense of inadequacy had come to the surface. Stasha bent down and placed her arm round Anne saying, 'You can buy me a box of chocolates.'

'You always want the last word, Stasha,' Anne remarked.

Stasha spontaneously bent over and kissed Anne on her cheek. Anne responded with a warm smile as she surveyed Stasha's outfit: a lemon coloured jacket and matching slacks. She looked sensational. Anne admired Stasha's impeccable dress sense.

But their animosity remained not far from

the surface; it was still there like a shadow in the water waiting for one or the other to disturb it. Both women knew when to row back from any confrontation and so the brief exchange was forgotten. They waited now for Belinda to turn up at the door and help Stasha take Anne down to the hotel reception area.

Once there, one of the hotel managers came across and asked if they were enjoying their stay. Stasha replied that it was 'a magnificent experience and a lovely hotel.'

The manager was pleased and said, 'If there is anything else we can do for you both, please let us know.'

Stasha nodded. Secretly, she thought she could get used to this type of treatment. She could certainly get used to having days that weren't crammed with worry and work.

There was no waiting around on this trip, and no sooner had Stasha and Anne arrived at reception than their vehicle magically appeared to take them the short distance from Piccadilly to Brompton Road in Knightsbridge.

Again, their transport was a luxury disabled taxi and Stasha was helped by the doorman to get Anne into the vehicle and securely positioned.

In mileage terms, the journey was short, but with West End traffic it took a good twenty minutes. Anne mentioned to Stasha that in years gone by she had walked from Piccadilly through Hyde Park to get to Harrods – a lovely, relaxing walk, especially in the spring or summer sunshine.

The Harrods building itself was as imposing as ever. Stasha had never really heard of Harrods, never mind seen it in real life. To her it looked huge, opulent and impressive, albeit somewhat irrelevant to her life. But that didn't stop her from taking a few photographs as they approached.

Their taxi drew up outside and she could not help but notice the array of expensive cars, chauffeur-driven limousines, taxis and doorman, all dressed in green, helping expensively clad customers enter and exit the store. Stasha was thankful that she looked smart, and Anne … well, she could go anywhere and be accepted. As the vehicle drew up outside, the Harrods doorman realised that there was a disabled passenger inside and immediately went to the side entrance, opened the door and said in a loud authoritative voice, 'Welcome to Harrods.'

A personal shopper was something new to

Stasha and she was starting to realise that the more money you had, the less waiting you did. As soon as Anne arrived at Harrods, this personal shopper was on hand to start the experience. Lucia was a beautifully dressed assistant. She approached Stasha and introduced herself to Anne. She was of Caribbean appearance – very well presented and very well spoken.

Lucia had already been briefed on Anne's disability and the relationship between Anne and Stasha, and this helped everyone to get off on the right foot. Lucia was friendly and obviously used to dealing with people, but Stasha got the impression that she was just a glorified sales girl wearing very posh clothes. The thought made her feel better.

The three of them sat down in their luxurious surroundings while Lucia tried to get a sense of the kinds of products they might be interested in, and what they might be looking for today. Anne remarked that they were here to browse the store and that they'd be interested in making a purchase if something took their eye. Stasha did not respond; she had not the money or inclination to purchase products in Harrods, although she would take great enjoyment in looking at what was on offer.

So they had decided on a tour of the store, visiting as many departments as they could. They started off on the ground floor and Stasha manoeuvred Anne through the famous food hall. The food was of a high quality and beautifully presented. They stopped and looked at various foods on sale.

'Does it make you feel hungry, Anne?' Stasha asked with Lucia listening.

'Makes me feel sick,' came the reply as Anne was pushed past the cold meat section. 'It's all too much,' Anne said, but Stasha had stopped at a large display of vegetarian food. It was beautiful and had obviously taken a great deal of time and expertise to create.

Anne glanced up at Stasha, looking for an opinion. Stasha wrinkled her nose before saying, 'Very nicely done.'

'If you like that sort of thing,' Anne replied and they moved on.

Then came the wines and spirits. Stasha deliberately paused around the gin bottles. 'Are you tempted, Anne?' she asked.

'If John was here, he would be, but I'm not.'

Lucia showed them different gins from around the world, but nothing made Anne put her hand in her pocket.

They both scanned all the bottles, which ranged from low to ridiculous prices. 'Who would paid that for a bottle of gin?' Stasha remarked.

Anne looked around. 'People must do it,' she said as they headed to the champagne section. Here there were all sorts of bottles, with prices ranging from fifty pounds to five thousand pounds.

'It's all slightly decadent,' Anne said.

'And off putting,' Stasha added.

These were not the words Lucia wanted to hear. She jumped into the conversation. 'You will be surprised how many people buy the expensive champagne.'

'I'm sure I would be, Lucia, but I won't be one of them today,' Anne replied, and Stasha laughed at her directness.

They moved on.

Next came the book shop; this was a large, comfortable and silent area of the store displaying numerous books on various different subjects. Some were beautifully illustrated with large picture books; others were more in depth. Anne asked Stasha to push her over to the philosophy section – it was a subject she had been interested in for many years.

There were plenty of books there and Anne could lose herself all day, but she found it difficult to pick up the books and scan their contents, so she merely looked at the titles and told Stasha to move them on to the next department.

They went up in the elevator. It was womenswear that came next. A floor dedicated to ladies fashion, with ridiculously expensive dresses, bags, blouses, hats and all sorts of other things.

'Are you tempted, Stasha?' Anne asked as she fingered one of the dresses.

'At one thousand five hundred pounds, I don't think so.'

Lucia showed Stasha an even more expensive dress costing twenty-five thousand pounds. Stasha shook her head; it was beyond her comprehension that anyone would spend such an amount on a dress that would probably only be worn once and never seen again.

Anne glanced around and observed the clientele. Although there were customers of all ages, they were mostly young and of Arabic or Middle Eastern descent. Some were buying, some were browsing. It was hard to detect who had money and who was just looking around.

Stasha assessed Lucia surreptitiously. Although beautifully dressed and well presented, to Stasha, Lucia was an equal, for despite the show she was no doubt another worker on a zero-hours contract, perhaps with a commission-based bonus.

Then came the department that Stasha had been looking forward to: the shoe department. This was every woman's dream: shoes upon shoes as far as the eye could see – beautifully displayed, beautifully lit, beautifully presented. There didn't seem to be any type of shoe this department didn't offer – it was a huge, opulent department with beautifully styled ceiling lights, bright displays, a highly polished floor and all the glamour and glitz you could wish for. Showcasing embellishments and intricate details aplenty, Stasha felt that her ultimate shoe collection would start right here. From vertiginous heels to ballet flats and ankle boots, this department catered to every occasion. Iconic style, or a love-in with lace-ups, statement-making platform sandals and expensive trainers.

Stasha took her time, looking carefully at the intricate designs and displays. Lucia noticed Anne's expression and smiled, for this department was every young fashionable woman's heaven, and it wasn't long before Stasha made her way over to a pair of shoes that had caught her attention.

It was a pair of Jimmy Choo crystal embellished sandals. Stasha held them up at Anne, saying, 'What do you think?'

'Very you,' Anne replied.

'Not my price range, I'm afraid.'

Anne raised her eyebrows and then Lucia stepped in, saying, 'Try them on, Stasha.'

Stasha didn't want to be tempted but it didn't take too much persuasion for her to sit down and remove her own shoes before sliding on the expensive Jimmy Choo's. She stood up and looked at herself in the special shoe mirror. They looked good.

'If only,' Stasha replied.

Lucia met Anne's expression, but Anne gave nothing away and Stasha soon replaced the shoes on the display and went back to pushing Anne around the department. She couldn't quite comprehend people spending over one and half thousand pounds on one pair of shoes, but then she didn't live in London or have a high-earning husband, and she didn't live in posh houses and have posh friends.

Anne considered whether to buy the shoes for Stasha. She thought quickly and carefully about the situation, then decided against it. It was the wrong gesture at the wrong time – she most certainly didn't wish for Stasha to feel in any way obliged to her, but more so she didn't want Stasha to feel embarrassed. And so they continued around the shoe department, enjoying some lively banter as they went.

'Shall we have a morning coffee?' Lucia suggested, and Stasha smiled in thanks, for she felt she could do with a sit down to take the weight off her feet. Somehow being in London made her feel very tired – all that spending she had done in her mind had exhausted her, so they made their way to the Roastery and Bake Hall situated in the Food Department. It was busy, but Lucia had managed to get a table. Stasha positioned Anne so she could observe all the busy happenings.

Stasha ordered what Lucia recommended, the Knightsbridge Roast Blend with a croissant, and Anne opted for tea with a shortbread biscuit, while Lucia had a coffee.

Without any inhibition, Stasha opened her bag and extracted Anne's ever-faithful plastic beaker, which she placed on the table like some expensive ornament for valuation. Once the refreshments were served, Stasha took the top off the beaker and poured the contents of Anne's tea into the plastic cup – she was used to this procedure, so she didn't spill a drop. Lucia watch the scene with interest, Stasha was competent and showed no hint of self-consciousness as she put the top back on the plastic beaker and handed it to Anne, who picked it up swiftly and swigged the liquid from the beaker like she was drinking from a bottle of spirits. Other customers noticed but did not react.

Lucia gave a reassuring smile to Anne, but it was not required, as Anne didn't care what people thought; she was thirsty and she wanted a drink.

'What is it like to work here?' Anne asked and Lucia shrugged.

'I get to meet some interesting people.'

Anne continued to suck at her beaker.

'Are you on commission?' Stasha asked.

'Basic wage plus commission,' Lucia replied.

'You haven't made much from us this morning,' Stasha turned to Anne and smiled.

There was a knowledgeable look in Lucia's

eyes as they met Anne's. Finally Anne said to Stasha, 'David arranged for the store to charge a flat fee for the use of Lucia.'

Stasha shrugged. So Lucia would get money after all.

'How long have you been caring for Anne?' Lucia asked.

There was an exchange of looks between Anne and Stasha. 'A few months,' Stasha replied.

Lucia had seen the exchanges, the hidden glances and the subtle touches between Stasha and Anne when they were in the store. 'You seem to get on well.'

Both Stasha and Anne laughed in unison; Lucia was obviously unaware of the difficulties they had experienced. Stasha didn't say anything, but Anne said, 'We get on well – now.'

Lucia was curious.

'We had words.'

It was all Stasha said.

Lucia frowned.

'Lots of them,' Stasha added.

Lucia sensed the atmosphere change; she couldn't quite put her finger on it, but whatever it was it lay there unsaid.

'We're good now,' Anne cut in, and Stasha

laughed, recalling Anne's confusion on hearing her use the phrase for the first time.

Stasha winked at Anne and Lucia could see the genuine warmth between them.

'And what made you come to London?' she asked.

'Change of scenery,' Anne said.

'Payback time,' Stasha gave a disarming smile.

'I'm always paying Stasha back, Lucia, I always put my foot in it,' Anne said.

'Two feet, Anne,' Stasha laughed.

Lucia suddenly couldn't read the mood, then Stasha placed her hand over Anne's. Anne's face broke into a smile.

Lucia notice the exchanges; there was a genuine warmth between the two of them, but there was also a hidden and unsaid sense of tension on the surface. Each clearly wanted to have a say over the other, and they seemed well matched, since both of them were so obviously outspoken. Maria searched for the phrase she would use to describe them, and then it hit her. These two women *appreciated* each other.

SEVENTEEN

London's theatre land, situated in Shaftesbury Avenue, was a short drive from their hotel, but it was not their destination this evening. London was having its usual chaotic, self-indulgent and excitable evening. The Novello Theatre, located on Aldwych, was a twenty-minute drive away and was showing the musical Mamma Mia. It was Stasha's preferred show and Anne had always liked the songs of the Swedish group Abba.

They had eaten in their suite. The room service had been efficient and the food wonderful. Anne had decided to have smoked haddock with some sliced tomatoes and French fries, while Stasha opted for a chicken salad with Caesar dressing. Their dinner together was quiet with relaxed conversation. Stasha was thoughtful and considerate and Anne made an effort not to say anything too controversial, even when a large Jamaican waitress came in with the trolley. Stasha looked at Anne and mouthed to her, 'Say nothing.'

It was an indication of how far the two women had progressed in their friendship that Stasha could read Anne's thoughts so quickly and be able to stop her from expressing her inappropriate opinions.

The hotel had arranged the transfers to the theatre, the tickets and the seating – which was near the front – so all Stasha had to do was get Anne ready and down to the hotel lobby at six forty-five and they would be magically transferred to the theatre. It was a long performance. Stasha had been concerned about Anne's stamina, but the production was so fast moving that the time sped along. Stasha was too young to remember all of the original Abba performances back in the 1970s, but she had heard of the musical, and it didn't disappoint; it was lively, entertaining, full of music and full of happiness.

Stasha laughed to herself as she remembered how, during one of the most poignant moments of the show, Anne had started to have one of her sneezing fits. She must have had ten sneezes in total, all of which were quite loud. Stasha had had to intervene, handing Anne a tissue and making sure she was kept presentable. Then came the interval refreshments, with Anne's infamous plastic beaker making another appearance. After pouring Anne's orange juice into the beaker, Stasha had treated herself to a glass of wine. Anne had an adapted aisle seat space and Stasha sat next to two American tourists. They were both jovial and entertaining. Stasha noticed that they were wondering about the relationship between her and Anne, and finally they asked.

'I'm her carer,' Stasha said, and the woman nodded.

'Oh that's lovely,' came the reply. 'She must think a lot of you.'

Stasha didn't offer any reply, but Anne cut in. 'She's wonderful.'

Stasha felt a glow sweep over her.

After the show, they got back in the taxi to return to the hotel. Stasha told Anne how much she had enjoyed the evening. When Anne had mentioned a trip to London, it had seemed far fetched and completely unattainable, but David had organised things so that there had been very little waiting and no confusion over the arrangements. The hotel had, as expected, been exemplary and Belinda had been thoughtful and caring – a great help to Stasha over the few days.

Stasha had enjoyed everything the two-day break offered; it had given her an insight into another way of life and how other people live. It didn't make her dissatisfied and it didn't make her unhappy. It just made her realise that there was great opportunity out there that she could capitalise on.

Stasha had proved she was good at her job and could face any difficult situation with a cool head and a calm mind. Yes, she had enjoyed these few days away from the house, but more importantly – and perhaps ironically – she had enjoyed Anne's company. It had been a refreshing break for both of them, but tomorrow at ten o'clock the disabled taxi would arrive and they would be back at home within hours.

Before they checked out, there had been a delivery from Harrods for Anne. It was twenty-five boxes of Christian Dior cookies, beautifully presented and exquisite. All were sumptuously wrapped.

'Who are they all for?' Stasha asked.

'For all the carers, as a gift, and of course Belinda,' Anne replied as she examined the product. A beautiful box containing three layers of cookies with some amazing decorations on them, including a dress and jacket, handbags, perfume bottles and many more things.

'Very nice,' Stasha said as she too examined a box. 'A nice gesture, Anne.'

Once home after a stress-free journey from London, Anne and Stasha settled back into their routines. The other carers had asked to see the videos and pictures that Stasha had taken on her phone; some were happy that the two of them had had a nice break, others said far more by being silent. All were astonished, if that was the right word, at the choice of hotel. It was now clear that they had vastly underestimated the cost of the trip. All the carers thought the Dior cookies were exquisite and were very appreciative of the gesture.

Predictably, there were a few occasional negative comments.

The coming weekend was Stasha's weekend off. Candy was returning, no doubt with a lot of questions and comments, but Stasha was no longer concerned about her. She felt that she and Anne were on a much stronger footing.

So the rest of the week passed without much incident. Anne had been sick a few times, Stasha had cleaned her up, then Anne had been sick again. On the Thursday, Stasha took Anne to another local garden centre for afternoon tea.

'I won't be here this weekend,' Stasha said

over dinner that evening and noticed the change of expression on Anne's face.

'Candy coming?' Anne asked.

Stasha nodded.

'With lots of questions,' Anne said and they both laughed.

So came the Friday and the start of Stasha's weekend off. Candy had arrived at four o'clock. She was her usual exuberant self and this time she brought a potted plant and placed it in front of Anne.

'Oh thank you, Candy,' Anne said.

'I've missed you, Anne,' Candy replied.

Stasha still got irritated that Candy had this thoughtful, manipulative streak in her. She was clever in her gifts, a potted plant would linger.

Candy kissed Anne on the cheek and asked if she had recovered from her London trip. 'Next time you can take me instead of Stasha,' she said.

Anne glanced across at Stasha, who raised her eyebrows but refused to make any comment on Candy's suggestion.

Candy went upstairs to unpack as Stasha was preparing to leave. Stasha placed Daisy in her cage and took her to the car. Then she went back to see Anne and said she would telephone her on Saturday.

'She has a slight chesty cough,' Stasha said, 'so don't take her out without her being wrapped up.' It was an instruction, not a comment, and Candy did not take kindly to it.

'I think I know what I'm doing,' was all Candy said.

Stasha said nothing but looked across at Anne. 'See you soon.' Candy heard the exchange and shrugged. Stasha left the house with an ambient goodbye to Candy, who stood at the lounge window and watched her drive off.

Candy turned round and faced Anne, who was sitting in her chair. 'I was so disappointed that you didn't take me to London, Anne,' she said.

Anne looked up, trying to think of the most appropriate reply. She satisfied Candy by saying a mere two words. 'Next time.'

That made Candy smile, and she went into the kitchen to make herself a cup of coffee.

It was Pollie's turn for the evening call. She got on well with Candy, for – like Candy – she was a good and caring mother and it showed in her care. Pollie always took charge and Anne never felt anything but comfortable with her.

EIGHTEEN

It was a strange feeling, but Stasha didn't really want this weekend off – it no longer appealed to her as much as it used to. She missed Anne, and that was something she hadn't thought she would ever say.

So Stasha's weekend was taken up with the obligatory cleaning and hoovering, and with generally sitting down and resting. She had taken her bicycle out for a ride, but her mind was back with Anne. In particular, she wondered what Candy was doing with her.

She had telephoned Anne's phone as promised on the Saturday evening, but it was Candy who answered. Candy told her that Anne was dozing and that she would not wake her, despite the sound of the television in the background. Candy was up to her old mind games again, but Stasha didn't worry, she simply cut the call and settled down to her evening watching some Saturday night TV with Daisy.

When Stasha returned from her break, Candy was not her usual self. Instead, she was quite friendly and considerate. She even asked how Stasha's weekend had been.

'Fine,' Stasha said in a monosyllabic tone, for it was now her turn to be uncommunicative.

Once settled in the house, Stasha made her familiar journey up the stairs to unpack her belongings.

'Anne is complaining of toothache,' Candy said to Stasha when she had returned downstairs. 'I gave her some paracetamol but she says it's quite troublesome.'

Stasha frowned, for she had never given dentistry a consideration. How would someone like Anne visit the dentist? It was a problem that had arisen out of the blue. Perhaps it was a nerve, or maybe something more serious that needed attention. Stasha went into the lounge and saw Anne asleep on her bed. Before she left, Candy came into the lounge and rested her hand on Anne's shoulder before kissing her on the forehead.

Anne held her hand out to Candy, saying, 'Thank you.'

Stasha made herself a cup of coffee in the kitchen before returning to Anne in the lounge.

'I missed you this time, Stasha.' Anne paused for breath. 'I missed your companionship, but most of all I missed your empathy.'

Stasha frowned, 'What does that mean?'

Anne was now fully awake. 'It means a sympathetic understanding of the situation.'

Stasha raised her eyebrows and Anne continued. 'It is not something Candy has in abundance ...'

Both women laughed.

'Candy's care can be sometimes be a little cold, although she always has my best interest at heart.'

Stasha quickly reflected on what Anne had said; it was almost a compliment, but not quite. 'I'm glad to see you too,' she said simply and they both smiled at each other.

It was a smile of two women who had started to acknowledge the benefits and attributes of each other. While they could still not really be described as friends, there was a mutual appreciation of each other, and in some cases that can be better than just being friends.

Anne noticed that Stasha was deep in thought; she had a glazed expression in her eyes and Anne asked what she was thinking.

Stasha wrinkled her nose. 'I was wondering what the future holds for me. I sometimes wonder if I made the right decision to come to

Britain.'

Anne took a sip of tea and munched on her biscuit. 'I'm glad you came …' she said and tailed off.

Stasha felt that the remark came from Anne's heart.

'How is your mother?' Anne suddenly asked out of the blue, and Stasha said she was suffering from a painful back, probably from doing too much work.

Then Stasha came up with a suggestion. 'Would you like to talk to her?'

Anne frowned, for she didn't comprehend the question. 'I don't follow you,' she said.

'We can arrange a virtual meeting with my mother in Poland and you in the dining room,' Stasha said.

Anne frowned.

'You can see her via the computer,' Stasha explained.

Anne raised her eyebrows and nodded in agreement. 'Why?' she suddenly asked.

'Mum wants to see you.' It was all Stasha intended to say.

Anne frowned and Stasha knew she had to go further.

'Because she just does.' It was all she wanted to say.

'Curiosity,' Anne summarised.

Stasha had often wondered about the prospects of a virtual meeting between her mother and Anne; it would certainly be an interesting encounter and she would telephone her mother tonight and tell her of the suggestion.

The rest of the day was taken up with tidying the house and putting things back to where Stasha liked them, since Candy had moved everything, and then the doorbell rang. It was an unexpected delivery. Stasha opened the door to see a man dressed in a courier uniform with a large box. He placed it down on the doormat and photographed it before picking it up and handing it to Stasha, who then came into the lounge and asked Anne what it was.

Anne shook her head in a dismissive gesture. 'Open it,' Anne instructed, and Stasha went to the kitchen to retrieve a large pair of scissors.

The package was extremely well protected and it took Stasha almost five minutes to remove all the sticky tape and extract the product from the box. From all the packaging, a new, lightweight, hand-held, battery-powered hoover emerged.

'But you've already got one,' Stasha said.

Anne remembered. 'I have given that to Candy.'

There was a silence as Stasha examined the new product and then looked at the invoice for four hundred pounds.

'Whose idea was this?' Stasha asked.

Anne felt she was being interrogated but said, 'Candy's hoover broke, I offered her my old one.'

Stasha bit her lip and said nothing, but she had to decide what to do. There was only one course of action open to her and that was to telephone David and tell him of the situation.

Their phone call lasted three minutes and, although Stasha implied that Candy had persuaded Anne to buy the new hoover and had used the credit card to pay for it, David made a judgement and told Stasha to keep the new hoover and let Candy have the old one, if that was what Anne wanted.

Stasha did not agree but she had no option but to abide by David's wishes. The rest of the afternoon was taken up with talking to Anne about what she had been up to over the past few days.

Tea and bed calls that evening were the duties of Emily and Dee, the two young sisters who came together. Emily had three children and Dee had one. Emily was a serene and harmonious person. She was self-deprecating, which made a refreshing change, and at times she came out with the most amusing remarks. Emily was eminently likeable, a real breath of fresh air and Anne loved seeing her. Dee was the younger of the sisters, a more serious character who could have a fiery personality when challenged. She cared for Anne in a proficient way and, like her sister, was easy to like.

Candy had been correct about Anne having trouble with two of her teeth, and this became a problem over Anne and Stasha's evening meal the following day. Anne had held her mouth and said her tooth ached, and Stasha had retrieved painkillers from the kitchen drawer and placed them in Anne's mouth with a glass of water on hand. Anne had managed to eat the meal and her sherry trifle, but the tooth was troublesome and she had asked Stasha to try and make an appointment with her dentist.

The following morning Stasha retrieved the dentist's details from Anne's address book and rang the surgery only to be told that, due to Anne's condition, it would be inappropriate for the dentist to carry out any procedure on Anne – that is, if they could even get her into the dentist's chair. It was a dilemma Stasha had never thought of – a disabled person such as Anne having dental treatment. She telephoned the office to ask for advice and they instructed her to ring the hospital that looked after Anne and ask them for their advice. This she did.

After being passed from pillar to post, Stasha was finally put through to the department that handled dentistry care for disabled people. This turned out to be nothing more than a helpdesk that provided the patient with the details of practices that were willing to come out to patients' homes. They sent Stasha the forms via email and she emailed them back that evening. It was two days later that Stasha heard back from a local dentist twenty miles away. She would come out with a nurse to carry out any procedure that was necessary. There were a lot of questions for Stasha and a lot of things to consider, and so she rang David and told him of the arrangement. Then there was further paperwork to fill out. Stasha did this in a diligent manner and an appointment was made for seven days' time.

'I don't know what I would do without you,' Anne said one afternoon as she glanced over the papers regarding the dentist's visit. 'You're like my right arm that I no longer have,' Anne said spontaneously with another smile; Stasha felt it was a nice way of saying how much she appreciated her.

Stasha, once again, reflected on the change of relationship she had experienced with Anne, and for the first time she admonished herself for being so awkward in the beginning. Stasha was starting to become aware that the two of them were beginning to learn lessons from each other, and she – for her part – knew that she would remember Anne for some considerable time.

The subject of talking to Stasha's mother had been on the calendar for some time, and Stefania was really eager to meet Anne. So one evening after dinner Stasha positioned her laptop on the dining room table. She had arranged to call her mother using the relevant software at the pre-arranged time. It was not long before Stasha was talking to her mother in Poland; the picture was clear and the sound perfect. Anne marvelled at the modern technology.

Anne had heard little snippets of information about Stefania from Stasha, but she was now intrigued to actually meet her, not in person, but virtually, for – in these modern times – this was the 'new normal'. Looking at someone virtually was interesting, but it only gave you a visual image of the person; it was not like meeting them in real life, where character and overall persona could be judged.

The internet connection to Poland via Stasha's laptop was immediate, and there on the screen was an image of a sixty-year-old plus lady. Stefania was well presented and carefully made up with gold earrings, a high neck blouse and a thin gold chain around her neck. Stefania had red lipstick on, and Anne realised that she had gone to some trouble to present herself in the best light. This surprised Anne, who hadn't thought it necessary even to run a comb through her hair.

Stasha started this somewhat awkward conversation. 'Mum, this is Anne,' she announced.

Anne leant into the screen as if it was making Anne closer to Stefania. 'What?' she said.

'Hello,' Stefania replied. Her accent was pronounced and her voice was distant, but clear.

Anne waved at her and Stefania waved back. Stasha was amused.

'You look very well!' Anne shouted at the screen. 'How are you?'

Stasha couldn't help but laugh.

Stefania was now shouting as well. She nodded, saying she was pleased to meet Anne.

Anne now nodded.

'You're lucky Anne,' Stefania said.

'What?' Anne replied.

'You have Anastazja looking after you,' Stefania finished.

Anne nodded. 'I know.'

Stefania nodded.

'She's wonderful,' Anne said as an afterthought.

'You don't need to tell me that,' Stefania said and Stasha asked her mother why she was shouting.

Stefania had started to talk but Anne didn't hear. She turned to Stasha and said, 'What?'

Stefania shouted something at the screen. Anne still could not understand so she turned to Stasha and said with incredulity, 'Why's she shouting?'

Stasha saw the funny side; this was like two blind women walking down a dark road.

'Nice girl,' Anne said.

'Who?' Stefania asked.

'Your daughter,' Anne replied. 'Very nice.'

'Thank you, Anne,' Stefania said.

'What?' Anne asked.

'You're lucky to have me looking after you,' Stasha said.

'Am I?' Anne remarked.

Both Stasha and Stefania laughed.

'Didn't start well, did it, Anne?' Stasha interjected.

Stefania said, 'You got under her skin, Anne.'

Anne nodded. 'Don't I know it.'

'She so enjoyed London,' Stefania pointed out.

'Me too,' said Anne.

'You're not what I expected, Anne,' Stefania said.

'What?' asked Anne.

'Thought you would be a bigger woman!' Stefania finished.

'A big woman?' Anne said and frowned.

'She means you're quite slight,' Stasha interrupted.

'You gave her a hard time, Anne,' Stefania admonished. 'She got quite upset.'

'I know.' It was all Anne wanted to say.

Stasha involuntary and affectionately placed her arm round Anne's neck and said to her mother, 'We're friends now, Mum.

'Life is too short to argue, Anne,' Stefania said.

Stasha asked her mother how she was doing, and what the weather was like, and what was happening over there. Stefania was an astute woman and they seemed a caring and concerned family. Anne wondered how Stasha's family felt about her going away and working abroad, and more importantly she wondered how they'd reacted when Stasha had told them of the hostile reception she'd received from this middle-class English woman. It was a dimension to their relationship that Anne had given no consideration, and not for the first time she regretted the hurtful things she had said – but you could not take words back.

Both mothers briefly spoke about their families and situations. Anne found that there was sympathy coming out of the computer screen from Stefania, and it surprised her. She was a pleasant and understanding woman.

When the meeting was over and the laptop lid was shut, Stasha put Anne back on her bed.

'Why don't you invite her over to stay with us for few days?' Anne said out of the blue.

It was a statement that completely threw Stasha. It was something she had not thought of and had never believed Anne would ask, but it was a heartfelt suggestion and something she would think about.

'Don't worry about the cost, Stasha, David will sort it all out,' Anne said as an afterthought.

NINETEEN

It had been on Stasha's mind for the last couple of weeks: should she tell Anne that her twenty-eighth birthday was coming up in ten days' time? In her training manual the care agency had made clear that personal celebrations should be kept to a minimum so that service users wouldn't be subject to any undue pressure or expense.

But everything had to be given suitable consideration and, after trips to London and Stratford, Stasha questioned whether she was working for a 'normal' service user who relied solely on a small pension. It wasn't that she wanted any gifts from Anne, it was just that she would feel disingenuous if she did not inform Anne of the forthcoming date. So the following morning, after breakfast, she dropped a hint that it would be her twenty-eighth birthday the following Wednesday.

'We must celebrate it, Anastazja,' Anne said.

Stasha frowned, for it was a long time since Anne had addressed her in such a way, but now it somehow didn't matter; there was now a caring tone in Anne's voice and Stasha smiled back.

'You don't have to, Anne, honestly. You have treated me to so much already.'

'I know,' Anne said, 'I will speak to David and he will arrange something.'

Stasha cleared away the dishes and prepared to move Anne into the lounge for the rest of the morning.

Lorraine, Anne's solicitor, had telephoned her mid morning. Stasha had answered the call and had passed the handset to Anne for her to have the conversation. Diplomatically, Stasha left the room and closed the door behind her.

The dentist appointment loomed large on the calendar and for some mysterious reason Anne's toothache had suddenly disappeared. This coincided with Anne's realisation that the dentist was going to be coming to the house to potentially carry out some work on her teeth.

'I feel fine now, the toothaches gone,' Anne tried to explain.

Stasha didn't believe her. 'Is that why you're chewing on your right side all the time when you're having your dinner?' Stasha was nothing if not observant.

'I don't have toothache like I used to, and I don't want any problems,' Anne replied.

'It's all been arranged,' Stasha said with a sigh, 'I can't undo it all.'

Stasha and the dentist had gone to a great deal of trouble to fit Anne in for an appointment quickly. To Stasha, it felt like the dentist had done her a favour in coming out at such short notice, and cancelling the appointment was unthinkable. She hoped that Anne would forget about her meeting with the dentist until it was too late.

In the afternoon Stasha took Anne for a short drive to get some petrol for the van, buy some flowers for the house and withdraw money from the cash machine for incidentals. Anne took up her usual position perched in the back of the van observing Stasha and the village. Anne remembered the village as a small, quiet settlement in the middle of England, but now – due to the ingress of multiple housing estates, new roads and supermarkets – it had all changed, and not for the better.

Anne had often mulled over the thought of moving house. She had mentioned this to David and he had found a suitable property down near Bournemouth, but Anne had procrastinated and now – as the years had gone by – she had become, primarily due to her stroke, far too frail to undertake such a move.

But Anne wasn't convinced she'd made the right decision. She had taken a strong dislike to the village – it was too busy and all the people she'd known had that either moved away or died off. It had become depressing seeing such a change in the place she and John had started their retirement. John would not recognise the area now. It had always been their intention to purchase a house in the Midlands, live there for a short while and then purchase another one down south, possibly in Devon, but this plan never came to fruition as both Anne and John quickly integrated into their life in the Midlands and time slipped by.

Anne had missed the boat, so to speak, but she had come to realise that you could not predict the future or indeed control it. Philosophically, and in today's unpredictable world, she was thankful to have a roof over her head.

David had never mentioned a care home; if truth be known, he had never even considered one, for Anne was not a person who would adapt well to those surroundings. David preferred to have his mother at home and looked after by one person only. He had visited once every few weeks. With Stasha, he knew he had found a good, compassionate carer; Anne could be difficult, but there were always two sides to an argument. David had said to his mother that he would only consider placing her in a hospice or hospital for medical reasons, or under the instruction of professionals.

Stasha had a phone call the following morning from a member of the local writers group that Anne used to be part of. Paul was a widower, and he asked if he could come round for a chat. Stasha placed her hand over the phone's mouthpiece and signalled to Anne that he wanted to come round and talk. Anne looked less than enthusiastic but suggested two o'clock.

So, after an early lunch, Stasha prepared Anne for the visit. Paul was in his late seventies – a rotund person with a balding head and the demeanour of someone used to management.

Stasha introduced herself and directed Paul into the lounge to sit at the top of the room, where Anne was waiting for him. Stasha had positioned the coffee table between Anne's chair and the other easy chair and, as Paul sat down, Stasha asked what he would like to drink.

'A black coffee would be nice, please,' Paul said. His manner was polite and assured.

Anne met Stasha's eyes. 'Tea?' she said.

Paul had worked hard in the financial industry and then moved to the village around twenty years ago, and he had become keenly involved in all activities related to the surrounding area and the village itself. He had been part of the writing group for a number of years and was a popular member. Anne had been the instigator of the group and was really the driving force behind it, but since her stroke she had decided that she would not return. Nevertheless, she was pleased that the group had carried on without her. Paul was now relating all the news of the various members and what they had been up to, but the real reason he was visiting was that he had just lost his wife to Alzheimer's, and this continued to weigh heavily on his mind.

'I suppose she has got release, she is no longer suffering,' Paul said as Stasha served the refreshments. Always polite, Stasha served Paul's coffee first and then served Anne.

She tapped Anne on the shoulder and said, 'Call if you want me.'

Anne nodded.

'She's nice,' Paul remarked and then went on to describe what he had been getting up to, with embellishments thrown in here and there.

Paul, who had without doubt had his wife's best interests at heart, had looked after her at home for as long as he could, then had moved her into a care home, which was local but expensive. After a year the bills became too much. Another care home had been located, and it had been there, shortly after his wife had moved in, that she had sadly passed away. Quite naturally, Paul was dwelling on the move to the new care home and was wondering whether it had precipitated her death. There were, however, no real grounds for these concerns, as many other factors had come into play by the time she'd been moved. Nevertheless, the guilt Paul was carrying, which Anne could see clearly in his face, was overwhelming to him.

Paul went on to say how hard it had been to look after his wife at home. Being the unseen carer to a disabled partner or relative was – at times – the hardest thing anyone could do.

Others found it rewarding and a privilege, but he had found it difficult.

The conversation made Anne reflect on her own position; what would have happened if David had instructed her to go straight to a care home instead of returning to her own home? The option had been available to him. After Anne's stroke, there was no way she could have been discharged from hospital without a suitable care plan or a reservation in a care home. But it wasn't something he'd considered.

Anne had often wondered whether she would end up in a care home. She had had to place John in one, although his care home had been miles away; a beautifully converted country house with staff that were familiar with looking after distinguished people. But even though it was large, spacious and very expensive, Anne still found the prospect of living there awful; she preferred her own home and she made that clear to David whenever he visited her.

Anne considered how she would cope in a care home. The thought still did not appeal to her; she felt they were anonymous places, where staff would have little insight into the people the residents had once been. They were sad, lonely places, since all the residents knew and accepted they were never going to leave.

Anne could hear Stasha in the kitchen as Paul babbled on and, not for the first time, she reflected on how she had treated her when she'd first arrived.

'Anastazja!' Anne called, and dutifully she came into the room. 'Come and join us,' Anne said.

Stasha went back to the kitchen and made herself a coffee then returned to sit next to Anne.

'A lovely name,' Paul said to Stasha, who smiled.

'David is thinking of moving to Cornwall,' mentioned Anne, and Paul went on to explain what he felt were the merits of living down south and by the sea.

'I want to move,' Anne suddenly said. 'Get away from the village, the traffic and all the memories ...' Anne paused. 'But David says no.'

'Listen to what he says, Anne,' Paul said gently, and Stasha nodded. 'The grass is not always greener ...'

Stasha frowned. She had not heard that expression before and Paul explained its meaning.

'Anne is very lucky having someone like you looking after her,' Paul said as he took a sip of coffee.

Stasha smiled at Anne and it was obvious to Paul that these two women had a good rapport and what looked like a strong friendship. Once again, he momentarily thought of his own wife; perhaps he could have had a full-time carer in, but the house wasn't suitable for that and his wife's mobile condition was nothing like Anne's.

Although Anne was paralysed, she was still reasonably astute and had capacity. That was the difference; when capacity is lost and the patient becomes awkward, disruptive and violent, and particularly when they're at risk of wandering off by themselves, then trying to keep them at home is always extremely difficult. Paul looked to the ground; he still felt guilty at what he felt were his own shortcomings.

'Do you miss your country?' Paul asked.

Stasha made eye contact with Paul but refrained from saying anything, for she anticipated what was coming next.

'Will you go back there?' Paul added.

Stasha paused. It was always interesting

that people thought that foreigners in their country would eventually go back to their native country; the implication was, 'after you have taken all you can from our country.' But she remonstrated with herself – perhaps she was a little sensitive on the issue.

Anne interrupted Stasha's train of thought. 'She makes a great contribution to our society and has helped me considerably.'

'Of course ...' Paul started. '... I didn't mean to suggest that I meant you would return to your family ...' but Paul was getting lost in his words.

Stasha gave a disarming smile and reassured him that she would be staying in England for the foreseeable future.

They continued to chat about all sorts, with Anne complaining again about how the village had been ruined and was now beset with traffic and parking issues. She pointed out that the line between village and city was becoming increasingly blurred; it was no longer a relaxing place to be. This brought Paul back to the subject of Cornwall.

'It wouldn't be the same, I suppose, moving on my own,' Paul eventually said. 'Like you, I waited too long ... but I need to downsize.'

When Anne was motivated to receive

Annette De Burgh

visitors, Anne enjoyed her talks with Paul; he was a stimulating person who gave her much to think about, as well as giving her inside knowledge about what was going on in the village. If truth be known, Anne missed a lot from her previous life, but she'd said to Stasha many times that there was no point looking back, for only the future was left. In one of the rare times she mentioned Michael, she would quote him, saying, 'What is the worst that can happen?' She would leave a pregnant pause before saying, 'Death, of course.'

TWENTY

Stasha was woken at six thirty on the Wednesday morning by Anne repeatedly ringing her bell. It made Stasha wake with a start and she looked at the monitor immediately to see that Anne was wide awake in her bed, restless and agitated. Quickly, Stasha got out of her bed, placed her dressing gown around her and went downstairs to see what was troubling Anne so early in the morning.

As soon as Stasha entered the room, Anne held her hand up to her in an attempt to make her understand what she was trying to say. Anne muttered something about the dentist.

'What about the dentist?' Stasha said with a frown.

Anne started to say something, but she was tired and couldn't get the words out. She shook her head, 'Don't come.'

Stasha deciphered what Anne was trying to say. 'You want the dentist cancelled, is that it?' There was a note of exasperation in Stasha's voice.

Anne nodded but she was confused.

'But they're coming this morning, Anne, at ten o'clock. It's too late to cancel them,' Stasha argued.

'Cancel them, please, I don't want them,' Anne pleaded.

'Is that what you have called me down for?'

Anne nodded.

Stasha sighed. 'But they're coming this morning in a few hours' time. I can't cancel, it's too late, it's all been arranged, the dentist is coming with a nurse,' Stasha said.

But Anne was not listening and she didn't want to be put off so she kept saying, 'Cancel the dentist.'

Stasha pulled the sheets back over Anne to make her warm and went back upstairs. She lay on her bed listening to the early morning news while contemplating exactly what she could say to the dentist at this late stage. Maybe she could even offer a payment for cancelling at such late notice.

It was a facet of Anne that carefully laid plans and arrangements could be cancelled at the last minute. Stasha suddenly thought of the trip to London and how it had actually gone to plan, but at other times – especially when visitors were coming to the house – things could be put off at the last moment. It was all becoming very awkward, and Stasha worried that visitors would think it was she who was putting them off, not the other way round.

Stasha checked her phone for the opening hours of the dentist surgery and noted that they did not open till nine o'clock, but she decided to ring the surgery anyway and leave a message saying she would ring back after nine and explain the situation.

Stasha need not have worried, for the receptionist at the dentist was more than understanding and implied that it was not the first time a patient had cancelled so late. In view of the situation, there would be no cancellation penalty, but the dentist did say that disabled people – particularly patients who could not get to the dental surgery due to mobility issues – often let their teeth go because they were scared of having procedures done at home. The receptionist's advice to Stasha was to quietly rebook the appointment for a few weeks' time without telling Anne first.

Stasha received a telephone call from David that afternoon explaining that Anne wanted to do something to celebrate Stasha's forthcoming birthday. David had given the matter some thought and had come up with the idea of having dinner at the house, cooked and served by a Polish catering company. Stasha could have the meal of her choice. Anne had requested that Candy join them, as well as a neighbour.

Stasha, not for the first time, was taken aback at the suggestion. It was an immensely kind and thoughtful gesture – a Polish chef to cook her native food – it sounded too interesting to miss and she agreed to it immediately. She asked David to join them as well but he declined, saying he was too busy. Once the conversation was over, Stasha went in to Anne and outlined what David had said.

'I know,' Anne replied, 'he told me the other day during our phone call what he was planning.'

'It's so very kind of you,' Stasha said and there was genuine appreciation in her voice.

'It's my absolute pleasure,' Anne said quietly.

It was a lovely early autumn afternoon and Anne had asked Stasha if she would like a walk around the park in a nearby town. The park was at the top end of the town and had multiple tarmac footpaths, a large lake and a cafe in the middle where one could sit out and enjoy the sunshine.

So the two of them set off after lunch on the eight-mile drive to the next town. Stasha parked the van efficiently, for she was now a master of doing this, and Anne felt very confident in Stasha's abilities. Once settled, they started to meander around the large lake passing other members of the public who were feeding the ducks. Others were with their dogs and young children. It wasn't particularly busy. Both Anne and Stasha usually made amusing remarks about the people they saw and today was no different; they finally reached the cafe and Stasha got one of the outside tables, made Anne secure and went into the cafe to order two glasses of orange juice. It was a refreshing drink for them both and, as per usual, Stasha had brought Anne's special cup with her and was carefully pouring the liquid into it.

Stasha sat back and observed Anne while enjoying the sunshine. Anne was a complex woman who had many sides to her; often she was good company, whereas at other times she was seemingly oblivious to the ways in which her comments could hurt and demoralise people. Stasha had come to the conclusion that Anne simply didn't know she was doing it and she wondered how she had got on with her younger children.

There was no doubt that David thought a great deal of Anne, for he had put in place some good quality care and never recoiled from any difficult decisions that had to be made. He had handled the initial argumentative side of Stasha and Anne's relationship with the correct judgement, and he had shown sympathy for Stasha, which she had appreciated. Whenever she spoke to him, he was quick to resolve any issues, and he had given Stasha the instruction that Anne must have anything she wanted, and that she was not to be unnecessarily upset by any carer.

'You never mention Michael, Anne?' Stasha asked.

There was a long pause from Anne and it looked to Stasha as if she was framing the answer to the question in her mind.

'What is there to say?' Anne eventually said coldly.

'I'd like to hear about him.' Stasha's tone was purposeful, for she had often wondered about Michael and his story.

Anne took more time to think about her answer. She took a long drink from her cup and carefully placed the beaker down on the table. 'He was my first born, so in that respect he was special.' There was a pause before she continued. 'Michael was at times a difficult character, very much misunderstood and very much misguided.'

Stasha frowned, willing Anne to continue.

'When he was younger Michael rarely put a foot wrong, unlike David, but while David had his feet on the ground, Michael often found it hard; he was a square peg trying to get into a round hole.'

Stasha her raised eyebrows, for Anne had used a good description. She could picture Michael a little better.

Anne continued involuntarily. 'Michael had the potential to be quite bright at school, but he had no motivation in him and that was a major part of his problem; he often admitted that he had no fire in his belly and that stunted a lot of what he was able to do. While David wanted to own expensive things and went about getting them, Michael was never like that; he had no use for personal or material possessions, he had no desire to have a lot of money, he had no wish to have expensive cars. So in that respect his outlook was somewhat limited and consequently he lacked ambition.'

Anne basked in the sunshine but she wanted to continue and give a balanced side to Michael.

'On the other hand, Michael was extremely well read and had hundreds of books in his collection, which he had read from start to finish. He was knowledgeable about the most unusual things. In the beginning he had something like a photographic memory, for he could remember the most odd incidents and recount them in agonising detail. He was not a fool – he was clever in his own way, and when he hadn't had a drink was very good company and quite humorous in a dry way. But like all alcoholics this was overshadowed by his habit. He couldn't seem to go a single day without drinking, and eventually his personality was eroded and he became lost in himself. It was very sad.'

'How did he get on with David? You said you had given Michael more attention.' Stasha asked.

Anne wanted to frame her answer carefully. 'As brothers, they didn't get on. I don't even think they were really friends to be honest. Michael often needed my support.' There was a pause as Anne remembered the analogy David often said with regard to Anne and

Michael's relationship; she related it to Stasha.

'If Michael had burned the house down, I would have blamed David because Michael would have used David's matches …'

Stasha frowned.

'I often think of that remark, as it is – unfortunately – so very true,' there was a note of sad reflection in Anne's voice. 'But as brothers, they had nothing in common. If you have nothing in common, there's no basis on which to build any type of friendship. After his death, we found Michael had written some truly awful things about David in his journals …'

Stasha looked aghast.

'Particularly hard as David had arranged and paid for some very comfortable palliative care for him …'

Stasha shook her head in astonishment, 'Was Michael resentful of David?'

Anne scratched her neck and thought of the answer. 'I think Michael would have been better as an only child, with the attention only on him. I'm not sure he liked having a sibling alongside him.

'I think, looking back, that Michael had a father complex. Most boys have a mother complex but I think Michael developed some kind of father complex with John. John was overseas for most of the year, but he was an authoritative man who saw things in a very black and white way. There was no in between; you were either good at something or you weren't, and Michael fell between those two stools. John would often quote, "*If a man shouts, his words no longer matter.*" Michael became overshadowed by John. Whereas David embraced it, Michael distanced himself from it and began to look for faults in people where none really existed; he became obsessed with certain past arguments that he would recall and put a different slant on things. But on the whole he was someone who was simply misunderstood. I often wondered whether he liked the family.'

'Do you mind telling me how he died, because he was quite young?' queried Stasha.

Anne smiled ironically. 'He died because I gave him a sip of my wine one night over dinner when he was eight years old; I remember he asked if he could try a little wine and I handed the glass to him and he took a sip and I think he liked the taste. Moreover, I think he liked the action of drinking. And that was the start of Michael becoming overly fond of alcohol.'

'Does David like a drink?' Stasha queried.

Anne shook her head vehemently.

Stasha paused before asking, 'And John, did he drink?'

'John was a regular drinker but he was also a social drinker; he drank with others and he didn't hide what he drank. When he was home, he would come from the office and he would have a gin and tonic and sit reading the paper while I got the meal. I suppose Michael witnessed all this and he thought it was the correct thing to do, but what he didn't appreciate was that John didn't drink after his meal, he went through the rest of the evening without touching a drop. Only in his later years when he was retired would he go to the pub for a pint of beer. But Michael was never like that, Michael became what I would call a dishonest, dependent drinker.'

Stasha decided to say nothing, for Anne was in full flow.

'I would ask, "Have you had a drink, Michael?" and Michael would shake his head and say no, but it was obvious that he had been drinking and he was only fooling himself. So in the end he took no responsibility for the amount of alcohol he drank because in his mind he wasn't drinking any.'

Stasha shook her head. 'Are you disappointed in Michael? It seems like he had a lot of opportunities?'

Anne thought of the answer. 'I don't think I am as disappointed as Michael would be in himself.'

'How exactly did he die?' Stasha asked gently, but it was a hard question for Anne to hear.

'He had liver failure, he had heart failure and he had water on his lungs. He was chronically anaemic and, as Michael would often say, it was all self-inflicted.'

Stasha sighed.

Anne was becoming upset as she talked, so Stasha changed the subject to people watching. It was something Anne liked to do and Stasha had taken it up as well, watching people going about their normal business, walking their dogs, talking to each other or just living their lives. Another of Anne and Stasha's new pastimes was going to the village in the van. Stasha would park in a particular spot, allowing Anne to observe people coming and going, for she enjoyed that, and for Stasha it was a restful half hour.

TWENTY-ONE

Whenever Candy was in the vicinity of Anne's house and there was a gap in her rota she would take it upon herself to drop by. She would walk in unannounced and make herself a cup of coffee, then she would go and sit with Anne and talk with her for half an hour. Stasha thought this was an annoying habit. Candy seemed to think it was her right to interrupt Stasha's day and that she could drop by to see Anne whenever she wanted; the problem was the warm welcome Anne always gave her. The two of them would sit together having a good old-fashioned chin-wag and, although Stasha was included, there was still a sense of her being on the periphery whenever Candy was talking to Anne.

It still got under Stasha's skin that Candy could immediately enjoy an easy rapport with Anne. They joked about what was on television, they talked about the food they had eaten, they commented about the other carers and they generally connected with each other in a way that Stasha and Anne simply could not.

For her part, Candy had started to become a little more cooperative with Stasha, mainly because Anne had wanted them to be friends – if only in her presence – but Candy was cunning and clever and always seemed to be one step ahead.

Anne did not always notice the interplay between Candy and Stasha, or if she did she chose to ignore it.

Today, Candy had a break in her rota, so she drove up Anne's drive, this time with a Battenberg cake. Stasha sighed. Candy went straight to the lounge, giving Stasha only a brief smile. Stasha chose not to respond.

Candy made some refreshments for Anne, and Stasha realised that Candy had timed her visit to coincide with Anne's afternoon break. So, with her coffee, Anne's tea and a thin slice of the Battenberg, Candy went back to the lounge, sat next to Anne and asked how she was. Stasha remained in the kitchen to clear up and she listened to the babble of voices from the lounge. Candy and Anne settled down to an easy and relaxed conversation, with Candy telling her some amusing anecdotes about what she had been up to at the weekend and Anne laughing at her tales.

Stasha stood in the hall and listened to the exchange between them. Candy was cheeky, even rude at times, telling Anne anecdotes with the odd swear word thrown in. Stasha joined them and noticed Candy's face drop, but she did not want to argue. She joined in the conversation and soon the three women talked together; their squabbles between them momentarily forgotten.

The 'model sisters' came to put Anne to bed on the Thursday evening. Maggie (the youngest) and Marie (the oldest) were probably the most composed and accommodating carers that Anne saw. Maggie was a beautiful young woman who presented herself in many different guises – her hair colour and style were all striking, as was her makeup. Her partner was an accountant and they had bought their own home, had two young children and were undoubtedly on the path to greater things. Maggie was posher than posh; she spoke well and was a considerate and courteous young woman.

Marie was similar, a bit older and a bit wiser, but with the same calm attitude. A more experienced carer who was thoughtful and consistent in her care. Marie was very high on Anne's list of favourites, after Stasha and Candy.

On the Friday evening Stasha decided to

have an early night, for it had been an extremely difficult and very stressful end to the week. She felt exhausted through concern and worry. With a semblance of order now in her mind, she was able to relive the events of her tumultuous afternoon. With Anne now fast asleep and snoring, Stasha managed to laugh at the events that unfolded only a few hours ago.

It all started when Stasha noticed an advert for a recently re-opened garden centre with a renowned tea and cake shop franchise on the premises in a town fifteen miles away. It was one of the few garden centres in the area that they had not visited. But what was meant to be an enjoyable afternoon jaunt around the plants and haberdashery turned into the afternoon from hell for Stasha.

With the help of the van's satnav Stasha was able to find the garden centre fairly easily and, once parked up, she got Anne out of the van and into the spacious and welcoming interior, which boasted a huge indoor shopping area. But Anne wished to go outside, for she enjoyed looking at the plants and breathing in the fresh air.

Stasha decided to take Anne to the rose garden section, for there were a few roses in

Anne's garden and perhaps they would buy another one which they could plant together the following day. The rose garden was situated at the far end of the business premises next to where the young trees were kept.

It was when Stasha was pushing Anne around the rose bushes that, suddenly and unexpectantly, the right rear wheel of Anne's manual wheelchair worked its way loose and detached itself from the chair's axle. The wheel rolled away and the wheelchair tilted heavily towards one side, like a ship listing at sea, and Stasha struggled to keep Anne level. She was suddenly petrified that Anne could tip out of her chair. It was an unthinkable prospect.

Stasha anxiously looked around for assistance but there was no one and the chair was starting to feel heavier. Stasha looked at the broken wheel and realised that this would not be a quick fix. And, as if this weren't bad enough, Anne was becoming more agitated and frightened.

'What's happened?' Anne asked impatiently.

Stasha struggled with the chair. 'One of the wheels has come off,' she stuttered, sounding out of breath.

'Well put it back on,' Anne instructed and Stasha rolled her eyes in despair.

'It's not that simple,' Stasha replied, and she was now really struggling to keep the chair level and Anne safe.

'Move me,' Anne commanded.

'I can't, there is no wheel on it,' Stasha's voice mirrored her anguish at this impossible situation. She looked to the heavens for some divine intervention, but none came.

Stasha had to think quickly. What on earth could she do? There was nobody about to help. She couldn't reach her phone and was at the very top end of the garden centre, which suddenly seemed deserted. The only saving grace was that it wasn't raining.

Surely somebody has to come by, Stasha thought to herself, but she looked around in vain – there was nobody.

In the distance Stasha spotted some large concrete blocks that had been stacked in one corner, next to some wood, but they were a fair distance from where she was. So, with an almighty effort and with as much strength as she could muster, Stasha lifted the back of the chair up and pushed it on its front wheels towards the concrete blocks. It was like guiding an out-of-control shopping trolley.

'What's happening?' Anne asked again, now with concern in her voice.

'Bear with me, Anne,' Stasha said and this time she sounded out of breath.

Eventually Stasha and the chair reached the concrete blocks and, with careful manipulation of the chair, she was able to position the rear axle over the block to support the chair evenly. The only snag was that Anne was almost halfway into the bushes.

'Stasha,' Anne complained.

'Be patient,' Stasha snapped.

'Don't leave me,' she could hear Anne shout as she ran back to the shop to get help, but she was frantic with worry that Anne's chair would move and she would fall out. She was out of breath and shaking, but she managed to obtain the assistance of two men, who ran with her back to where Anne had been abandoned.

To Stasha's utter relief, Anne's chair was still upright. She quickly calmed Anne down. The men surveyed the damage as Stasha went to retrieve the wheel that had rolled some distance away.

'Your granddaughter has asked us to help,'

one of the men said.

'I'm her carer,' Stasha replied as she was phoning David.

'Oh, I see,' the man replied and suddenly there was a change of attitude. 'Don't worry,' the man said to Anne, 'we'll sort it out.'

Stasha now looked at the ceiling of her bedroom and then back to the CCTV monitor, observing Anne in bed and thankfully restful. She closed her eyes, knowing how devastated she would have felt if anything had happened to her.

Her mind went back to the events of the afternoon. It was decided that the garden centre would lend Stasha a wheelchair to take Anne home in, but then came the thorny issue of how to transfer Anne safely and without injury from one chair to the other while at the garden centre. There were no hoists here. Added to that, Anne was starting to get cold.

Stasha rang the office to ask for advice and they advised her to get four men, two for Anne's legs and two for under her arms, and quickly and efficiently transfer her to the other chair.

Two other men volunteered to help, and the four men carried out the procedure quickly and efficiently. Now, lying back on her bed in the peaceful surroundings of her bedroom, Stasha could allow herself another laugh at the total absurdity of the situation, but she was pleased with herself for handling the unexpected dilemma so well.

The icing on the cake was Anne's comments to her once back at home.

'You did well, Stasha,' Anne said, and Stasha knew the statement was meant.

Stasha's birthday dinner had not been spoken about since her conversation with David. But behind the scenes, all the arrangements for the dinner had gone smoothly and a Polish chef and his waitress had been booked.

If truth be known, Stasha was not a great one for these types of occasions but she felt it would be churlish to turn down what had been planned. Curiosity had got the better of her and she wanted to see what David had arranged.

After dinner that evening, when the evening news finished, Anne and Stasha were sitting in the lounge when Anne suddenly asked, 'Will you bring your family over eventually?'

The question was innocently asked but it

still made the hairs on the back of Stasha's neck stand on end. As with all Anne's questions, it merited a thoughtful answer, and she pondered for a few seconds before responding. But her irritation got the better of her.

'What you mean is when can my family come over and sponge off your economy? That's what you're asking.' Even to Stasha's ears it sounded harsh.

Anne raise her eyebrows for she had thought the bickering about Stasha's origins had been put to bed, but it was obviously still there lurking beneath the surface.

Stasha, with a frown on her face and annoyed at herself for snapping, said, 'We wouldn't be able to afford a house that would be suitable, and my parents certainly couldn't live in mine, and who would employ my father. He's very happy where he is, thank you, Anne.'

Anne did not say anything but Stasha had found herself a spade and was determined to keep digging.

'We don't all live in houses like this with empty bedrooms.'

There was suddenly a whisper of the old arguments resurfacing. Anne wasn't sure what had triggered Stasha's defensive response, but she quickly realised that Stasha's resentment had not gone away completely – it had merely been hidden. Anne was surprised at the outburst but it was hard for her to read Stasha's expression behind her dark glasses.

'I'm sure you'll get there in the end, Stasha.'

It was a peaceful statement and one which took the wind out of Stasha's sails. She could only nod in agreement.

Then it was Anne's turn to stir the pot, saying, 'What is it you like about our country?' She waited for Stasha to rise to the bait. She was not disappointed.

Stasha sighed, 'You're telling me it's your country now, are you?'

But before Stasha could continue, Anne deliberately had the final say. 'I wish to be on my own please.' It was a cold statement from Anne that harked back to previous times.

Stasha had been dismissed. She got up and walked slowly out of the room. There were the beginnings of an argument and she would have relished the chance to answer Anne's provocative questions regarding immigration, as she never liked being on the losing side of a disagreement, especially with Anne. That was probably why there had been such antagonism between them, for essentially they had the same qualities. Stasha loved to have a final say, but this time it hadn't worked; Anne had wisely seen trouble ahead and decided to cut it off at the pass.

Stasha went to the kitchen to clear up. She gazed out of the window, placing both hands on the kitchen counter and bowed her head. She knew she was in the wrong – being awkward, snapping at Anne – for this time Anne had done nothing wrong other than ask a perfectly normal question and Stasha, for no reason, had taken exception to it. She knew she had to go back into the lounge and apologise.

Once in the lounge, Stasha bent down next to Anne's chair and said 'sorry' and was rewarded with an understanding but tear-filled smile from Anne.

'We're good,' Anne replied with a smile.

Stasha smiled at the turn of phrase and the incident was forgotten.

TWENTY-TWO

Autumn was suddenly mediocre weather-wise, but it had improved dramatically over the past few days. Gone were the rainy afternoons and cloud-covered mornings and in their place had come welcoming sunshine.

'An Indian Summer,' Anne had said, but Stasha did not understand the statement. They had started to discuss the things that they would like to do together throughout the remaining days when there was still light. Although Anne was frail, she was always willing to leave the house and travel in the back of the van.

Over the last few weeks the two women had stared at the greenhouse in the rear garden and they had both commented that it should really have a coat of paint. To Anne's surprise, Stasha had suggested painting it in a brighter colour – she would get the paint and do the job herself on a suitable afternoon.

Today was that day.

After lunch Stasha propelled Anne out into the rear garden. She secured the wheelchair by switching the power off and then carefully set about preparing the greenhouse for painting.

Stasha had painted a section of the rear garden fence earlier so painting was not alien to her. She placed old bed sheets around the base of the greenhouse and carefully loosened the door lock and handle before brushing down the exterior of the greenhouse with a soft brush and wiping down the windows.

Anne watched the diligent manner in which Stasha applied herself to the task. 'Looks like you've done this before,' Anne commented.

Stasha looked round at Anne, struck by the absurdity of the statement. 'I can't afford decorators, Anne.'

Anne said nothing.

'You get a sense of satisfaction by doing the job yourself and sometimes on a nice afternoon like this it's better than staying indoors,' Stasha continued.

Anne nodded but she was secretly glad that it was not her who was about to paint the greenhouse. In the past, she had painted the odd wall, but she was thankful those days were behind her.

Stasha had finished brushing down the exterior and now did a final wipe over the windows. The greenhouse was by no means large and the job wouldn't take that long. The two women had had a discussion about what colour to paint it; Anne had wanted green but Stasha had suggested something a bit lighter, so they settled on a sort of grey-silver colour using outdoor paint that would protect the wood and require just one application.

Anne remained amused that Stasha would undertake the task of painting the greenhouse while still wearing her sunglasses. She had tied her blonde hair back into a ponytail but had seemingly forgotten to remove her sunglasses. Over the months this had become something of a trademark for Stasha; Stasha without her dark glasses was simply not Stasha, and whenever Anne asked her to remove them they were quickly replaced. They were not really sunglasses, per se, more tinted spectacles and Anne had tried to find out why Stasha constantly wore them, for she had lovely, inviting eyes that certainly should not have been behind dark glasses. Anne eventually accepted it after hearing that Stasha was susceptible to frequent headaches and that the dark glasses helped to prevent them.

Anne marvelled at Stasha's enthusiasm, for the afternoon had become quite warm. While Anne was enjoying basking in the sunshine, it was perhaps getting a little too warm for strenuous work, but Stasha carried on undeterred. Anne admitted that the colour Stasha had chosen was appropriate and that she applied the paint in a diligent and conscientious manner.

Stasha went back into the house and emerged a few moments later with the step ladder from the garage. She positioned it adjacent to the greenhouse and then, with impressive agility, she climbed to the top step with her tin of paint and paint brush and started to paint the top window frames without hesitation.

'Be careful,' Anne said, and Stasha smiled inwardly for she was touched by Anne's concern.

'Who would look after you if I fell?' Stasha teased and she could see a frown on Anne's face.

'Don't fall, please don't fall,' Anne answered and there was a note of worry in her voice.

Stasha turned around on the step ladder, saying, 'I thought that's what you wanted,' and the moment she said it, she regretted it.

Anne's face dropped and Stasha knew her remark was uncalled for. She stopped painting, came down from the ladder and went across to Anne, who was sitting in her chair with her head lowered. Anne had heard the remark but had chosen not to say anything. It was Stasha who knelt down, once again, by the side of the wheelchair, saying, 'I'm sorry, I didn't mean that.'

Anne pursed her lips, 'An understandable reply Stasha.' There was no malice in Anne's voice and Stasha got up and went back to resume her painting. As she reached the greenhouse, Anne called to her and she turned round. Anne was pointing to a section of the greenhouse. Stasha frowned and shrugged her shoulders.

'You've missed a bit,' Anne said mischievously, and they both laughed together before Stasha resumed her work.

'What do you think of the colour, Stasha?' Anne asked from the garden, seeing now the contrast between the light paint and the original colour it was replacing.

'It makes a change.' Stasha was non-committal.

Anne continued to watch Stasha paint. Suddenly she thought she could do with a drink. 'Wouldn't mind a drink,' Anne suddenly announced.

Stasha turned around from her task. 'Seriously Anne ...?' Then she gave a small shrug. 'You want me to get you a drink in the middle of painting the greenhouse?' There was a note of exasperation in her voice.

'I'm quite thirsty,' Anne persisted.

Stasha took a deep breath, methodically placed the paintbrush down, removed her rubber gloves and walked back to the kitchen to get some warm water from the kettle. She put it into the plastic beaker and went back outside to Anne. Stasha stood over Anne and watched her drink it. In all fairness, Anne drank all the liquid and handed the empty beaker back to Stasha, who smiled and then affectionately ruffled Anne's hair before resuming her painting.

Ever since the incident at the garden centre, Stasha had been left with only the electronic wheelchair to use. David had sent a large taxi to retrieve Anne's broken chair from the garden centre and return it home, and it was now away being repaired – apparently the wheel had been unknowingly overtightened by the gardener when he tried an earlier repair.

The electric wheelchair was not ideal. Anne had a habit of switching the machine on and moving herself to wherever she wanted, sometimes with disastrous results. She had knocked and cracked the screen of the television, she had smashed into her hoist and she had scratched all the inside doors with the chair's wheels, as well as towing her bed from one end of the lounge to the other by inadvertently latching on to it in a careless reversing manoeuvre. An accomplished operator Anne certainly was not.

Now, mischievously, Anne switched the electric wheelchair on and started to proceed to the top of the garden.

Stasha sighed. Another distraction. She wished Anne would stay in one place. Stasha had no choice but to remove her gloves for a second time, and she strode over to Anne. At the top of the garden there was a deep pond under a large, old oak tree – a misjudgement by Anne could have dire consequences, with the aftermath too horrible to think about.

'Anne,' Stasha said gently, 'come back and watch as I finish painting.'

Begrudgingly, Anne swivelled her chair around and went back to her original position. Stasha continued to paint.

Daisy appeared from nowhere. First she went to Stasha to examine her work, and then she had a quick look round the pond before coming back to Anne, leaping on to her lap and snuggling down for a quick nap.

It took Anne's attention away from trying to move the wheelchair again, for she was now quite happy to monitor Stasha's painting while gently stroking Daisy, who was lapping up the attention.

'She has her favourites, doesn't she?' Stasha said.

'She's a lovely cat,' Anne replied and looked into Daisy's eyes, saying quietly under her breath, 'Who can believe there is no soul behind those luminous eyes.'

Stasha continued to paint and, in just over one hour, she had completed the task. The paint was applied evenly and carefully, and Anne admitted that the greenhouse now looked good.

'Jack of all trades,' Anne said to Stasha.

'What does that mean?' Stasha queried.

'It means you're good at everything.' There was a hint – but only a hint – of admiration in Anne's tone.

It was a compliment Stasha took because she was pleased with what she had done. She carefully put the paint away, washed the paintbrush, gathered all the bed sheets together, took the step ladder back to the garage and then took a garden chair and sat next to Anne in the sunshine, enjoying what was left of the afternoon.

By early evening Stasha was feeling tired. She might have been a young, fit twenty-seven-year-old but standing on a ladder, looking after Anne and clearing up in the afternoon sun had taken its toll, and she was feeling exhausted. There was the evening meal to make, two more calls for Anne and tidying up to do before she could eventually let herself have another early night. Anne had adapted to these early nights quite well; in the beginning she was still awake every night at midnight waiting for Stasha to make her comfortable, but now it was lights out at ten thirty, and Anne would be fast asleep by eleven. Stasha remained thankful that Anne could still sleep right through the night, and it was still very rare that Anne would wake Stasha in the middle of the night.

Now, lying back on her bed, Stasha reflected on the afternoon. She remembered painting a section of Anne's fence earlier on. Anne had been a little critical of the job, but that was in those early, difficult days; today had been pleasant, there was laughter and jokes and a most unlikely connection continued to form between them.

Stasha delved deeper into their relationship. She felt it was she who had perhaps changed the most. Anne had frequently told her that she had a chip on her shoulder. She reluctantly admitted to herself that caring for Anne had started to give her the satisfaction she had been looking for. Stasha felt she was genuinely making a difference to someone's life, and that in itself could have no price. Praise from Anne was equal to praise from three other people, given that she gave it so rarely.

Stasha had now mellowed, possibly from experience. She knew how to deal with Anne and with difficult situations, and she found that she had grown in terms of her personality, character and stamina. For that, she silently thanked Anne, but it had been a hard lesson.

TWENTY-THREE

It was the day of Stasha's birthday dinner. David was adamant that everything would be taken care of, so tonight Stasha could sit back and watch others work around her.

Anne had had an early evening call with Cian and Leigh and had been freshened up. Candy had been invited and was due at six, and Maureen from the village would also arrive at six.

Maureen was an elderly lady from the local church, who seemed to know all the goings-on in the village. She was an educated lady, a retired head mistress of a local girls' school who had her principles and opinions, and who knew a large number of the residents in the village. She had lived for most of her eighty years in the surrounding area and had subsequently seen significant change.

An interesting evening lay ahead.

The chef – who was named Marcin – was a tall, friendly, confident figure who arrived in a white van at five, together with his waitress (who was also his girlfriend). Stasha let them in and they both immediately set themselves up in the kitchen, with the waitress laying the table in the dining room very elaborately. Anne could hear the chef talking to Stasha in Polish; she could not understand what was being said but it sounded quite jovial and happy, with a few laughs thrown in.

Maureen arrived at the house just before six; she came in a taxi that David had arranged and greeted Anne in the lounge. She had brought with her a small bunch of carefully chosen flowers.

Anne introduced her to Stasha saying, 'She's wonderful.'

Stasha was all too keen to take Anne's words as a compliment. Maureen turned round and nodded a greeting to Stasha, who quickly showed her one of the easy chairs to sit in.

'How long have you been caring for Anne, Kasa?' Maureen asked as she settled herself in the chair.

Anne and Stasha looked at each other.

'Her name is Stasha with an S,' Anne said.

'Stasha?' Maureen queried and she looked at Anne for confirmation that she had pronounced it correctly.

'It's short for Anastazja,' Stasha felt obliged to say.

'Really?' said Maureen looking puzzled.

Stasha explained to Maureen that saying her full name to people sometimes proved difficult, not only because of the spelling but also the pronunciation, and that it was only her mother who really used her full name. Anne remembering only too well this bone of contention from their early days.

Maureen listened, noting the waspish comment from Stasha.

'It's such a beautiful name,' Maureen said, 'it suits you.'

Stasha blushed as Maureen asked again how long she had been looking after Anne.

'I have been here for months now ...' Stasha looked at Anne in what Maureen thought was an affectionate manner.

Maureen knew only too well how uncompromising Anne could be, and she again looked at Stasha from beneath lowered eyelids. This young, slim, blonde girl in her twenties was attractive – even sexy! Maureen found it hard to imagine Anne and Stasha living together under the same roof. Her mind momentarily boggled.

Maureen quickly assessed Stasha. She seemed comfortable around Anne and vice versa. Stasha adjusted Anne's chair to make her more comfortable and straightened her cardigan; there was a definite rapport between them, with a lot of eye contact, and Maureen realised that their relationship was close. That surprised her, for if she'd had to guess what Anne's carer would be like, she would not have imagined someone like the young, attractive woman in front of her. Perhaps that was the reason her curiosity had been piqued.

The waitress, a slim brunette of small build, came in and asked Maureen if she'd like a drink. Maureen opted for a small sherry.

'Is Candy here yet?' Anne asked, and Stasha shook her head.

'She's texted me to say she's on her way.'

'Candy?' Maureen asked.

'Another carer,' Stasha replied, 'one of Anne's favourites.'

Maureen raised her eyebrows, wondering what she would be like.

Stasha took her seat next to Anne and they faced Maureen, with the spare easy chair reserved for Candy. A highly polished coffee table was in the centre and the waitress came in and brought the drinks on a silver tray. She handed the sherry to Maureen, a glass of iced orange juice to Stasha and what looked like fruit juice to Anne. Maureen realised she was the only one drinking alcohol so she sipped her sherry self-consciously.

Stasha checked her phone after receiving a text message before placing it back on the table.

'They spend a lot of time on their phones these young ones, don't they, Maureen?' Anne remarked.

Stasha laughed and Maureen asked why Anne wasn't having a sherry.

'I'd love to join you, Maureen, but with my medication I can't,' Anne explained.

'I'm sure a little one wouldn't do you any harm. In any case, Anne, how are you doing?' Maureen asked.

'I get by, Maureen. It is not the life I had, but I'm alive and I'm thankful. I have good days and bad days. Mostly good days, thanks to Stasha here.'

'And where are you from, St-, St-, St-, Stasha?' Maureen stuttered.

Even to Anne's ears it sounded like an age-old question, and she momentarily closed her eyes hoping Stasha would just answer the question and not be overly defensive.

Stasha had caught Anne's expression saying simply, 'I come from Poland.'

Maureen raised her eyebrows. 'Do you like

it here?' she asked.

For the first time Anne could understand Stasha's point about the overly curious British tradition of asking where people are from. This was the second time she had witnessed it. It was something she had not thought of before but now Stasha had pointed it out, it was quite evident that Stasha faced more discrimination than Anne had originally thought. Not that Maureen was being discriminatory – she was just being friendly, but it was so predictable.

'I like your country,' Stasha said. The emphasis on the word 'your' was deliberate. Stasha quickly glanced at Anne, who winked. There was no option but to smile at Maureen, who had witnessed the interplay between them.

'And how do you find Anne?' Maureen fired the question at Stasha.

'It's been interesting.' It was all Stasha wished to say.

Maureen laughed. What she would have given to have been a fly on the wall when the two of them were introduced.

'What made you go into care?' Maureen's questions kept coming.

'I wanted to make a difference, I worked in

a factory and the work was the same day in, day out, and I had no satisfaction. With this job I feel I'm doing something. I'm improving Anne's life and that is quite a nice feeling.'

It was a thoughtful answer and Maureen was impressed with Stasha's insight.

'She's lovely,' Anne interjected.

Stasha raise her eyebrows at Anne's statement, remembering the vitriolic comments that had come from that same person in those early days.

Stasha noticed a car coming up the drive.

Candy let herself into the house and entered the lounge carrying a large colourful bunch of flowers; she went immediately across to Anne and kissed her on her forehead, asking how she was before turning to Stasha and handing her the flowers.

Maureen observed the interplay.

'Happy birthday,' Candy said.

Stasha frowned, for it was an unexpected gesture and one that took her by complete surprise. Stasha could not help thinking there was some sort of ulterior motive behind the gesture.

'Thank you,' Stasha said in astonishment and got up from her chair, 'I'll put them in water.'

Anne introduced Maureen to Candy, explaining that this was her other carer who stayed with her on Stasha's days off.

Candy said hello before going back into the hall and removing her jacket. The waitress asked her what she liked to drink and Candy replied cautiously saying, 'Just a lemonade.'

Maureen was now alone with Anne in the lounge and could not resist saying, 'Some nice girls you have looking after you.' But it was more of a question than an observation.

'Who would have thought it, Maureen,' Anne replied. 'Me being looked after by such young women.'

'How do you find them?' Maureen's voice was nothing but a whisper.

Anne paused. 'I would genuinely be lost without them, or probably in some sort of awful care home.' Anne raised her eyebrows. 'These two in particular are absolutely wonderful. I can't fault either of them. They are so different in personality, but there's other carers as well who come in and assist.'

'How many?' Maureen asked.

'I think I have about twenty,' came the reply.

Maureen's face dropped. 'Twenty?' she repeated.

'Oh yes, girls of all ages and all abilities, all of them as dedicated and professional as the next. I have no complaints whatsoever, and between you and me I'm absolutely astounded by the good grace and behaviour they show me.' Anne paused. 'I think I am the only one who can sometimes be a little curt.'

'Not you, Anne.' Maureen smiled. 'Have you got your favourites?' Maureen asked with a wink.

'Anastazja is my favourite because she's here all the time and we have come such a long way in our relationship. Candy I've always said is Stasha's perfect foil,' Anne said.

Candy came back into the room with her glass of lemonade and sat down next to Maureen. 'How long have you known Anne?' she asked.

Maureen went on to explain that they had gone to the same church when Anne had been mobile, but since Anne's stroke their meetings had become infrequent, so it had been a very nice surprise to be invited this evening.

'It's Stasha's evening,' Candy said as Stasha re-entered the room. 'She will be forever twenty-eight.'

Stasha recognised the challenge and said, 'Can you remember that far back, Candy?'

Anne laughed, for it was rare that Stasha showed moments of humour. The remark was well received by Candy, who sat back in her chair, crossed her legs and relaxed.

'It's a Polish dinner,' announced Anne, 'we have a Polish chef.' Anne was repeating herself, and they all nodded and started to discuss the merits of foreign food and what they did and didn't like.

'Fish and chips for me, any time,' Candy said, 'or a hot curry.'

'A good old roast dinner,' Maureen replied. 'Lamb with mint sauce.'

Anne announced that she mostly now ate mushed up food but would try something different this evening, while Stasha boasted about her trim figure.

'Just salads for me.'

Candy laughed. Maureen was becoming more intrigued by every passing minute with these two young women.

It was then time for photographs. It wasn't like the old days where you would whip out the family album and go through various pictures – these girls had thousands of pictures on their phones, and it was Candy who started by showing Maureen pictures of her young children. Maureen nodded her approval at the happy pictures, then it was for Stasha to show Maureen pictures of her parents, their house in Poland and the general store where they worked, along with a few other pictures of her in her native country. She also showed her pictures from her and Anne's trip to London and of their various trips to local garden centres. Candy showed a picture of Anne at one of the U3A meetings surrounded by fellow members.

'You went to London?' Maureen said, and Anne nodded.

'Stayed at the Ritz,' Stasha said.

Candy was quiet, for she was still a little miffed that she had not been invited.

'The Ritz?' Maureen said in utter astonishment.

'Can't tell you what it was like. Another world. Took in a show, went to Harrods,' boasted Stasha.

Maureen listened. She wasn't entirely comfortable with what was being said. Was Anne being taken advantage of? She thought it unusual for a disabled woman to take her carer to London to stay at the Ritz and go to Harrods. It was certainly not the usual state of affairs with a live-in carer and an elderly patient, and she wondered who was instigating all these happenings. Instances of carers taking advantage of their patients, stealing and being abusive were often in the news, but she knew this wasn't the case here – the interplay between the three of them was very jovial and good-natured and she said to herself how lucky Anne was to have two lovely young women looking after her. Maureen was also glad that Anne had David to look out for her, for she knew David would not let anyone care for Anne without careful scrutiny.

It was then that Maureen noticed the cameras positioned on the walls. Anne was reading Maureen's thoughts, so she had no option but to explain.

'David looks after everything, phones me every day, and he arranged the trip to London. He scans and pays all the bills that come into the house. As you can see, we are surrounded by cameras and I know he'll probably be looking in on us sometime this evening and hoping we're having a good time'

Maureen felt reassured.

TWENTY-FOUR

They had chosen their preferred dishes and could hear the chef busily preparing them in the kitchen. Ironically, both Stasha and Candy seemed to have become temporary friends. Candy asked Maureen about her charity work for the church, which involved taking a group of parishioners to Lourdes every autumn. Candy was a little unsure about this, so Anne reminded her that Lourdes was the spiritual and religious site in France which is famed for healing and miracles.

'I'd like to go myself,' Stasha said, 'perhaps sometime in the future.'

Maureen replied that everyone should go at least once in their life, but she suddenly felt her statement was too Christian and quickly added, 'If they want to, of course.'

Candy gave a disinterested shake of her head. 'I have enough trouble keeping my head above water without worrying about where I'll end up.' She made it sound funny, and everyone laughed.

Religion was never a safe conversation topic over dinner so they temporarily moved on to the cost of living crisis, with Stasha somewhat flippantly saying, 'Have you heard of that, Anne?'

Maureen picked up a slight note of resentment in Stasha's voice and she looked across at Anne who had also raised her eyebrows.

Anne gave the matter some thought before saying, 'When John and I originally moved to Scotland we occupied what was called a company house; it had no central heating, or even any type of heating. We had to survive many Scottish winters with just a small back boiler for heat and a tiny log fire, so I do know something about being cold in the winter.'

Stasha was not to be deterred. 'But John had a good job didn't he, so you could have food in the fridge and nothing to worry about.'

Maureen sat back and witnessed the interplay. She was unsure of what to make of it. Maureen was not picking up a vibe of dislike between them – more a mutual exercise of having the last say. It was interesting that Stasha felt secure enough in their relationship to challenge Anne's opinions; it was in fact a refreshing change and didn't seem to worry Anne.

'You have preconceptions of my life, Stasha, that are at times misplaced and misguided, if you don't mind me saying,' Anne retorted.

Candy was relishing the exchange between them. Stasha listened.

'You seem to think the older generation have had it easy and that we don't know about poverty, hardship, starvation and all the things that younger people feel they have experienced for the first time.'

Stasha shot back, 'I'm not saying you've had an easy time, I'm saying that the generation today have it equally hard, and that sometimes older people don't generally acknowledge that.' Stasha was her old self, like a dog with a bone.

But Anne was not to be outdone. 'The young today want the wealth of the old without the work in between.'

'You sound condescending, Anne,' Stasha said, and the reply surprised Maureen.

Candy listened, thinking they were not surely going to have one of their infamous arguments tonight.

Anne looked across at Maureen who was sitting listening. She was wondering how Anne was going to deal with the situation.

Stasha continued. 'All I can say is that working for the minimum wage is not very pleasing. There is little hope and gaining the next step on the ladder is very difficult.'

Anne thought about a suitable response. She finally said, 'I want you to think about your annual salary Stasha before you pay tax, and I want you to think of Candy's annual salary before she pays tax, and I want you to add them both together. The figure you arrive at would still not be enough to pay my annual income tax bill. David has also had six-figure tax demands, so the older generation – who have seemingly had it so good – still contribute to society more than is immediately apparent.'

Stasha was momentarily silenced and Candy allowed herself a small smile at Anne's victory.

Maureen also gave the win to Anne, on points at least, but what was more intriguing was the undeniable love–hate relationship between Anne and Stasha. There seemed no malice in either statement, their body language was friendly and the vibe was not unpleasant, but there was a hidden connection between them that made the verbal sparring all the more interesting to listen to. Maureen came to the conclusion that Anne and Stasha must have had many similar exchanges. It made for a very good and stimulating situation, something that Anne needed. Maureen had imagined Anne's carer as a middle-aged woman fussing around, but Stasha brought a youthful outlook as well as a sense of compassion. Maureen's assumptions had been turned upside down. Everything about Stasha was in technicolour, and Anne was so lucky to have that.

There was general hush in the room, with Stasha eventually saying, 'Okay, Anne, you win that one.' Stasha could not help but smile. She got up and walked across to Anne's chair and knelt down beside her, placing her arm around Anne's shoulders to give her an affectionate hug.

The gesture took Maureen by surprise, but it was Candy who voiced her thoughts.

'Thick as thieves, those two.' It was a genuine observation, meant with no criticism. Maureen gave Candy a quizzical expression and Candy continued. 'They love arguing with each other.'

The waitress entered the lounge and announced that the evening meal was ready to be served. Maureen struggled to her feet and it was Candy who helped her into the dining room, while Stasha watched Anne manoeuvre her chair from the lounge to the dining room. She took her place at the head of the table.

Stasha sat next to Anne, with Maureen on the other side and Candy at the end of the table.

The table had been beautifully laid with a crisp, white linen tablecloth, two small vases containing flowers at either end and some very nice cutlery. The glassware was beautiful and the whole ambience was one of a quality. It reminded Stasha of her time at the Ritz.

The waitress came in and, in an act of solemnity, placed each plate down in front of the diners. Anne was served first, then Stasha, Maureen and Candy. The chef came in with a bottle of chilled white wine and poured Maureen a glass before filling up Candy's and Maureen's. The chef then asked if Anne should have a glass, but Stasha gently shook her head.

Anne had no option but to comply, although Maureen felt it was a little over-protective. But she didn't know the whole story and she allowed herself a taste of the wine. It was lovely.

Candy said it was beautiful wine and raised her glass to Stasha, saying, 'Forever twenty-eight, Stasha, am I right?'

Stasha laughed before saying. 'Well, you

should know.'

They all joined in the toast and took a sip of their respective drinks. The food was exquisite, served on pristine white plates accompanied by beautiful cutlery; it generated a nice atmosphere and they all began to tuck in to their starters. Stasha got up from her seat and helped Anne cut her food into small pieces. Maureen observed under lowered eyelids.

Candy relished the taste. 'If you have food like this back home, Stasha, why are you living over here?' She devoured what was on her plate as if she had never eaten before.

'Taking your jobs, Candy, Anne knows all about that.'

Fortunately Anne laughed this off, saying, 'Okay, Stasha, you win that one.'

They all laughed.

The four of them talked with jollity on a range of subjects from contraception and inconsiderate partners to the pros and cons of living in high-rise flats, not to mention the perils of getting old.

Anne held her glass up. 'We should toast Stasha's birthday.'

Dutifully, they all held their glasses up and gave a toast to Stasha, but Anne wanted to say something that had been on her mind.

'Unusually …' she stumbled at the start, for she was getting tired, but she managed to get the words out. 'It was no secret that Stasha and I did not get on in the beginning.'

Stasha gave her a warm smile as Anne carried on.

'I condemned Stasha unfairly and too harshly with my criticism, and I lacked compassion. And for that I am sorry.'

Maureen momentarily wondered what had gone on in those early days. She listened as Anne continued.

'So I say tonight once again, in front of you all, that I regret the friction that was caused …' Anne was beginning to choke with emotion, which – to Maureen – suggested that Anne's comments came from the heart.

For the second time, Stasha got up and knelt down beside Anne's chair. She placed an arm round her, saying, 'I am glad I've known you, Anne.'

Candy was surprised at the remark and offered a small smile towards Maureen, who looked at Anne.

Their main course was equally appetising and went down very well, and even Anne commented on how tasty the food was, despite her small portions.

They discussed holidays and where they'd like to travel to. Maureen had recently returned from America and Anne recalled some of the holidays she had enjoyed there, particularly in Florida. One of her favourite hotels had always been the Pier House at Key West, where she and John had enjoyed memorable relaxing holidays.

Candy suggested that a weekend in Blackpool was more for her pocket. She could not see herself doing any overseas travel for the foreseeable future – not because she didn't want to but because, as she said, 'I haven't got the money to do it.'

Stasha was more measured. She still wished to see the world, find out what it had to offer, experience different cultures and grow as a person, but like Candy she said, 'It's never going to happen,' and shrugged.

Anne quickly realised how limited their horizons were, and it was not through lack of ambition. They seemed a sad generation with nothing but multiple happy pictures on their phones. She had already had a discussion with Stasha about saving money, and Stasha had responded by saying, 'How can you save money when you haven't any money to save?'

John had always promoted careful money management and she always remembered her mother's frequent refrain of 'turn a pound over twice'. David had the same ethos as his father, saying, 'There's plenty of rainy days in Britain.'

Their conversation moved on to Anne's village and how much if it changed. Maureen recalled stories of living there fifty years ago when most of the village was fields. She had slowly witnessed the building of the new estates and fast food outlets which had encroached on the village.

'Never liked this house,' Anne commented. 'Never liked the village really either,' she added, and Candy asked why. 'It's neither a village nor a town. It's too busy, too much traffic. I miss Scotland.'

Stasha had been shown pictures of Anne's former house in Scotland and she had seen the picturesque countryside and the general feeling of space. She had seen images of the atmospheric winter months, with the thick frost on the cars and the snow-capped mountains. There was a general sense of affluence in the pictures.

Anne said she always found her current house too small.

'Small?' Candy said. 'It's a lovely, warm house.'

'Terraced houses like mine,' Stasha said, 'are small. You don't appreciate how crammed they are until you live in ones with space.'

They quickly moved on from the village and Maureen asked Anne how she felt she had coped since her stroke.

Anne gave a self-deprecatory shrug. 'Going from being independent to dependent is almost impossible to imagine unless you have lived through it. I went from one day organising and chairing committee meetings and writing novels to being looked after by complete strangers. It was a steep hill to climb.' Anne paused before adding, 'Sometimes even the carers do not readily appreciate or understand that.'

Candy frowned. 'I'm not with you, Anne.'

'A lot of the concern is for the carers and how they go about their duties and how difficult it is for them. But there seems little consideration given to the mental health of the patients themselves, as patients. We are not light switches who can go from one life to another quickly and effortlessly; there is a element of humanity in all of us, and while I acknowledge that being a carer is a difficult job, one has to walk a mile in the shoes of the patient to understand their predicament.'

'Are you saying we're not caring enough?' Candy asked.

Stasha listened carefully, for this was the second time Anne had touched on this subject and she wanted to be clear, in her mind, about what Anne was trying to say.

'Explain what you mean,' Stasha said.

Anne took a sip of her coffee. 'It's nothing to do with the care. It's nothing to do with the attitude of any carer. It's to do with the patient and their frame of mind, like I said, going from being independent to dependent and from having a perfectly normal life – being seen in public and being acknowledged by people who know you – to being looked after by strangers in the most intimate way. It would seem that the patient's journey is given little thought when care teams stroll up to new customers.'

Stasha disagreed as Anne knew she would. 'We are here to look after you because you asked us to come.'

Anne shrugged. 'I never said I didn't, but what I am trying to get across is the dramatic change that some patients have undergone, both physically and mentally, before you even walk through the door in the first place.'

Stasha frowned. 'We didn't give you enough consideration. Is that what you're saying?' There was a crispness in Stasha's tone.

Anne was on a roll and she looked at Stasha. 'Consideration can work both ways. I never gave you the respect that you deserved when you initially looked after me, but at times I felt some of the care team lacked consideration when looking after me also.'

Candy still didn't understand the point Anne was trying to make. Maureen said nothing.

Anne was getting tired. 'My point is that it's a traumatic life change to go from being an independent person to relying entirely on carers. This should be – and probably is – mentioned in your training. We're not sacks of potatoes. When we ask you to come, it's because some of us have gone through a dramatic, life-changing event. This should be considered when care work is taken up and when you're trained.'

There was a silence around the table. Anne continued. 'Nobody ever asked, until now, how I was coping with the situation.'

Stasha remembered those early days. Perhaps she was just obsessed with Anne's cruel and disparaging comments. She remembered being polite, but try as she might she could not recall asking Anne how she was *coping*.

Maureen sagely nodded her head. 'Anne has a point.'

Candy also gave a slow thoughtful nod, saying, 'It's something I haven't taken into consideration, but I will in future.'

Stasha sat back, for Anne was still full of surprises and she always seemed to be able to teach her a thing or two about life, and getting through the obstacles it presented. She was interesting and stimulating, and Stasha knew that even if she stayed in care it was probably unlikely that she would ever meet someone like Anne again, and that saddened her.

The three of them soon moved on to talking about more jovial subjects. Stasha's birthday dinner had been a success; they had all enjoyed the delicious food, the exemplary service from the chef and his waitress, and the stimulating conversation.

Now, with the house cleaned and Anne back in bed and snoozing – not to mention snoring – Stasha sat alone in the sitting room texting her mother about how the evening had gone.

Stefania said that there was perhaps a grain of truth in what Anne had said over dinner; there was perhaps – in the care sector – a lack of concern about the mental health of clients. But her mother also pointed out that she was not a counsellor, she was a carer, as her job title said. Stasha pondered; when caring and comforting patients, should she also consider their mental health, as well as their physical health and comfort? It was a dichotomy; there was not really any answer, but she knew that she – and probably Candy as well – would not forget what Anne had said.

It had been a point that Anne had made well.

Annette De Burgh

TWENTY-FIVE

The usual routine resumed in the following days. The doctor had spoken to Stasha and asked for the district nurse to visit, and she arrived on the Wednesday morning promptly at ten to take Anne's blood pressure and a sample of her blood. The blood pressure reading was fine and the blood had been taken without fuss.

Daisy, however, had been odd during the past few days. She had taken to sitting next to Anne's chair, rather than on her lap or on the chair itself when empty. This was not something she'd done in the past, and Stasha also noticed the opaque, reflective starring of her orange eyes whenever they looked at Anne. Stasha made a mental note that perhaps Daisy wasn't well. It was, however, soon forgotten when Daisy's meal time arrived; then she would desert Anne and head straight for her feeding bowl.

Stasha had been planning what to do in the next couple of weeks; there was another interesting talk at the U3A which Anne had wanted to go to and another member of the local book group had wanted to come and visit. These things were written on the calendar so Stasha would not forget.

'Let's go to the park this afternoon, Stasha,' Anne announced a few days later. 'I could do with some fresh air.'

The village, for all its downsides, had a nice, green recreation area – this consisted of a man-made pond with numerous footpaths and seating areas, and a children's play area. It had been built by the house builders to compensate the village for their ever-increasing intrusion on to the green belt.

Stasha and Anne had enjoyed a leisurely stroll around the various footpaths before settling down on a bench to enjoy the afternoon sunshine.

'You look pensive, Stasha,' Anne remarked.

Stasha frowned. 'That means thoughtful, right?' Stasha said, remembering how Anne had used the word in the past. 'My mother wants me to visit her,' she sighed.

Anne raised her eyebrows. 'Oh, you must go to see her, have a few days away, ask her to come over and see me.' There was encouragement in the tone.

Stasha said jokingly, 'You trying to get rid of me.'

'No, you deserve a break,' Anne soothed. 'Your mum misses you, I bet.'

Stasha agreed. 'It's just a question of when, and of course there is the airfare and travelling expenses to think of, as well as Daisy. It is not as simple as just jumping on a plane and going.'

'I will pay for you to go. Daisy can stay with me,' Anne said.

Stasha gave a reflective sigh. 'Oh, Anne, I know you would but it's too much to ask.'

'Pfft,' Anne replied. 'You let me know when and I'll get David to see you're okay.'

Stasha placed a comforting hand on Anne's leg. 'It would be nice to see her, but it would be a good five days away.'

Anne shrugged. 'Have a break Stasha, go and see your friends.'

'You'll no doubt have Candy to look after you,' advised Stasha and there was a hint of a smile on her lips.

'It could be worse, couldn't it?'

Anne winked at Stasha and they both laughed before Stasha voluntarily held Anne's hand for a brief moment and squeezed it. Silence engulfed them as the two women were lost in their own thoughts.

A woman with a border collie dog came up to Anne and introduced herself as someone Anne had known before her stroke, a well-spoken lady who asked how Anne was. Anne was courteous in her reply, ending with, 'I would not be here if it weren't for Anastazja.' Anne introduced Stasha to the woman.

'What a beautiful name,' the woman said.

'And it suits her.' Anne gave her usual reply and Stasha smiled. It was a caring thing to say about her and she was momentarily touched by it.

The woman wished Anne well and they both watched her as she strolled off with her dog. It wasn't long after that Stasha decided to return home, put Anne in the conservatory and serve some well-deserved afternoon tea.

Some months later ...

Stasha looked out of the rain-splashed window, it was February and the miserable weather had set in for the day. She turned round and surveyed the small but homely living quarters and slowly walked back to one of the caravan's two bedrooms.

The residential caravan park, or park home as they are sometimes referred to, was designed for pensioners who were either alone or widowed, or who had downsized their homes to something smaller, more manageable and more easy to maintain. There was a community and there were friendships, but it was nevertheless a reminder of what life could become when you get old – downsize after downsize until you ended up in a static caravan surrounded by similar identical homes on wheels.

Stasha went to check on her patient and, as she did, she caught her reflection in the glass of one of the kitchen cupboards. Gone, today, were the sunglasses that she often wore. While her eyes had not lost their attractiveness, they had a hint of fatigue about them. Stasha went into the small bedroom, passing the Zimmer frame, wheelchair and commode as she did. Her eighty-year-old patient was fast asleep. Realising there was little to do, Stasha went back into the living area and sat on the couch to browse her phone.

It been four months since Anne had passed away and, after the funeral, Stasha had spent two weeks with her mother, surprisingly and unexpectedly grieving for Anne and trying to rebalance her life. Upon her return, the agency had offered her another live-in role, this time for Janet, who had dementia, mobility problems and – at times – behavioural problems. She had a family but Stasha had never met them. Janet's caravan was situated at the far end of the park. It was one of the smaller ones, and it comprised a kitchen, sitting area, small bathroom and two very small bedrooms.

Stasha's work schedule was very similar to her schedule at Anne's. She would have a weekend off every now and then, but it was not Candy who replaced her, for she had left the agency.

Instead, it was either Whitney or Zoe. Whitney was a young mother of two, competent and confident, who lived with her partner who was a decorator. Zoe was nineteen years old; she was new to the agency; a good carer and enthusiastic about her job. Both would take it in turns to look after Janet for the three or four days while Stasha was away.

Stasha's afternoons were now often long and the days, all similar in their routine, often stretched out interminably. The living conditions were somewhat restricted and, with the caravan park not allowing any animals, she could not bring Daisy for company. Janet would spend most of her time making no sense, rambling on about nightclubs she used to visit when she had been younger and – inappropriately – the sex life she'd had with her husband. Stasha, always polite and considerate, was not really interested in listening to all that.

This afternoon, with little to do, Stasha sat down with a cup of coffee and went through the hundreds of images on her phone. She came across some pictures of the time she visited London with Anne. She appraised each photograph; it was such a happy time for her and she could still remember the experience of that splendid afternoon tea she had so much enjoyed, especially with Anne's irreverent behaviour. Other photographs sprang into view: a selfie of them both in the conservatory, another with Anne next to the van at one of the parks they'd visited, and another of her, Maureen and Candy enjoying the birthday meal that David had arranged for her. Stasha was frozen in time. She looked carefully at the images and, as she did so, quickly wiped away the beginning of a tear that had appeared in the corner of her eye. While Janet was a sweet and confused old lady who meant no harm, the truth was she missed living in Anne's house, she missed having Daisy with her and she missed going out in the van for afternoons. But above all that she knew, deep down, that she missed Anne and the life they had shared so briefly together. She had come to appreciate the stimulating and sometimes abrasive arguments they had. She gave an inward laugh. How absurd that she should be thinking about how much she missed Anne – it showed just how wrong first impressions can sometimes be. What Stasha wouldn't give to hear the ringing of Anne's bell right now.

It had been a tremendous shock on that particular morning to come down as normal to find Anne unresponsive in bed. Part of

Stasha was glad that Anne had passed away in her sleep, a bigger part of her was grateful that the preceding day had been joyful and happy. An even bigger part of her was glad that Anne had passed away in her own home and not some sterile hospital room.

Stefania knew her daughter was upset at Anne's passing and had immediately asked her to come home for a few weeks. It was apparent on meeting her daughter that the toll of Anne's sudden death had hit her badly, but after a week or so the clouds had lifted and the real Stasha had started to return. Stefania had asked whether Stasha wished to continue in this line of work, and after giving it a great deal of thought Stasha had decided to return to the UK and continue. Having a break and being with her mother had done her the world of good. Everything had been put into perspective.

Stasha had not heard from David since a phone call on the day of Anne's passing, and she remembered how she'd had to leave the house for good that afternoon, with Daisy and all her belongings. She'd returned to her own home. The care agency had said they would be in touch with her for some rota work on a daily basis to keep her employed.

Curiosity had got the better of Stasha one afternoon and, two months after Anne's death, she had driven down the lane to Anne's house. As she approached the drive, she slowed down and looked up towards the house. As she did so, she noticed that the gates were open and that the gardener's van was parked halfway up the driveway. Involuntarily, she stopped the car, got out and walked up the drive to speak to the gardener, who she had known during her time at the house. He recognised her and welcomed her with a smile, and she asked what was happening.

The gardener shrugged, saying, 'I still come every week and Mrs James comes every Monday, but there's nobody here.'

'Have you seen David?' Stasha asked and, as she looked round, she noticed that Anne's van had gone.

The gardener shook his head and exchanged a few more pleasantries before returning to tidying up one of the flower beds. Stasha felt a compulsion to walk up to the house and look through the windows but the blinds had been closed so there was little point. The house, although still well presented, looked like there was nobody living in it, so she returned to her car and drove off.

So Stasha's life as a live-in carer continued in the same vein, albeit under different circumstances. She had absolutely nothing against Janet, who was a kindly old lady living out her remaining years as best she could, but there was no spark or human interest. Stasha, being the ultimate professional, gave the same standard of care to whoever she was dealing with and there was no doubt that Janet appreciated all her efforts.

But that extraordinary relationship she had experienced with Anne was missing.

Friday was the start of her two-day break. Whitney was coming to look after Janet for the weekend and she arrived at Janet's caravan by taxi at four. It was odd, for the resentment she felt when Candy looked after Anne was not present with Janet – this made Stasha think of the ambiguous text she had received from Candy earlier in the week. She had not answered it but now glanced at her phone and scrolled back through the various texts she had since received – then she found Candy's and read it again.

CANDY > STASHA
Have you got what I got?

It still didn't mean anything and she was not going to show her curiosity by replying.

Stasha eventually said her temporary goodbye to Janet, got in her car and drove home.

Once she was back at home, she set about opening her house, feeding Daisy and putting on some heat, for the house was cold. She unpacked before deciding on what she was going to have for dinner.

Her meal was spaghetti bolognaise and, after eating it half-heartedly, Stasha sat back on her couch and relaxed, wondering what she was going to do for the weekend. She telephoned her mother and was deep in conversation when her front doorbell rang. Stasha ended the call and got up to open it. The neighbour who had collected her post over the past few weeks needed to hand it to Stasha. It was taken without interest and put on the table.

It was then that Stasha decided to have a warm bath, so she put the immersion on and waited a while before enjoying a relaxing soak in her tub with a glass of red wine. She came down to the lounge in her nightwear, made herself a small snack and enjoyed another glass of red.

While watching some rubbish on television, she reached forward and sifted through her mail. There was nothing of interest but then she noticed a white premium-looking envelope. It looked like it had been hand delivered. Stasha retrieved it from the table and proceeded to open it. It contained a letter and a QR Code. Stasha read the letter, it was from Anne's solicitor, and her eyes rested on the word 'beneficiary'. She then read the instructions for the QR Code.

She retrieved her phone and scanned the code.

Suddenly, Anne jumped at her from the screen. The video had been shot in the dining room of Anne's house, presumably when Lorraine had called round that morning all those months ago. She listened to what Anne had to say.

'Stasha, as you are watching this we must presume that I have died and peace and tranquillity have returned, once more, to your life! You often talked about your desire to travel to all those wonderful places and the pipe dream, as you called it, to have a deposit for a house, buy a new

car, *to settle down and build roots here in the UK.
I said, never chase your dreams, for they will find
you. I wish to give you the opportunity to fulfil all
those dreams as I am so thankful that we met; my
remaining weeks were never black and white for
you colourised those days. But more importantly
Stasha I want you to be happy, because you once
said to me; "if you're not happy then nothing else
matters." We move on, someone always has to be
the first to go, so don't miss me too much as death
is but my next great adventure.'*

The video ended.

Stasha replayed it.

Again.

And again.

And again.

Then, involuntarily she stopped a tear
forming in the corner of her eye and through
blurry eyes she telephoned her mother.

It's not the goodbye that hurts
it's the flashbacks and memories that follow.